The moral right of the author has been asserted. A CIP catalogue record of this book is available from the British Library

First paperback, hardback, ebook, editions November 2021
Book design by Susan Krupp
ISBN 978-1-7399294-2-8 (softback)

c1f15e41f71433a9efb9b6ec0034e828e40e15bebaeb8e087109dfe3eb45f8c3

www.ryanharperjones.com
comments, thoughts, reflections gratefully received at
info@ryanharperjones.com

A Council of Ghosts

Ryan Harper Jones

Contents

~ 1 ~

Samuel Rufus

A loud crash filled the forest. Snow and smoke swirled around the trees as birds fluttered away and rabbits fled in panic. Steadily the snow settled, and the smoke cleared to reveal the vague outline of a dark spectacled pale-faced man. He smacked his long coat vigorously as if dusting himself off. Then he removed his hat and smacked it against his leg several times before placing it firmly on his head.

He stepped forward unsteadily, found an opening in the forest, dropped his bag and staff on the floor, and then sat down, tired and resigned. He was out of breath. There were three scratches and a bruise on his face, it had been a perilous journey. He had crossed hundreds of miles through untold danger to be here.

The moon shone quietly across the countryside surrounding Edgings Burrow. For a while, Samuel Rufus sat and admired the peace and solitude he found himself in. He watched the snow falling steadily, spreading a beautiful white blanket across the horizon. What a relief, he thought, to be in the safety of Edgings Burrow.

A while later, he set off towards the small lonely lanes, his long staff casting small indentations in the snow next to his footprints. A layer of snow gathered on his brimmed hat and shoulders. He raised his staff. Magically, the snow flew off.

Rufus arrived at the house of Jones the bank clerk. He tapped his wooden staff softly on the cottage door.

Jones opened the door looking flustered. "Ah, good evening."

"The keys," said Rufus with a tired hoarse voice.

Jones glanced at him for a moment, noting the dark round spectacles, and the cuts and bruises on his left cheek. *There's probably a black eye behind those glasses. He's been in a fight again,* thought Jones.

"We expected you last month," complained Jones.

Rufus sighed, reached into his pocket, and pulled out a crumpled envelope. "Just the keys please." Jones smiled at the money and produced a set of keys from his pocket.

"How long will you be staying this time?"

Rufus did not answer. He took the keys, turned around and walked away leaving Jones muttering something about rude tenants and dark spectacles in the winter.

Rufus entered Ten Gibbets Lane, closed the door, and trotted resolutely to the window. He looked out searchingly in one direction, and then the other. The road was still and quiet, nothing stirred. He was pretty sure he had not been followed.

Rufus sighed, turned on a table lamp and lit the fire before sinking into the armchair. Now and again, he stroked his pointed beard softly and glanced out of the window just to be sure.

*

Ten Gibbets Lane was a beautiful cottage with a small mature bushy garden at the front, and an overwhelming view of the countryside and the forest at the back. A street lamp highlighted the cottage's warm features.

Rufus' strange habit of standing at his window for hours on end, peering out macabrely through his ever-present dark spectacles made him the object of idle gossip.

The lamp and the fire in the front living room were always on. They were on in the day, in the evening and through the night. When the chilly winter made way for spring and then summer, the lamp stayed on emanating a soft glow through the living room. The tell-tale smoke rising from his chimney at all hours of the day and night indicated that the living room fire was also constantly on.

*

A year after Rufus arrived in the village, the village was paying less attention to him. The weather had turned cold. The frost settled in each night leaving a distinct chill in the air. Soon the countryside was covered with a white frosty flutter which looked beautiful every morning as children walked into school.

On the bitterly cold night of Halloween, of all the nights in the year, two more strangers entered the village and reignited the fires of gossipy fascination.

One of them was a tall lean man with a long thin white face and a pointed nose. He wore a high collared long coat and walked through the village with such an air of grace and slender that he seemed to be gliding across the snowy lanes. Now and again, he smiled courteously revealing a set of thin teeth that sent a chill through the already frozen bones of passers-by.

The second was a chubby round-faced man with an upturned nose and two large mouse-like front teeth protruding downwards from behind his upper lip. His untidy hair came down to his shoulders.

"And then I caught him," hissed the tall man as they approached the village square.

"The slithery snake," muttered the chubby man. "I hope you made him pay Arak."

"Oh yes Trenton, I did. He paid very dearly... for a few days," Arak smiled.

They stopped at the square seemingly unsure of where to go. Arak looked around and sniffed the cold air. He turned towards another village lane before eventually arriving at the doorstep of Samuel Rufus.

Arak crossed his long skinny fingers, closed his eyes, and sniffed the air again. More assured of himself, he knocked on the door and stood back a few paces tapping the tips of his bony fingers together and looking straight at the door. He swayed back and forth on his feet.

There was no answer, not even the customary ruffle of the curtain followed by Rufus' face peering through to see who had ventured the indecency of disturbing him. Arak knocked again. Arak and Trenton became impatient. Arak turned his left ear to the door and listened intently.

"I know you're there you dog, I can smell you," he hissed quietly through the door. "Just open the door."

"Are you sure this is the right house?" asked Trenton kicking small flurries of snow into the air.

"Yes," said Arak sniffing the air again. He banged furiously on the door. "You can't keep hiding Rufus. *You're only making it worse for yourself!*"

As this happened, Saul, who lived opposite the cottage, Ruby, and Henry, his two best friends, returned home from school. They turned into Gibbets Lane, approached the cottage, and gasped quietly when they saw Arak and Trenton. Arak's frozen white face sent a chill through their bones.

"Don't stop walking," urged Ruby through gritted teeth. "Let's wait by the corner and see what happens."

"We haven't got long," urged Trenton. He pulled out a chain-watch from his long coat and fumbled around with it realising that he was holding it upside down. "Seventy minutes left."

The children walked inconspicuously to the corner of the Lane. Then, sure they were out of sight, slipped behind a thicket of snow-covered bushes, knelt down, and watched Arak and Trenton.

"The window," whispered Henry excitedly pointing at the cottage.

The curtain moved gently to reveal the shadowy figure of Rufus peering out cautiously.

"We'll have to let ourselves in," hissed Arak. He walked around the side of the cottage into the garden. Trenton kicked the snow around impatiently.

"Trenton! Over here quick!"

Trenton slipped and scampered to the back.

"Stand back!" shouted Trenton.

There was a crash of glass and then a brief silence, broken by a frenzy of shouting and screaming. The children gasped as the front window crashed to reveal the chubby fat figure of Trenton flying into the street and landing in the snow with an almighty tumbling thud.

Arak scurried around from the back. His face bruised, his lower lip bleeding, and his left eye black and sore. One arm of the coat was ripped, smoke rose softly from a burn mark on the coat.

"Get up you imbecile!"

Trenton clambered to his feet and clenched his fists angrily. *"Let's go back and teach the dog a lesson!"*

"We can't take him on," said Arak. "We need more people," he added quietly. Without another word, Arak and Trenton turned away into the distance.

*

The children were left dumbfounded by the sequence of events.

Henry sighed slowly. "That was—"

The children turned around sharply. The front door had opened. They peered intriguingly through the bushes and saw Rufus step out of the cottage. He walked up to the gate as calm as a feather and turned to look at the broken window.

"Stupid... dumb... animals," he mumbled in a hoarse voice. Rufus turned to walk into the cottage. He stopped abruptly and turned to look quizzically at the bush. The children gasped and did not dare to move.

"Henry, Saul, and Ruby?"

How did he know their names? What now? Should they stay hidden behind the bush? Ruby got up, picked up her wet bag and patted the snow off her clothes.

"Err yes."

Saul and Henry followed her nervously.

"Could you come in for a moment?"

This was the last thing any of them expected. They waited a moment before Saul nodded and led Ruby and Henry into the garden towards the door.

The children stepped through the corridor. They furnished a nosy glance at the front room as they walked past. The light had finally gone out, and the room was a chaotic mess. Furniture had fallen over. Two wall paintings lay on the floor. The room at the back was no better. The window was broken, glass littered across the floor and furniture lay upside down. Most strangely however, there was a black burn mark strewn across the wall opposite the fireplace. The children stood glued to it for a moment as Rufus disappeared into the kitchen.

"What do you think happened here?" Henry asked quietly.

"A fight obviously what do you think?" muttered Ruby. "Didn't you see what—"

"A… err fire," proposed reappearing with a brush and shovel. He looked up disappointedly at the wall.

Instinctively, Henry and Saul helped to stand the furniture up allowing Rufus to sweep up the glass beneath it. All the while, they stole curious glances at Rufus. There were two cuts to his cheek, his glasses were still glued to his face. But despite the skirmish, he conducted himself around the room with a remarkably calm demeanour.

Sometime later, both rooms were tidied. Rufus drew the curtain over the broken window, lit two wall lamps, and then lit the fireplace.

"Now listen," began Rufus. "I have to leave, but there's something you need to know. Arak, Trenton, and anyone else that accompanies them are very dangerous. If they ever return, you are never, I repeat never, to speak to them. Do you understand?"

The children nodded.

"Don't even look at them. Just stay away. Do you understand?"

They nodded again.

"You're leaving?" queried Henry.

"It's for the best," replied Rufus quickly. "Arak will bring danger to the village. It's me he's after. I should go while I can."

Rufus led them to the front door. "Now remember what I said," he said before closing the door behind them.

*

That evening, Saul and Mr Humphries sat in the living room contemplating the sequence of events at Ten Gibbets Lane.

Mr Humphries sat in his armchair carrying a worried expression. He was reading a book while Saul browsed through his homework trying hard to conjure up the will to begin working on it. Maths was his least favourite subject, and the array of questions in front of him made him feel nauseous and dizzy. He had a poor attention span at the best of times, and that evening's strange drama gave his concentration a lot of latitude to wane and lose focus.

Saul's gaze affixed itself on a photograph on the wall in front of him. He had never paid much attention to the photographs and paintings around the house. He recognised David Murray and Jefferson Hardy, Ruby and Henry's fathers. He also recognised his aunt and uncle, Sarah and Thomas. But that was about it.

The photo on the living room table was an old photo of Mr Humphries, Murray, and Hardy standing next to two strangely dressed friends. It was taken outside the mansion many years ago when the Lord of the mansion still lived there. What was particularly strange about it was the whiteness surrounding a man wearing black, a result of *over-exposure* proposed Mr Humphries. *It used to happen quite regularly with older cameras,* he had explained. Saul preferred his personal theory, that the man in black was a ghost.

~ 2 ~

The Lamp

A month later, Ten Gibbets Lane lay spookily empty. Speculation had spread through the village about a *fight* at Ten Gibbets Lane and Rufus' sudden departure.

The weather turned cold. Soon it began to snow relentlessly. The snow came down in persistent downfalls throughout the day and well into the night. Heavy blizzards battered the village and the biting wind howled through the narrow lanes sending a deep chill through the village.

The children walked home from school one afternoon. Their hands plunged deep into their pockets and warm puffs of air floating upwards from behind the scarves loosely hugging their cold faces.

The walk home led them through picturesque windy country lanes, hugged tightly on both sides by the beautiful countryside. Along the way, they passed two farmhouses, and at the outskirts of the village, they walked around the great mansion.

The mansion had lain empty for nearly forty years after the death of the last Lord, Edgar Tanbrooke. His grandson Harold was a banker in London, and although he had inherited the mansion, he rarely visited it.

The mansion sat in ten acres of once beautiful gardens, now overgrown into a mess of grassy weeds. An imposing stone brick wall surrounded the gardens, and thick wild hedges, bushes and trees grew along the inside of the wall. Here and there, the trees and bushes climbed wildly over the wall adding to the air of abandonment.

A coat of arms sat on the gate announcing the rich and honourable lineage of the *Lord of the Manor*. A long time ago it had imposed itself proudly on all visitors, but today, the rusty coat of arms was barely visible through creeping twisting ivy which covered the gate.

The gate opened to a long path leading to the great mansion. On a bright summer day, the mansion could be seen from the lane. It occupied three floors and was built of old stone brick with a welcoming porch leading to a huge wooden door.

"Let's cut through," proposed Henry as they reached the mansion grounds.

Now and again, they took a shortcut through the grounds. A hundred yards from the main road, the wall had deteriorated into a state of disrepair. A few layers of brickwork had fallen away. At the far end of the grounds, a clutch of bushes hid another deteriorated section of the wall leading back onto the lane.

"There's probably three feet of snow in the grounds Henry," complained Saul.

"I know but it'll save ten minutes and it's freezing cold," replied Henry, shivering gently as he looked over the wall.

Saul and Ruby looked at the dark path ahead and then the white unbroken snowy grounds of the mansion. Saul walked to the wall and climbed into the grounds. Twenty yards into the grounds, almost knee-deep in snow, Saul and Ruby wondered why they had listened to Henry.

The mansion grounds were beautifully lit by the steady moonlight. A beautiful blanket of unbroken snow lay across the middle. Small shrubs and trees cast long sporadic shadows across the edge of the grounds.

As they passed the front of the mansion, Saul slowed down and stopped to a standstill.

"What's up?" asked Henry.

"Hold on," muttered Saul, eyeing the mansion carefully. He pointed his gloved hand up. "Look up there."

"I can't see anything. What is it?" asked Ruby, sinking her cold hands deep into her coat pockets.

"The window to the right above the door. There's a light on."

Ruby and Henry looked carefully at the grand stone-faced windows above the entrance.

"Why yes…" said Henry squinting his eyes. He removed his glasses, wiped them, put them on and looked again more carefully. "That's strange. It's been empty for years. Has someone moved in?"

"No, we would've heard about it," suggested Ruby. The cold wind swept across the mansion grounds and threw up a flurry of snow. "Maybe they're having some work done."

"Well ours are the only footsteps," said Saul surveying the snow-covered grounds. "Is there another entrance into the grounds?"

"Only the main gate, and that's been locked for years," replied Ruby. The gates to the mansion had been held together by a huge rusty padlock and chain for as long as anybody could remember.

"Let's walk around to see if there are footsteps going in," suggested Henry.

Despite his small frame, timid nature, and his glasses, which were the object of fun for two school bullies, Henry was fearless, sporty, and seemed to harbour an endless reserve of energy.

"Whoever it is must have gone in before the snow came in yesterday morning."

"There's only one entrance, and unless someone else knows about our shortcut, there's no other way of getting in," said Ruby. "And anyway, it's not our business is it?"

"It is if someone's broken in, right?" proposed Henry.

"And turned on a lamp for everyone in the village to see?" asked Ruby sarcastically. "Even if someone's broken in it's not our business Henry. It's cold and dark and I just want to get home."

Ruby's dark black hair waved gently into her eyes from under the hat. She was shivering gently.

"Let's go," said Ruby.

Moments later, the children had climbed out into the lane.

*

The light in the mansion played on Saul's mind all night. He tossed and turned for more than an hour and struggled to sleep. Outside, the wind howled, whined, and whistled fiercely through the small lanes and streets. Flurries of snow fell from cottage rooftops, and occasionally, the wind pounded and rattled against the window in Saul's bedroom sending a shiver through his body.

As Saul lay in bed, the incident with Rufus, Arak, and Trenton, and the light in the mansion slowly merged and drifted into a strange dream. The Lord of the mansion had returned after decades. He stood looking out of the mansion window wearing dark spectacles and holding a lamp. The lamp then merged into the illuminating glowing spectre of the ghost of the wandering lady, a popular Halloween story in Edgings Burrow. She seemed to glide aimlessly past Saul's house letting out an agonising whining and moaning which intertwined itself with the wind as it whistled past the bedroom window. The scene changed again. Now Arak was banging on Saul's front door, and then a moment later, one of the men from the photo in the living room stood terrifyingly at his bedpost. It was a frightening sight. Saul wanted to cry out but was stuck in that strange debilitating dreamy state where the sound just would not leave his mouth.

The banging at the door became louder, and then, suddenly, there was a loud crash. Saul awoke with a judder. He jolted upright and sat as straight as a rod. He was sweating, his heart was pounding uncontrollably. The wind had stopped, and the room was shrouded in silence. The light from the street lamp shone lazily through the window casting a warm glow in the room.

Saul realised quickly that while everything else had been a dream, the banging sound was real. Something had fallen inside his room, and it was not the first time this had happened.

He looked around carefully. Nothing had fallen off the dressing table. There were no books on the floor. The mirror was intact, and his school bag sat untidily where he had left it. Thankfully, the two paintings were still on the wall. Finally, he looked at the bedside table and saw that the empty tea mug lay scattered in pieces at the foot of the bedroom wall. There was a mark on the wall, somehow, strangely, the mug must have hit the wall as it fell off. Saul sighed wondering how it could possibly have travelled from the table to the wall.

Saul sighed again before sinking into his pillow and drifting back into a more uneventful sleep.

*

"Maybe it was the wind," proposed Henry on the way home. "Was the window shut?"

"Of course it was shut. I mean it's freezing, why would I leave it open?"

"Couldn't it... well... have opened in the middle of the night?"

"No, it was firmly shut."

"A... poltergeist perhaps?" proposed Ruby. It was difficult to tell whether she was being serious or sarcastic. "Well, it's happened a few times before, right?" Ruby asked. "I mean *stuff moving around and—*"

"The light's on, look," interrupted Saul. They had reached the mansion and were standing at the foot of the gate.

"Children," came a cheery voice which made them jump.

They turned around to see Jonah Hudson, Ruby's uncle, trudging through the snow towards them. His hands were sunk deep into his pockets, a warm colourful scarf hugged his face. Jonah lived alone. His wife had died four years ago, and Saul, Ruby, and Henry were the closest he had to children.

"Has someone moved into the mansion?" asked Ruby after exchanging pleasantries.

"The mansion? Why no," Jonah glanced across the grounds. "Why do you ask?"

"Well, there's a light on in the upstairs window. We thought maybe someone had moved in."

Jonah looked carefully at the grand building. "You must be seeing things," he asserted dismissively. "But no. Nobody's moved in. They need to do something about the mansion, that place is running into ruin, it's—"

"The window on the first floor," interrupted Saul pointing through the gate. "There's a bright light, you can't miss it."

Jonah looked again. "Must be the reflection of the street lamp. Mind how you go and don't forget to remind Jefferson about tea on Sunday," he added before walking away.

"That's weird," said Henry when Jonah was out of sight. "Are we seeing things or something?"

The children stood looking fixedly at the light in the window. They felt a peculiar sensation urging them to discover the reason for the lamp. Somehow, strangely, the light seemed to be emitting an inviting pulsating call.

"I reckon we should go around and… well, just have a look around to see if any windows are broken," proposed Saul.

"That's the most sensible thing you've said all day," said Henry cheekily.

"Do one of you have a torch?" asked Ruby.

"A torch?" quizzed Henry.

"I wouldn't count on the lights being on, or even working."

"Good thing I came prepared," said Saul. He pulled out a torch from his bag and then turned it on and off.

"Yes," sighed Ruby. "I suppose there's nothing more to it."

They climbed into the grounds and trudged through the snow towards the mansion.

"I can't believe nobody else has noticed it. I mean it's so bright," said Saul quietly.

"Yes," began Henry. "And I don't see why Jonah couldn't see it and why nobody else in the village has said anything about it."

They reached the porch and stopped for a few moments to admire the spectacular building.

Saul stepped onto the porch. A stone statue of a huge dog sat on one side of the front door, seemingly guarding the entrance. On any other day, the statue would have felt tame, perhaps even charming, however, this evening it adopted an aggressive and unwelcoming demeanour and added to the anxiety of the occasion.

Saul raised his eyebrows and reached for a brass knob on the door. He turned it softly. It did not move.

"Let's try around the back," suggested Henry.

They walked along the front and then turned a corner into darkness. Saul turned the torch on and passed it quietly to Henry.

At the back, Henry stopped at a small window sitting at head height. He pulled himself to his toes, waved the torch through and looked through into a dark corridor.

"Seems empty. Let's have a look inside, what do you think?"

Henry gritted his teeth and tried to push the window open. It jerked open easily, and for a moment, they stood frozen to the spot. They had got this far, were presented with easy access to the mansion, but nobody seemed to know what to do next. Saul clasped two hands together and looked up at Henry. "You first."

"Thanks," whispered Henry sarcastically. He passed the torch to Ruby, stepped onto Saul's hands, and climbed through the window onto a wooden floor. Saul and Ruby followed and joined Henry in a cold corridor.

Ruby shone the torch around to reveal a collection of small paintings lining the walls on both sides. The paintings depicted an array of scenes from village fairs, hunting expeditions through the forest, and what appeared to be large family gatherings with groups of children running riot in the grounds while their parents picnicked under the shade of the trees.

Saul and Ruby followed Henry through a door at the end of the corridor into a spectacular hallway. The walls were lined with paintings and a small collection of statues sat against the walls. The front door of the mansion sat on one side, and at the opposite end, a magnificent staircase led up to a balcony.

"Look," said Ruby pointing up to a faint light on the balcony. "That's where the light's coming from."

"Let's have a wander around first," proposed Henry. "The light's not going anywhere is it?"

They settled in front of one of the walls and admired a warm portrait of a lord and lady of the mansion, both seated in armchairs next to each other. Two children were playing on the floor in the foreground, toys were scattered around the floor and a servant stood by pouring tea.

"That's beautiful," whispered Ruby mesmerised by the painting.

Next to it on either side and underneath it, sat a collection of portraits of lords and their ladies dressed in their finest regal outfits.

"Lord Curchester," said Ruby pointing at one of them. She recognised it from their history classes, which a year ago, had examined the colourful history of the three villages.

"And his wife the Lordess Beatrice," suggested Saul.

"Lady not Lordess," corrected Ruby. Saul frowned sarcastically.

Some of the paintings were more disconcerting. One of them depicted a war-torn town beset with ruined buildings. The streets were a chaotic mess. Smoke rose from burnt buildings in the background, bodies lay strewn across the street, and on one side, lines of people were walking away from the ruins. Most poignantly perhaps, a woman sat at the forefront with her hand on her head crying in grief. A small girl, probably two or three years old, stood next to the lady. One hand covered her mouth, wide open in shock, the other clung to a small teddy bear. The painting held such rich vivid detail that it made the children feel they were standing at the foot of the scene.

"This is devastating," said Saul who like Ruby and Henry, stood captivated by the painting.

Suddenly, a howling sound tore through the mansion. The children gasped in horror and Ruby fumbled with the torch as it nearly fell from her grasp. For a moment, they stood frozen in silence, not daring to move or make a sound.

"We should have closed the window," whispered Henry. *"Hello!"* he shouted suddenly.

Saul and Ruby jumped in panic.

"What are you playing at you idiot?" hissed Ruby.

"It's obviously empty," whispered Henry consolingly. "If anybody heard the window, they'd be here by now."

"Look…" began Ruby nervously. "At least we know we can get in and out. Let's come back another day."

"That's… that's not a bad idea," replied Saul nervously.

"We've come this far, let's have a quick peek," whispered Henry. Saul and Ruby thought for a moment before agreeing reluctantly. Without another word, they followed Henry towards the stairs.

It was a solid wide staircase, wide enough for them to walk side by side. A beautiful warm red carpet ran up the middle and both ends were lined by richly decorated balusters topped with a solid thick wooden bannister.

A small landing sat at the top of the steps. An assortment of small statues rested firmly against the wall. The landing parted into two staircases, each leading to opposite ends of the balcony. The children took one of the staircases. Ahead of them sat two rooms. The door to the first room was ajar, the light was coming from this room.

Saul took a deep breath and pushed the door. They walked in.

An oil lamp sat in the window spreading a comfortable glow across the room. The room was warmly furnished. Two armchairs sat on either side of the fireplace and a small coffee table was tucked up against one of them. A small clock and a selection of statuettes lined the top of a beautiful fireplace. Although the mansion felt and looked completely abandoned, the clock, the lamp and the layout of the room suggested that someone was living here.

"The clock's ticking," said Ruby nervously.

"Who'd light an oil lamp in an empty house?" asked Saul with a knotted brow.

"Indeed. Who'd do a thing like that?" said a hoarse blunt voice behind them.

~ 3 ~

The Council

Saul, Ruby, and Henry turned around sharply and froze in horror. A bald ragged looking man stood at the doorway. A black patch covered one eye. His eyebrows were lowered disapprovingly.

"Poking your nose in other peoples' business hey?" he grunted. "Well, we have ways of dealing with nosy rats. *Out!*" his harsh voice boomed off the mansion walls causing the children to shudder. *"Down the corridor. Move!"*

Saul's scattered brain tried to think quickly. Could they escape down the staircase? Would the one-eyed man catch up? He might catch one of them but not—

"You found them Junus," said the calmer voice of a tall slender dark-skinned man walking up the stairs. "I didn't expect children."

"Surprised me too Damian."

"What shall we do with them?"

"We'll have to hold them until we decide. *Are you deaf?"* grunted Junus turning to the children. "Down the corridor."

A steady murmur of conversation, probably coming from one of the side rooms, became louder as they walked into the darkness. At the end of the corridor, Damian trotted in front and opened a door. He gestured for them to enter. They walked into a dark room. A tall strong muscular man stood inside the door, his arms folded, resembling an executioner standing determinedly over his miserable task.

"Mills, scout the area and make sure there are no more." The tall man nodded and walked out.

It was a warm room beautifully decorated with red velvet wallpaper. Articulate coving met the ceiling all around and a beautiful chandelier hung at the centre of the ceiling. Warm flames danced wildly in a fireplace at the centre of the room casting long shadows around the room.

A strange group of characters sat on sofas and armchairs around the fireplace. It was too dark to see them properly, but the children noticed seven men and three women eyeing them suspiciously as they walked in.

The light of the fire flickered eerily over their strange faces. There was something *not right* about them, thought Saul. Their clothing was strange and some of them looked as if they had walked out of a Victorian play. A few of them wore cloaks like Rufus and all three ladies wore shawls. But it was not this that had caught Saul's attention.

"These… brats," began Junus, "were wandering around in the lamp room." An unsteady murmuring filled the room.

"Quiet," said the soft voice of a bald man sitting in an armchair close to the fire. He wore thin round glasses which sat below a thoughtful wrinkled brow. "Who are you?"

"I…" Saul gulped nervously, "I'm Saul, this is Ruby and Henry."

"And you were in the room with the lamp?"

"Y…yes," said Saul nervously.

"Was the lamp turned on?"

Nobody answered for a moment.

"Yes sir," replied Ruby quickly before the man could ask again.

"You saw the light and it lit up the room?"

"Yes."

"Speak up girl and stop mumbling we can't hear you," said another lady with short hair. Her lips barely moved as she spoke.

"Yes!"

A wave of murmuring spread through the room.

"Something's gone wrong," muttered an elderly lady almost to herself. "Nobody else has ever seen it."

"Who sent you here?" asked the lady with short hair.

"Why have you come here?" added Junus amidst a crescendo of noise.

"N... nobody sent us," replied Henry nervously. "We saw the light from the lamp and became suspicious, we thought someone had broken in."

"We didn't mean to be nosy or anything," added Ruby.

"Well, it's too late *not to be nosy*," berated Junus.

"Please let us go, we won't say anything," pleaded Ruby.

"I don't think we can do that. You've heard and seen too much," said Junus.

"This is nonsense," said a familiar voice. The children gasped as Rufus walked in. "I know these children. They live near the cottage I've been staying in. They're not spies. I've been living opposite that boy's house for months," he pointed at Saul, "I would've realised that he's a spy by now wouldn't I?"

"If they're not spies, how did they see the lamp?" grunted Junus.

"I don't know. Maybe Ambrose Dunster can answer that," said Rufus impatiently.

"Rufus is right," said the bald man. "Let's not waste time with these children. We've got more important matters to attend to," he added to the relief of the children.

"Get off home," began Rufus, "but not a word about this to anybody, do you—"

"Ryder, they've heard too much," urged Junus turning towards the bald man. "They could jeopardise the plan."

Ruby was trembling and did not notice that Saul and Henry were right next to her, looking just as scared.

All the while, Saul was looking fixedly at each person in the room, particularly Ryder and the lady in white who were both sitting in front of the fire. There it was again, something uncannily strange about them, thought Saul. They all had pale faces and white hands.

"I… I can see through them," he muttered incomprehensibly.

Was the light of the fire playing tricks or could he really see through them? He looked around at each one, and realised frightfully, that each person in the room looked just like...

"Ghosts," muttered Ruby. Her eyes were wide open. "They're… ghosts," she added almost choking on her words.

Ruby was right. The light was not playing tricks, and as the children glared at Junus and the lady in white standing in front of the fire, they saw the wild flames right through their bodies. Saul turned to look at Ryder sitting in the chair near the fire. Was that the back of the leather chair he could see through Ryder's chest?

The realisation that they had been talking to a group of ghosts, that one of them had been living in their village and that two of them were roaming the countryside around their village was too much to bear.

"They've seen and know too much," said Junus. "We can't just let them go home. They'll start talking."

"They could be agents of the dark lord," proposed the short-haired lady. "How else can they see the lamp?"

Dark lord? thought the children at the same time.

"Are you mad?" Rufus asserted.

Without realising it, Ruby and Henry had come into a huddle next to Saul.

"We have to make for it now," whispered Saul, his lips barely moving. "When I say, just turn around and run for it."

Henry nodded nervously but Ruby was a nervous wreck, she was trembling, and Saul worried she would not respond promptly.

"Did you hear me Ruby?" asked Saul putting a reassuring hand on Ruby's arm. Ruby nodded nervously.

"What are you suggesting Junus?" asked Ryder.

"They need to *forget*. Forget they came here, forget about Rufus... everything in fact."

"Memorixia? That's extreme. We don't use the—"

"Now!" cried Saul.

The children turned in unison and ran for the door.

"Stop them!" someone shouted.

For a moment it felt like one of his worst nightmares. He was desperate to run, but his legs would not move fast enough.

There was pandemonium in the room as the ghosts tried to catch the children. Chairs were thrown back and two of the ghosts tried to head off their exit. A moment later, the children were in the corridor leaving behind a chaotic commotion.

The children jumped down the staircase two steps at a time. As they turned to run down the last section, they were horrified to see Mills standing menacingly at the bottom of the stairs. They turned sharply to run back up but saw Junus Palfrey standing threateningly at the top. Instantly they tore up the opposite staircase into the opposite corridor. Saul prayed that one of the rooms in the corridor had a window that opened, maybe they could jump out and chance it. Strangely, he noticed, the corridor seemed to be covered in a soft barely visible mist that ran up towards the ceiling.

"No don't!" screamed a voice.

BANG!

There was a flash of light. They felt an agonising pain that felt like a lightning bolt had torn through them. They were jolted from side to side, and then felt they were drowning and choking into the depths of an ocean. All the while they felt paralysed, unable to move, breathe or scream. It had been a frightening, terrifying, deathly experience.

Then they landed on the floor writhing in pain and agony.

~ 4 ~

Another World

Saul, Ruby, and Henry lay curled up, clutching their chests and groaning with pain. They were breathing uncontrollably. Their hearts were beating frantically. They were overwhelmed by a terrible feeling of shock, dizziness, and nausea, in too much pain to move or talk.

After a while, Henry opened his eyes wearily. He saw Saul and Ruby lying on the floor next to him, both clutching their chests and groaning quietly. Saul was curled up in a ball, his mouth wide open in agony. Ruby was grimacing in pain, tears trickled softly down the side of her face. Henry felt a strange surge of relief realising that they were there with him, and most importantly, were alive.

It took a while for the paralysing feeling to recede. Steadily, Henry opened and closed his hand. Saul stretched his legs. He took slow and controlled deep breaths. A while later, Saul got up, but his legs felt like jelly and he nearly fell with dizziness.

Where were the ghosts he wondered?

"Henry... Ruby…" he began hoarsely, "we're … we're not in the mansion," he added looking worriedly around him.

"This isn't right," Ruby muttered deliriously, holding her head with both hands. Nothing that had happened so far, not the realisation that the figures in the mansion were ghosts, nor the horrible feeling of paralysis or even the hellish jolting and sinking, could have prepared them for the shock they now faced.

They were not standing on a hard carpeted floor in a cold dark mansion. Instead, they were on rough mossy ground in a strange unwelcoming forest. Tall thick trees and strangely coloured bushes surrounded them. The atmosphere was not cold, dark, and dank, but warm and humid. A strange strong *foresty* smell filled the air, one which they had experienced occasionally on a hot day in the forest of Edgings Burrow.

Suddenly a loud deep crowing sound shot out above them. The forest was coming alive with a plethora of unfriendly, loud, and confusing sounds. Another crowing sound responded behind them followed by a horrendous screeching to their left. Now they were surrounded by a cacophony of tweets, whistles, screeches, and croaks. Without realising it, the children crept closer together and stood in a frozen frightened huddle.

Saul, Ruby, and Henry looked around the forest to discover the source of each noise. The tweets and whistles were beautiful and welcoming, but the screeches and croaks, accompanied by a rustling sound in a nearby bush or a tree were disconcerting.

"I want to go home," sobbed Ruby quietly.

Henry reached out and put his arm around her to console her. His lips were pursed together tightly.

"Where are we?" Ruby asked.

"What happened?" asked Henry.

"I'm not sure. We ran across the balcony into the corridor. There was that grey mist, and then the flash," replied Saul looking up into the trees to find the source of an unnerving screeching sound. "And then that drowning feeling."

"I want to go home," said Ruby again, she was shaking softly.

"Let's rest here until we can figure something out," suggested Saul looking around carefully and gesturing for Henry to sit down.

Time passed, and steadily they became more comfortable with their surroundings. The threatening world around them became more friendly. Ruby nudged Saul and Henry and gestured towards a large black crow-like bird which croaked loudly and flew down with a flutter onto a bush. The bird surveyed the space around it, pointed its long beak in every direction, before flying off with another deafening croak. A green squirrel-like creature with a long tail and an almost equally long neck scurried out of the bushes. It reached up to some berries before scurrying away.

A while passed. The forest became dark and eerie. The sounds around them changed and the high-pitched tweets gave way to lower-pitched croaks and screeches.

"Hand over your bags and empty your pockets," said a loud voice. Ruby screamed and all three children jumped to their feet.

Nobody had noticed three men creep up to them. One of them was pale-faced, lanky, and skinny with hard determined features. The second man was black, bald, and bearded, he seemed big enough to pick all three up with one hand. Two thick chains sat around his neck, a ring was nestled on each finger. The third man had a dark complexion, a stubble, and eyebrows that seemed to meet between his brow. He pointed a sword at Ruby.

"Are you deaf?" asked the bald man. "Your bags and your pockets."

Instinctively, Saul turned and ran in the opposite direction. Ruby and Henry tore after him. Moments later, they were ducking and diving through bushes, around trees and under branches. It was a desperate run, each one of them feeling increasingly tired and breathless.

Suddenly there was a huge bang!

"Just keep running!" shrieked Ruby.

Saul turned to see what was following him. He caught a brief glimpse of three figures.

"Oww!" Saul had hit a heavy branch in front of him as he turned around and fell flat on the floor. *"Don't stop!"* he shouted clambering to his feet.

Suddenly Henry cried out loudly. He had been grabbed from behind and was pushed down onto the mossy floor. A moment later, Ruby was down, and before Saul knew it, his hands were grabbed from behind him.

"Got you!" shouted a familiar voice.

"We've found them!" shouted another.

"Where are we?" asked a third familiar voice amidst what was becoming a tangled mix of shouting and calling.

"I don't know but let's set up camp here," began the familiarly calm voice of Ryder, "we'll find out where we are tomorrow morning."

"Who's got the camping equipment?" asked someone.

"Over here."

Two people busied themselves with a huge bag while another started a fire. A hive of activity surrounded the children as the space that was once the forest steadily turned into a camp.

"You've got into a right old fix haven't you?" said the unhelpful voice of Junus Palfrey as he lifted Henry to his feet. "I'm gonna let go of you but don't you try to run on me. You're not in Edgings Burrow now. Ain't no point running, there's nowhere to go. Do you understand?"

Henry murmured an agreement.

"The same goes for the rest of you, there's nowhere to run. It's dangerous out there and you have to stay with us," continued Junus. "Let them go."

The three children huddled closer together and watched the activity around them in shocked disbelief. The ghosts they had tried to escape from, were busying themselves setting up a camp.

"Now that was stupid," said Damian sternly as he walked up to them. "Why did you have to do something silly like that?"

"S... silly like what?" asked Saul quietly.

"Walk through the portal of course, how will we—"

"Where are they?" queried the frantic voice of Rufus.

"We've tied them up and—"

"Not them, the children."

"They're fine, don't worry we—"

"Thank goodness you're safe," Rufus sighed running up to the children.

"Doe Festers is setting up a tent," Ryder announced. "Take them to it when it's ready. And for goodness sake don't let them out of your sight."

Mills walked up with a few stools. "Wait here until the tent is set up."

The children were surrounded by an organised tangle of busy activities. Lamps were lighting up, travel bags were being piled up by a clump of trees, and people were walking around busily.

"Have you noticed we can't see through them now?" asked Henry quietly.

"Yes," replied Saul.

"Maybe our eyes were playing tricks on us," suggested Ruby.

"We all saw it," asserted Saul.

The children thought about this for a while. They looked around, squinted their eyes but could not see through the figures around them.

"Where are we Rufus?" asked Saul after a while.

"In another world," announced Rufus.

"Another world?" asked Saul and Henry at the same time.

"Yes, this'll be quite difficult," He moved his stool a bit closer to the three children. "It's like this. You accidentally passed through a portal, which was opened for us to return to our world, that's this world. But you got through ahead of us."

"Portal?" queried Saul.

"Was that the white foggy misty thing in the corridor?" asked Ruby.

"Right."

"That's crazy. How's that even possible?" quizzed Henry.

"Well look around you," said Rufus firmly. "You're not in Edgings Burrow. All you need to know is that you're safe. Nobody here will harm you and—"

"Wow!" exclaimed Henry suddenly, nearly falling off his stool. Rufus, Saul, and Ruby turned suddenly. "How… how's he doing that?" he asked, his mouth wide open.

Doe Festers had curly dark blond hair, a round face and small eyes. He was dressed in a red velvet coat and wore a colourful striped jumper, with an equally colourful scarf around his neck.

To the children, he looked like a maverick showman, perhaps better placed in a funfair. But it was not his eccentricity that had caught Henry's attention.

Doe Festers was standing upright and waving his hands in the air slowly from one side to the other. As he did this, a white tarpaulin sheet raised itself magically into the air up to the leaves of a tree and then landed softly on a set of poles in the ground. A moment later, the empty space had become a tent, leaving the three children completely speechless.

"That's the other thing I need to explain," began Rufus hesitantly. "The err... easy answer is that we're sorcerers."

"Sorcerers?" asked the three children almost at once.

"You mean like *magicians*?" asked Saul.

"No not magicians. Magicians can't do real magic, magicians play simple tricks, but sorcerers are born with special powers, I mean *real* powers," Rufus noticed they were getting even more confused now.

"You mean that Ryder, Mills and all those people are sorcerers, I mean they have… powers?" quizzed Ruby raising her eyebrows. Her eyes were fixed on Doe Festers setting up another tent further away.

"And... are you ghosts?" Saul asked nervously. "I mean when you were in *our world*—"

"The Upperworld," interrupted Rufus.

"Upperworld?" asked Saul. "Err, right the *Upperworld*, you looked like… well *ghosts*, but you seem… fine now," the words came out without Saul realising what he was saying, he had a habit of doing that.

Rufus smiled. "We're not ghosts. The reason we looked a bit *strange* in the mansion is that our bodies aren't adapted to conditions in your world, we often have unpredictable reactions. Most of us just fade like ghosts," he said. "In my case, my iris becomes a pale white colour. That's why I always wore my glasses. Over time we adapt, and you wouldn't be able to tell the difference."

"Your tent is the second one on the right there," interrupted a voice. They turned around to see Doe Festers standing behind them pulling a set of poles out of a bag.

The tent was laid out tidily. It was warm and well-lit by a set of large candles which flared up wildly around a surprisingly large space. Four makeshift beds lay invitingly on the floor. The children surveyed the space before dropping their school bags and coats on the floor and settling down tiredly on the bed.

"You must be hungry," An elderly thin lady with shoulder-length grey hair walked in carrying a tray of food. "I'm Althea Gimble," she added, placing the tray on a small table. "Some bread, soup, and juice. We haven't had a chance to cook anything fanciful yet."

"Thank you," said all three children almost at the same time.

"Get comfortable. Find me if you need anything," Althea stopped at the exit and turned around. "Oh, and one more thing. Given your earlier experience in the forest, I'm sure you don't need reminding that the forest is a dangerous place. Don't leave the tent please."

As they ate, they experienced a strange combination of relief and anxiety.

"The way I see it," whispered Saul eating his bread. "If they'd wanted to harm us, they would've done it by now."

"I know but I don't see why we can't just go home," said Henry. "Can't we just go to that spot in the forest and… I don't know *magic* our way back or something?"

"It probably doesn't matter whether we go tonight or tomorrow. Whenever it happens, we're in deep trouble," said Saul quietly.

"We'll be grounded for a year," murmured Ruby in agreement.

The thought made them feel anxious. For a while longer, the children sat and watched busy shadows walk past the tent. Doe Festers returned to light more candles, a beautiful warm glow spread through the tent. The wild sounds of the forest and busy voices filled the air around the tent, and the fire cast a mesmerising warm glow in the tent as it flickered and flared away.

*

Saul, Ruby, and Henry were awoken by a steady hubbub of chatty conversations, the clanking of metal pots, and the rustling noises of people moving around.

Henry opened his eyes, closed them again and then reopened them, realising firmly that yesterday's events were not a dream. Eventually, the children dragged themselves out of bed and made their way nervously out of the tent.

The camp was hectic. People moved around busily. Althea Gimble prepared the food while the short-haired lady, who seemed to refer to them only as *boy* or *girl*, organised the table.

"Good morning," she said abruptly. Her manner reminded the children of a strict headmistress. "Come. Sit."

"I'm Mistie Herma," she announced sharply. "And you are?"

"Saul."

"Ruby."

"Err… Henry."

"*Errhenry?* That's a name, is it?" Mistie asked rhetorically, her lips barely moving as she spoke.

"Henry," came the response more assertively.

Breakfast was served and a secretive murmuring of conversation surrounded the table.

"Winfred, Stergo, and Kayla have tightened their grip over Petonia," began someone. "They're ruling it with an iron fist. There are famines in part of Petonia, hundreds and thousands are still homeless."

"It's all brewing up to another war if you ask me."

"Is the master really alive?"

"The Dark Lord is building an army."

"And may he fail miserably," said Rufus walking up to the table and seating himself next to Ruby.

The children ate their breakfast nervously.

"How do we get back home?" asked Saul quietly after a few moments.

"Well sending you back isn't quite straightforward."

"Why not?" asked Henry rudely. "We didn't want to be here."

"It's not that we don't want to get you back home," began Rufus, "it's just that getting you home isn't easy." The confused looks on their faces prompted him to continue. "You got here through a portal which was opened to get us, the Council, back into the Netherworld, that's this world. That *misty space* on the balcony was a portal.

"That portal got you into the Netherworld, but we can't use the same portal to get you back. We have to find one that opens into your world.

"A portal is a gateway, a secret passage between the Netherworld and the Upperworld. We've been using them for centuries. We go through a portal into your world. Sometimes we can come back through the same portal. Otherwise, we have to come back through a different portal."

All around them people were either seating themselves or moving away from the table. A steady murmur was broken now and again with the clunking of pots and pans.

"The only person who can open a portal is Ambrose Dunster. Unfortunately, he's gone to the Upperworld to close the portal that Arak has been using. Ambrose wants to be sure Arak and Trenton get back to the Netherworld. They're dangerous, we can't have them roaming around your world."

"But there's a *portal* nearby somewhere right?" asked Henry anxiously.

"Not that we know of," replied Althea Gimble coming into the conversation. "We don't know where the nearest one is, only Ambrose can find one, and if he can't then he has to open one."

"Portals are a strange phenomenon," continued Althea. "Occasionally portals just materialise for no apparent reason, nobody knows how or where one might open up. The worrying thing is that you shouldn't have been able to walk through the portal, people from your world shouldn't see them let alone walk through them.

"Portals have a time limit, sometimes an hour, sometimes a day, and quite often we just don't know what the time limit is."

"But what's really worrying," said Rufus. "Is whether Arak has found someone who can open portals into the Upperworld. The ramifications of that are unthinkable. He's a terrible piece of work you know." Saul pulled his lips together in agreement.

"And nobody else can open a portal?" asked Ruby.

"No," replied Rufus. "Ambrose Dunster is the only person we know that can open portals and control their parameters."

"Parameters?" asked Ruby.

"Yes, the precise time that one enters your world, how long the portal is open for and where it opens," Rufus replied.

The children pondered this for a few moments as the table slowly cleared around them.

"Hold on," said Ruby excitedly. "Do you mean Ambrose can get us home just before we left?"

"Of course," replied Althea smiling. "Just in time for tea if you want."

Saul raised his eyebrows and Ruby smiled. If this were true, they would not get into trouble. Their predicament seemed quite straightforward, the sooner they could catch up with Ambrose Dunster the sooner they could get home.

"Don't worry, you're perfectly safe with us." Althea said reassuringly. "We want to get you home as soon as possible. Now eat up, we have to leave soon."

"Pinch me," murmured Saul a little while later.

"What?" asked Henry dreamily.

Ruby and Henry followed Saul's gaze to see Doe Festers bringing the tents together. His arm was stretched out in front of him, his palms faced upwards, and as he lifted his hands, the tarpaulin rose upwards from the poles. He brought his two hands together in a single slow clapping motion, the tarpaulin came together and then fell softly to the ground as he dropped his hands. He repeated this a few times, now bringing the poles out of the ground and then back down onto a pile at the edge of the forest.

Sometime later, Junus Palfrey approached the table and perched himself on the bench next to Ruby.

"Kirby Hall's a day from here," he said to Rufus. "We'll be there by the evening."

His presence made the children uncomfortable. Ruby noticed two thick gold rings on his left hand. The word *kill* was tattooed onto the knuckles.

"Once we get there," he continued gruffly, "we can figure out a way of getting rid of these brats."

"Ignore him," said Rufus apologetically. "He's a little rough around the edges but quite soft inside. Generally, he means no harm."

"Generally," murmured Ruby.

A little while later, there was a busy tangle of activity as the group gathered themselves and set off on the long walk through the thick forest. Steadily, the group headed through the dense forest.

*

An hour passed away without the children realising how long they had been walking. The forest became thinner, the trees were wider apart, and the bushes were thinning out.

Ruby nudged Henry excitedly and pointed up at the trees. In all the tumultuousness of the day before, they had not noticed that the leaves on many of the trees were blue, and as the branches reached further upwards, they became purple. All around them beautiful birds chirped, tweeted, and flew between the trees.

They emerged from the forest and were met with a breathtaking landscape. Far in the distance, and in every direction as far as the eye could see, there sat a wonderful hilly terrain, brightly covered with large pockets of orange, purple, and blue. The hills rose, fell, and blended mesmerizingly into the horizon.

Henry stopped suddenly and stood wide-mouthed, looking up at the sky. Above them, three suns shone gloriously in the deep blue sky. One of the three suns was like the orange sun of the Upperworld. The second sun was much redder and larger, and a third green, much smaller sun, sat to the far right of these.

"Solarius, Surius, and Senerius," obliged Ryder. "Solarius is the big bright sun, a bit like the sun in your world. Surius is the red sun and Senerius the blue one."

"Looks green to me."

"If you look at it long enough, which you shouldn't of course, you'll see it's blue," suggested Ryder. "I think you'll be quite stunned by the six moons."

"Six… moons?" gasped Saul.

"Yes. We'd better catch up," said Ryder noticing that the rest of the party had moved further ahead. "There's a lot of ground to make up and no time to marvel at the scenery I'm afraid."

They had taken well to Ryder. His composed persona and soft manner was warm, friendly and welcoming.

"Excuse me sir, but what's Kirby Hall?" asked Saul.

"Kirby Hall is an old mansion belonging to a dear friend," Ryder began softly. "It's in a beautiful hilly part of the Netherworld known as Turnton Walden. Whenever there's a crisis, we meet at Kirby Hall."

"Crisis?" queried Saul worriedly.

"Hmm, yes," replied Ryder gravely. "The Netherworld seems to be heading towards a terrible war. But you needn't worry about that, you'll be gone well before then."

"We're answering the call. That's an urgent message sent to the council when there's something critical and important to the Netherworld.

"Do they know what this *call* is for, I mean what they've been called for?" asked Saul.

"For twelve years, our leader Rabin was presumed to be dead. The rumour is that Rabin was imprisoned all that time and that he's escaped," Ryder said this with an infectious smile on his face.

"He's asked the council to meet at Kirby Hall. It's a bit tricky though. Many of us haven't met in thirteen years and many of the council don't believe he's alive. No doubt we'll find out when we reach Kirby Hall."

~ 5 ~

Kirby Hall

The strange and wondrous sights and sounds of the journey kept Saul, Ruby, and Henry so energised and excited that nobody noticed it getting dark. Surius and Senerius had disappeared inconspicuously, and Solarius, the largest of the three suns, was setting lazily over the horizon.

The light faded and some of the sorcerers banged their staffs onto the ground, instantly a steady glow spread out from the top. The glow grew brighter, and soon the journey ahead of them was illuminated perfectly. The children watched on in wonderment, now and again looking up at the end of a staff to find the source of the light.

The shadows around them drew longer, and the landscape and wildlife that came with it changed quite curiously. The beautiful bright purple, orange and blue shrubbery and flowers around them were duller now, and the cheery tweets of birds gave way to the sporadic squawks and screeches of the previous night.

A flock of wide-winged birds floated towards them in the distance. They squawked with a low guttural sound causing Saul, Ruby, and Henry to look up nervously.

"Deirons," announced Doe Festers.

"Are they dangerous?" asked Ruby looking up nervously.

"No. They're scavengers. A bit like vultures in your world," said Doe. "Scavengers never attack living prey."

Despite Doe Festers' assurances, the children looked up anxiously now and again and continued to do so until the deirons disappeared into the distance.

"Here we are," announced Althea Gimble suddenly. "A bit later than I'd hoped, but at least we're here in one piece."

Ahead of them lay a white pebbled path lit up on either side by bright lamps sitting on the end of poles. The path led up to a beautiful brightly lit white building.

The building was surrounded by a beautiful garden. Numerous stone clad windows lined the walls of the building and a grand entrance greeted the travellers.

They were led through a set of huge oak doors into a magnificent busy lobby. A handful of people rushed towards them excitedly, and momentarily, the lobby was awash with small groups busily greeting each other with cordial handshakes and hugs.

"Welcome to Kirby Hall my friends," called a tall blond-haired man from inside the hall.

"My dear Conrad," responded Ryder taking Conrad's arms and embracing him.

"You haven't changed in the slightest my dear," said someone.

"Oh, we really should have made more effort."

"Isn't it remarkable that the great master is alive and well?"

"Is it true? Is he alive or is it just another rumour? Listen, have you actually seen him?"

"Yes, he is. No, I haven't seen him, but he'll be here tomorrow night. Well at least I've heard he'll be here. Can you believe it? Never in my wildest dreams."

"Did you hear about the escape? Only the great master could have enacted something like that."

The children became overawed and felt lost amidst the hubbub of activity. Steadily, they edged away to the side of the lobby.

Henry nudged Saul and gestured to a staircase at the centre of the hallway. A small scruffy boy, probably about their age, sat quietly on a step. He had oriental features. His hair was roughly cut, and he wore a black shirt and a loose pair of trousers. Henry walked over to him.

"Hello," said Henry in a quiet friendly tone.

The boy looked up and nodded.

"I'm Henry."

"Jordan," replied the boy looking down at his hands.

Saul and Ruby edged over and introduced themselves.

"Busy isn't it?" asked Henry trying desperately to strike a conversation.

Jordan nodded softly.

"Are you from around here?" asked Ruby.

Jordan shook his head. "No. Nickle Mansley."

"Is that nearby?"

Jordan shook his head. Had he been here long? He shook his head. Did he know many people here? A few. And so it went for a little while before Henry sighed quietly and gave up. Jordan was hard work, and it was difficult holding a conversation with someone who only responded with a yes, no, a nod, or a shake of the head.

"We seem to have forgotten about you," said Althea apologetically as she walked towards them. "We have a room for you and some fresh clothes," she added gesturing for them to follow her. "You too," she added turning around at Jordan. "You can sleep in the room when you're not working at the stables Jordan."

"Stable boy. I could've guessed," muttered Henry under his breath. "Ouch!" he added as he felt Ruby's shoe at the back of his shin.

Althea led them up the stairs, through a bright long corridor into a beautiful spacious living room. The room was comfortably laid out with two sofas and an armchair, set out welcomingly in the middle. Two bedrooms led off the living room each with two beds and a separate washroom.

"There's a change of clothing in the wardrobes. Dinner is served in an hour, don't be late," she added before walking out.

It did not take long for the children to settle in. Henry had agreed grudgingly to share a bedroom with Jordan. He had not fancied the prospect of muted conversations, but by the time he and Jordan had organised themselves in the bedroom, Jordan was steadily emerging from his shell. Now and again, Henry saw a soft smile and a look of excitement on Jordan's face. Occasionally, Jordan's responses extended beyond a frozen *yes* or *no.*

"Are you alone?" asked Henry after a little while.

"No, my father's with me. He's in the stables," replied Jordan. "What about you?"

"We're alone." This was the easiest answer. Later on, perhaps tomorrow, they might explain the extraordinary sequence of events that had led them here. "Did you arrive today?"

"Yes."

"What does your father do in the stables?"

"He looks after the krays and—"

"Henry, Jordan, look at this!" exclaimed Ruby excitedly from the living room.

Henry and Jordan scurried to the living room and found Ruby and Saul sitting on a balcony overlooking the gardens.

An enchanting scene greeted them. The gardens were beautifully lit up in warm colourful lights. A plethora of busy activity flowed through the garden, and an assiduous conversational hum filled the air. In the background, sporadic lights were scattered against the countryside as tiny twinkling lights marked out the distant villages.

But perhaps most breathtaking of all was the glorious night sky. Six moons, each one a slightly different colour, sat warmly in the sky against an array of twinkling stars.

*

Dinner was a magnificent affair. The grand dining room was warmly decorated. Dozens of candles sat in an elaborate candle holder at each table, collectively lighting up the hall warmly and filling the air with a strangely spooky aura.

A conversational hum and an air of nostalgic sentiment filled the room. Many of the people had not met for thirteen years, and for most of them, this was the *fortuitous* reunion they thought would never happen.

"This way children!" invited Damian who seemed to appear from nowhere. He led them to four seats at the front of the hall.

Dinner was served, and an array of starters, were followed by a temptingly wide selection of mains, and then a spoiling choice of desserts.

When dinner was finally over, a continual musical tone tickled the air. The sound came from the garden.

"The druidic quartet," helped Jordan leading them out into the garden. "They're really good."

Bright lamps graced the edges of the garden and warm sparkles rose up magically from the flowery trees. Three women and a giant bearded man sat on a platform at the edge of the garden playing a set of strange stringed instruments, unlike anything the children had seen before. The man bowed a long thin cello-like instrument. His left arm stretched up to reach some of the notes and his head bobbed from side to side to the rhythm of the music.

Two of the ladies played a huge harp-like instrument, much taller and with many more strings than a normal harp. As they plucked each string, a vibrating musical drone spread through the air sending a shiver through the body of everyone in the audience. A warm feeling filled their hearts and a soft smile spread across their faces. Then, one of the ladies began to sing a splendid, beautiful, and uplifting song. Her voice carried itself through the night sky and mesmerised Saul, Ruby, and Henry who stood listening with a dreamy look on their faces.

*

"We can't just sit in the bedroom all day," began Saul the following morning. It felt as though half the day had already passed by the time they woke up. Glorious sunlight drooped into the bedrooms making the children feel tired and lazy.

"Let's explore the Orange Forest and go down to Kirby Lake," suggested Jordan. "And if we have time, we should go to Turnton Valley, the views from there are spectacular."

"The Orange Forest?" queried Saul.

"You can see it from the balcony," helped Henry. "It looks fantastic."

Kirby Hall sat at the peak of a large hill. On one side a thick dense orange-leaved forest spread itself for miles, and on the other, lay swathes of open land marked with splendid thickets of greenery, flowers, and shrubs. In the distance sat Kirby Lake, twinkling invitingly whenever any of the three suns beamed down on it.

The children went over a crisscross of streams and reached the forest, densely packed with massive thickets of bright orange-leaved trees and darker orange bushes.

Later, the children sat lazily on the bank of Kirby Lake for over an hour, kicking the water now and again, still struggling to comprehend the wonders of the netherworld. The feeling of the water patting against their legs was strangely therapeutic.

"W... what was that?" Henry jumped away from the water in a panic and stood eyeing the lake carrying a dumbfounded expression.

"What was what?" asked Saul lazily.

"Something just swam past. Look, there's something in the water."

A hundred yards into the lake, a large black shape was moving steadily closer towards the bank. Suddenly, a long slimy snake-like creature, five times the thickness of a tree trunk, swam across just beneath the surface. Saul and Ruby dragged themselves backwards in a frightened panic and moved away from the lake to join Henry at the edge of the bank.

"A kherk," announced Jordan nonchalantly.

The children stood watching the black shape swim across the bank. Suddenly there was a splash.

"What are you doing?" cried Ruby emphatically.

Jordan had jumped into the lake and was swimming quickly towards the kherk.

"Jordan!" screamed Ruby. "Get something to pull him out!"

It was too late. Jordan was too far for anybody to reach him.

"Oh no," murmured Ruby helplessly as the slithery figure of the kherk moved closer to him.

Henry gasped suddenly, *"Bloody he—"*

"Jordan!" screamed Ruby.

"It's… it's pulled him down," muttered Saul deliriously. In an instant, Jordan had vanished leaving a frantic ripple of water behind him.

"We have to do something," began Henry, "I don't know what but—"

"Shall I go in and find him?" asked Saul. "We can't just stand here, he's—"

The children gasped as the water erupted to reveal a large black serpent-like head shooting upwards out of the water. Two dark eyes looked out towards them, and a thin mouth opened softly to reveal a line of thin teeth. Most remarkable, however, was the sight of Jordan perched behind the head of the great beast, his arms wrapped tightly around the kherk just below the head. A beaming smile across his face.

"It's a bit like an overgrown snake. It looks scary, but it's very friendly and wonderful to play with!" Jordan screamed in a strange gargled voice before disappearing back into the water.

Moments later, the kherk shot upwards again. *"Come in, it won't hurt!"* screamed Jordan before disappearing again.

"Saul!" cried Ruby and Henry together. To their horror, Saul had jumped in and was swimming away from the bank.

"Saul, get back here now!" screamed Ruby. "Henry! Get some help!"

"What do I—?"

"I don't know, use your brain for once, go and get Rufus or someone!"

"Do you even know how far Kirby Hall is?" asked Henry looking up at the top of the hill. "It'll take an hour there and back."

Saul swam away slowly through the refreshingly cool water. Suddenly he stopped. What a ridiculous idea, he told himself.

What had he been thinking? *I must get back.*

As Saul turned back to the shore, he saw a soft commotion in the distance behind him. He looked back around and nearly screamed at the sight of the black slimy scaly figure of the kherk moving steadily towards him, its huge tail swishing gently from side to side behind it. It looked frightening! The kherk edged closer, and now Saul could see its huge wide head tearing through the water. The beast was much larger than it seemed at the shore.

Saul was frightened. Horrified. He could not believe what he had done. He swam frantically towards the shore, all the while consoling himself with Jordan's words, *it looks scary, but it's very friendly.* Behind him, Saul heard the sound of parting water.

Stay calm Saul. Just… stay... calm, he repeated to himself. His heart was beating frantically, his arms splashing through the water wildly. *Just… stay... calm.*

He desperately wanted to turn around to see how far the kherk was but dared not. Suddenly, the water pushed against him and shunted him sideways. Saul jerked as the frightening slithery figure of the beast swam underneath him and ahead of him. Saul would rather it was still behind him than filling the expanse in front. A moment later, it vanished leaving nothing but clear water.

Now's my chance, he thought swimming harder than ever.

"It's fine!" he cried looking up out of the water towards Ruby, Henry, and Jordan. *"I'm alright!"*

Once more he felt a powerful wave of water push against his body, and once again, he saw the terrifying figure of the kherk slide past his body, this time so close, he could have reached out. In that instant, a strange relief filled Saul. The kherk did not harm him. It did not scratch, bite or attack him. It probably could have, but it didn't.

Ruby and Henry stood in the near distance watching on incredulously. *"Come out Saul!"* Saul heard Ruby screaming. *"Grab this!"* she added. Henry raised his eyebrows as he watched Ruby waving a feeble branch around in front of her.

Saul was a hundred yards from the shore when he felt the familiar wave of water pushing against his body. Saul kept surprisingly calm. He saw the dark slithery figure of the kherk swimming towards him. Again, it slipped past him. Saul stretched out his arm just in time to feel the scaly body of the beast as it swam past. An indescribable warm feeling surged through Saul's body. But as soon as the kherk had passed, Saul shivered gently as he felt the cold water around him.

Saul changed his mind, he would not swim to the shore, but would *stroke* the kherk a few more times before heading out of the lake.

The kherk came closer. It slid past, turned in a circle underneath Saul, came back up towards him, and before he knew it, the kherk's head was underneath Saul. For a long time afterwards, Saul did not know why he did what he did next. He pushed both arms forward, put them around the creature's head and held tightly. Again, that strange warm feeling surged through his body. But then, to Saul's horror, the kherk swam downwards at a dizzying pace. Saul panicked, he had to let go! He had to swim back to the roof of the lake. But for some unknown reason, he could not bring himself to let go.

The kherk went down deeper and deeper into the lake. Saul had left it too late. He could not hold his breath any longer. It was now or never, he had to let go and swim back up. But how far was the roof of the lake?

Saul coughed desperately. Instantly, water filled his lungs! He was horrified. He *had* to get to the top of the lake.

But what was this? He should have been choking but he wasn't. He was not struggling to breathe. Instead, the water felt warm and soothing inside him. Saul exhaled the water out. This felt strange. Saul sucked in some water and a moment later exhaled it out again.

He was breathing water!

Saul was so preoccupied with the strange sensation he did not notice that the kherk was shooting upwards. Suddenly, Saul felt the water break above him as warm air hit his face. An instant later, the kherk shot back into the water. Saul was living and breathing water again. He looked around him to see bright clear blue water all around.

There's something magical about this lake, thought Saul. How else could he possibly explain what was happening? The kherk swam down deeper into the lake, turning this way and that and occasionally tearing through the water at an exhilarating pace.

I have to get back up, thought Saul. Suddenly he felt a jerking sensation as the kherk changed direction and moved upwards through the water.

Did I just do that? To the left, he thought, the kherk moved left. Saul was stunned. To the right, it moved right. Down, up, left, right, up, slow, fast.

Saul lost track of time. He had rarely had so much fun in his life. He could do this all day, regretfully, he had to go back.

Finally, Saul let go of the kherk but realised immediately that this was a mistake. He should have guided the kherk to the top of the lake. No sooner had he let go than he felt he was drowning. Now the water did not feel warm, instead, it seemed to freeze in his lungs. He felt a horrible choking feeling as he coughed out the water. Saul swam towards the roof of the lake in a panicked frenzy.

His head cropped out of the water. He coughed and spluttered out more water while swimming frantically to the shore. Once there, he dragged himself out and lay on his back coughing profusely.

"Saul!" screamed the voice of Ruby. *"Are you.?"*

"That..." Saul coughed. "Was absolutely… *cough*… brilliant."

He coughed a few more times and then sat up slowly. He was greeted by the sight of Ruby standing with her hands on hips carrying an angry look on her face.

"Brilliant?" asked Ruby rhetorically. "Do you know how worried we were? What on EARTH were you thinking?"

Saul coughed sporadically. "Listen—"

"You could've been killed, is that what you want?"

"List—"

"What would we say to your parents?"

"Listen. Just *listen!* The kherk isn't dangerous. I know it looks all frightening and beastly. I can't explain it. I mean… *cough!* I was holding onto it and I had this really strange feeling in my body … *cough!* I can't explain it, but... I could breathe underwater. Actually, breathe. Honestly—"

"If it likes you, the kherk bonds with you," said Jordan helpfully. "And then—"

"You can breathe right?"

"Yes. Did you guide it?"

"You mean like *tell* it where to go?"

"Yes."

"Yes, that was amazing. It was surreal and…" Saul stopped and turned back to Ruby and Henry. "Trust me Ruby, it wasn't dangerous, it was perfectly safe, you should… *cough*… try it."

The last few words came out without Saul realising what he was saying. When he saw Ruby's pursed lips, the narrowed eyes, and the knotted brow he realised instantly that he had gone too far.

"Really?" began Ruby in a terse tone. In that one instant, Saul admitted afterwards, he felt just as scared of Ruby as he had of the kherk.

"Oh. I should try it as well?"

Henry looked at Ruby and then Saul and then back at Ruby again wondering what would happen next, all the while expecting Ruby to quite simply explode.

"I meant—"

"We've just had the fright of our life Saul and all you can say is I should—"

"Guys! Break it up," interjected Henry. "Look it was a mistake. Saul, promise you won't do anything... err... *stupid* like that again."

Saul murmured something in tentative agreement.

There was a long silence. Nobody dared to speak. Jordan, not used to Ruby's occasional outbursts, dared not utter a breath.

"You need to have a bath," said Ruby eventually.

Saul and Jordan raised their eyebrows.

"I think it's the lake," helped Henry. "There's a strange *pungy* smell... we'll meet you in the garden."

~ 6 ~

Twins

After a quick bath, Saul and Jordan headed for the garden. They sped through a maze of corridors, each one looking the same as the one before it. As they approached the head of a staircase, Saul froze at the sound of an eerily familiar voice.

"I know that voice," he whispered. "That sounds like—"

"*Lying cretin!* You know a lot more than we give you credit for."

Saul put up his hand as Jordan came running behind him. The voice came from around the corner. Saul edged gently towards the voice. He pressed himself against the wall and peeked around carefully.

"One last time. What do you know about them?"

A shiver shot through Saul's spine as he saw Arak holding a small chubby bearded man by the scruff of his neck against the wall. He had a balding head with a short tuft of hair around the edges and a short stubby beard. The man had been lifted off his feet, he was trying frantically to reach the ground.

"I'd never betray our plans. I… I haven't met any searchers. You have to believe me," choked the frightened man.

"*Liar!* You'll tell me everything you know otherwise *your* little secret is out. Nobody knows how you got out of that prison, do they?"

"I... I escaped, fair and square, there's nothing to know."

"That's not quite true, is it? You had help and–"

"Th… that man," muttered Saul quietly. "He's the one that visited Rufus with… *what's-his-name…* Trenton."

"What are you talking about Saul, that's—"

"Quick, follow me," Saul tore off back down the corridor and then down the main staircase into the lobby. He charged through a small crowd, bumping wildly into two people, out of the front entrance, through the garden and then stopped sharply when he reached Ruby and Henry, both sitting quietly at the back of the garden.

"Arak!" he shouted breathlessly. *"He's here! Upstairs… We have to tell Rufus or someone!"*

"Saul are you sure?" asked Ruby, her eyes wide open in shock.

"Saul!" cried Jordan running into the garden.

"Yes! He was arguing with one of the—"

"Saul, listen to me," panted Jordan as he caught up.

"He was a short guy, I don't remember seeing him before, but Arak was threatening him, something about a *secret* or something. But if we're not quick—"

"Saul that wasn't Arak!" screamed Jordan. A couple of people looked around suddenly. "Stop… panicking," he said in a calmer voice. "I'll explain."

"Explain? What is there to—"

"Shut up and listen to me," said Jordan sharply. "Let's sit down somewhere quiet," he proposed looking around embarrasedly.

They walked to a bench at the far side of the garden.

"That wasn't Arak, it was—"

"What do you mean it wasn't Arak, I saw—"

"That wasn't Arak," said Jordan, nearly losing his temper, "it was Siraf, Arak's twin brother."

Saul, Ruby, and Henry stood looking at Jordan with eyes wide open in shock.

"His—" began Saul.

"His twin brother," repeated Jordan slowly. "Yes, they're twins. Siraf is one of us, the *good guys.* He's been with the council for years."

"But he looked just like—"

"Because they're identical twins, idiot!"

"Twins?" asked Saul, his mouth wide open.

"Yes."

"Are you sure?" I mean—"

"Of course I'm sure."

"So, let me get this right," helped Henry. "Arak is with the… well, *bad guys* and Siraf is good, he's with the council, right?"

"Right."

"Is he," began Saul trying to select his words carefully. "Well, a—"

"A vampire?" prompted Jordan raising his eyebrows. "Yes."

Ruby gasped, Saul and Henry opened their mouths in shock.

"A real vampire?" quizzed Henry.

"Yes, real," replied Jordan. "They're both vampires, Nordic vampires."

Saul, Ruby, and Henry were quiet for a moment as they tried to absorb this.

"*Nordic* vampires?" asked Saul.

"So he… drinks blood?" asked Ruby, before Jordan could respond.

"Err… yes, but it isn't as easy as that."

"What do you mean it isn't—"

"Well, unlike Dwarkan vampires, Nordic vampires can be weaned off drinking blood, Siraf doesn't drink human blood anymore. We're not sure about Arak though," replied Jordan casually.

"They're really vampires?" asked Ruby.

"Well, it could be worse," said Jordan almost jokingly.

"How could it possibly be worse?"

"Well at least they're not werewolves."

"You're taking the mick now," said Saul.

"Taking the mick?"

"Yes, you know, just joking right?"

"No. Haven't you ever seen a werewolf?"

"Of course we haven't seen a bloody—"

"Have Arak and Siraf always been vampires?" interjected Ruby throwing a disappointed look at Henry. "I mean were they born like that or were they… well, you know *converted* or something?"

"They were converted when they were children."

"Children?" gasped Ruby.

"Quite a sad story really," continued Jordan. "They've ended up on opposite sides and they're both always trying to get the other to join them. Let me explain…"

Arak and Siraf lived in a lonely forest with their parents. They were a nondescript family, living their lives rather peacefully, content with everything they had in life. That was until they heard rumours about 'the herd'. A group of Nordic vampires were terrorising villages many miles away. Every day the news became more worrying as they moved closer and closer to the forest. Now the family wondered whether they should leave for a city, at least until the herd passed by. But the father was adamant that the forest was too big, and anyway, the herd was more interested in villages because they had more humans, they would never bother a lonely home in a forest.

But one fateful night, the herd reached the forest, eventually arriving at their home. They killed the parents and attacked Arak and Siraf. It took a while for the transition into vampirism to complete, and when it did, their vampiric instinct led them to seek the *father herd*, the herd that had initiated them. It was a long journey, one which led them through many forests, villages, and towns. One day, they met a group of sorcerers who wanted to help them. The sorcerers began to wean the brothers off blood. It took a long time, but it was working.

But one night they had a terrible disagreement. They argued bitterly all night. Arak wanted to move on, but Siraf wanted to stay with the sorcerers. Arak left angrily in the morning. He never found the father tribe but instead became involved with the Gorans and spent the rest of his time as one of their many henchmen.

For a while longer, Jordan told Saul, Ruby, and Henry about the ways of the vampires, the horrible weaning process that Rabin had continued with Siraf to get him off human blood, and Siraf's incessant longing to reunite with his brother.

*

Saul and Jordan sat at the window looking out at the splendid countryside. Henry was asleep on the couch, and Ruby had disappeared to explore the halls.

At the foot of the hill, a small group of travellers appeared like a line of ants. Steadily they wound their way up the path. They were followed by a bigger party of eight or nine people, and within half an hour, around forty or fifty people had climbed up the hill towards Kirby Hall.

A hawk floated over the garden for a few moments before shooting upwards and away into the sky. In the distance, a herd of osseri, long-necked long-eared horse-like creatures, gathered around the lake giving out loud trombone-like calls as they drank water.

"What… is that?" gasped Saul.

A carriage climbed slowly up the windy path. Two men dressed in black cloaks sat at the front of the carriage, two rode a horse at either side and another two behind it, indicating that the carriage carried a very important passenger. But this was not what had grabbed Saul's attention.

Four black leathery six-legged creatures, much bigger than a horse and with a frightening long bony face, pulled the carriage up the hill. The animals grunted and puffed now and again revealing a set of sharp fangs.

"Steragon," offered Jordan.

"They're frightening… look… they... they have red eyes."

The clatter of hooves and wheels became louder as the carriage came closer. Soon it reached the top of the hill, passed by the balcony, with Saul and Jordan watching with bated breath, and disappeared inconspicuously around the back of the hall.

"That must have been Rabin," whispered Jordan in awe.

*

That evening, a long table was laid out on the stage. Seven chairs sat behind it and a grandiose throne-like chair was set in the middle.

"There's Siraf," muttered Henry unnervingly.

The tall thin frame of Siraf spoke busily to Damian at the far side of the room. Damian turned around searchingly. His gaze stopped at the children and pointed towards them. Siraf nodded, thanked Ryder frenetically before turning towards the front of the hall.

The children sat in frozen silence as Siraf came closer to them. He was a few yards away. He smiled, revealing his thin sharp teeth and sent a chill through their spines.

"You met my brother Arak," he began in the same hissing voice that his loathsome twin had announced himself with in Edgings Burrow.

"Yes," replied Ruby slowly.

"Was he well?"

"He was well… err, very healthy and… just very well I suppose."

"Did he return?"

"I don't know, I mean we're not sure, he—"

"Where did he go?"

"Huh?"

"When he left your world, where did he go?"

"I'm not sure where—"

"He's back," interrupted a sorcerer sitting at a table next to them.

"Do you know where he went?"

For a few moments, Siraf and the sorcerer were engaged in conversation. All the while, the children could not take their eyes off him. A distant lonely look filled his face. His face was fuller and redder than Arak and did not seem as white and frozen.

"Why is he so concerned about his brother?" whispered Henry a moment later. "He's on the bad side, isn't he? I mean I'd denounce my brother if I had one, and he turned over to the bad side."

"It's not that easy," replied Jordan. "He probably still cares for

Arak, maybe even misses him. Just because someone's on the other side it doesn't mean we have to hate them. Lots of families were torn apart by the war and some ended up on opposite sides. Anyway—"

"*Master!*" screamed a voice.

~ 7 ~

Rabin

The room erupted into a rapturous frenzy. Chairs were pushed back, everyone shot to their feet and turned sharply to the entrance of the hall. The sound was deafening. The atmosphere was maddening.

Henry nudged Ruby and gestured towards a lady wiping tears from her face as she clapped and cheered wildly. An elderly man stood a few yards away from them, his gaze transfixed on the entrance and his lips pursed tightly as he also struggled to hold back his tears and emotions. They were not alone. The whole room was consumed by a torrent of happy, joyous emotion brought about by the genuine realisation that their great leader, long presumed dead, was well and truly with them.

The children stretched out to see a short elderly bearded man walking into the great hall. He held a staff with one hand and Rufus' arm with the other. His squinting twinkling eyes were barely open as he walked along. His wrinkled face wore an infectious smile. A strong magical presence surrounded Rabin.

Ryder, Doe Festers, a short bald man, and a tall, elegant man followed slowly behind Rabin. The six guards that had arrived with the carriage, trailed behind them.

Now and again, Rabin nodded or raised his hand at someone to his left or right as he walked past them. Twice he stopped and turned to someone standing at the side, said a few words and continued his walk through the hall.

Now he was yards from the stage. As he walked past the children, they felt a tingle spread through their spines.

Presently, the great sorcerer climbed onto the stage, closely followed by his entourage. Ryder pulled back the chair, and Rufus took Rabin's staff and stood with it militarily at Rabin's side. The six guards stood watchfully at the back of the stage, not smiling, flinching, or showing any reaction to the emotional commotion.

Rabin stood behind the table; both his hands laid out flat on it. The beads on his right wrist straddled on the table and two rings on his left hand twinkled now and again in the light. Eventually, he raised his arms to acknowledge the rapturous applause and cheering that still boomed through the hall. He sat down, but the cheering did not stop.

Although the children did not know Rabin or fully appreciate the importance of the occasion, the mood was infectious, and they became drawn into the excitement. They began cheering loudly.

After a few moments, Rabin raised his hand, the room went quiet. He gestured for everybody to sit down. The atmosphere sunk into excited pin drop silence.

Everyone waited excitedly for Rabin's first words. He looked around the hall, seemingly recognising and quietly acknowledging the presence of each and every person in the hall. Presently, his gaze stopped at the four children perched nervously at the front of the room. Ruby took a sharp intake of breath, and Saul, Henry, and Jordan felt a surge of excitement flow through their bodies.

Rabin turned his gaze to the gathering of sorcerers. "My friends," he began in a hoarse tired voice. A collective thrill flooded the hall as the voice permeated through the hall.

"My friends," he repeated. "I never thought I would see you again. I spent twelve years in the dungeons of Warin. Steadily my will and sorceric powers were eroded. Day by day, the sorceric spirit edged away from me, and I became increasingly desperate to get out of that dungeon. Then through one last effort, I managed to expedite every last ounce of my sorceric energy, and through the ingenious efforts of Eisen Roth, Conrad, Nicholas Darby and Caleb, I was able to escape and be reunited with you."

"That's my dad," whispered Jordan pointing proudly at the tall man. "On the left," he added.

"Many of you have undergone arduous and dangerous journeys to get here. Some have even had to escape the clutches of death to get here." Rabin looked around searchingly. "More than once," he added with a smile, his gaze settling on a thin grey-cloaked sorcerer.

"That's the wizard Callius," helped Jordan.

"A wizard?" began Henry. "What's the difference between—"

"You're all anxious to know why we sent the call," continued Rabin. "These are troubled times my friends. We don't know who our allies or enemies are. We're steadily meandering towards the crossroads of another war. Continual agitation, plotting and squabbling have blinded Petonia and Goran. Neither side will see reason. Both nations are locking horns and positioning themselves against each other for what they believe will be *the war to end all wars.*

"But this will just be another endless war that solves nothing. How easily they've forgotten the savagery and suffering of the great war. This war will be deadlier than any the Netherworld has ever seen. Those dark days when nation was pitted against nation, when families were made homeless, and mothers lost their husbands and children will soon return."

The enthusiastic ambience of the room sunk from the heights of frenzied excitement into a sense of darkness, doom, and disaster. Worried looks spread across the faces of sorcerers around the room.

"A dark force has risen in Goran and is fanning these flames of hatred. Baron Von Valak has—" an outpour of murmuring and chatter suddenly spread through the hall. "Baron Von Valak," repeated Rabin above the noise, "wants to rule Petonia." The room went quiet. "It won't end there. Once he takes Petonia, he will move for the three southern continents and claim total rule over the Netherworld.

"He is preparing a huge army. He's building a battle fleet that will bring thousands of soldiers over the Black Ocean and he is building powerful and deadly weapons driven by the latest advances in alchemy.

"But there is hope. Two moons from now, Goran and Petonia will meet in the Palace of Petonia to negotiate another peace treaty. A treaty to rest all notions of war.

"We've gathered here to begin our preparations for the potential failure of those negotiations. Theran, sorcerer general of the Kerack army, and Grandon Smith, our chief commander and master searcher, will be formulating our plans. As many of you know, Theran led Petonia's campaign in Kerack, the last and only state that remained standing at the end of the war, and Grandon of course, needs no introduction."

A strong tall muscular man stood up as Rabin sat down. He bowed his head to Rabin and then the captivated audience. He wore a brown cloak and black boots and carried an imposing presence.

"In the last year of the war, Petonia had the upper hand," began Theran in a sharp authoritative voice. "My troops were preparing to drive out the enemy and win the war for Petonia.

"However, as you know, we were betrayed. During the purge, many of our friends were captured and imprisoned, many fled into hiding and many more were killed.

"The prisoners were too important for the Gorans. So important they were kept alive. Their captors hoped to gain their allegiance and learn something about our sorceric powers. Sadly, many of our friends made those traitorous alliances, either with the noblemen or with the Gorans.

"Our mission is to rescue those friends that still swear allegiance to the council. There aren't many sorcerers left in this world, but by jove, we'll save every one of them wherever we can." A huge cheer filled the room.

"We've discovered where most of our friends are being held, and we've narrowed our focus to five prisons. There are more, but these are a priority," Theran pulled down a large map on the wall behind them. Five large red dots, one green dot and four orange dots were marked around the map. An array of lines linked the dots together.

"We're going to form seven missions. Grandon Smith, our finest searcher, has planned the escapes," there was loud applause as a tall thin wide-mouthed thick moustached man stood up and bowed his head to Rabin and then the audience.

"Each mission will raid one of these locations on the first moon of Lunam-Pras, in the still of the night when the moon is highest," began Grandon in a booming army general like voice.

"Midnight," helped Jordan looking at Saul, Ruby, and Henry who looked lost. "I wish I could hear the rest of this but I'm late."

"Late?" queried Saul.

"I have to feed the krays, I should've been there fifteen minutes ago," he added getting up and walking out of the hall.

"Each team will enter their target and locate our friends," boomed Grandon. "You'll be armed with weapons and enough explosives to bring the whole prison down. Use them carefully." A few people around the room raised their eyebrows.

"Nicholas Darby will meet each team and provide guidance on how to prepare the explosive," continued Grandon. "You are reminded that following the centiwar, the Senate and the Council signed the accursed Arkan decree. We agreed we wouldn't use sorceric powers under any circumstances," a sporadic murmur of reluctant disagreement trickled through the room.

Grandon pulled down chart after chart of prison after prison and described the layout of each one. He described how strong the walls were, how many prisoners were inside and how well protected it was. Occasionally, he pointed to a chart that outlined the layout of a prison and marked out the entrances.

"By the second moon of Lunam-Pras you will all gather in Fort Delmar at Port Newton," Theran continued, standing up. "Once there, we will recoup and plan the next step. Be there on time. We can't wait longer than a week before we move on. May the druids guide your hand."

Rabin stood up and brought an end to proceedings. Slowly, the sorcerers exited the great hall, and Saul, Ruby, and Henry were left to stroll out of the hall quietly.

"Hey, where did Jordan go?" asked Saul as they approached the door out of the great hall.

"He said he had to tend to the *krays*," replied Ruby.

"What are krays?"

"Children," called a voice behind them. Theran trotted towards them, his boots thudding gently on the wooden floor. "The master would like to speak to you," he said turning back towards the stage.

A tingle spread through their spine. They walked back nervously to the stage, climbed up the steps and stood meekly a yard in front of Rabin's chair.

"My children," began Rabin looking at them in turn.

There was a powerful mesmeric aura about his presence. It felt magical and enchanting, and each time he smiled, the children felt a strange heart-felt warmth.

"It's regrettable that you entered the Netherworld. That should never have happened. We must get you back safely to the Upperworld. We can't risk you becoming embroiled in our problems. Rufus." Rufus turned attentively. "Has Ambrose been instructed?"

In all the tumultuousness of the last few days, the children had completely forgotten about Ambrose Dunster.

"Yes, but it's a bit awkward," began Rufus hesitantly. "Ambrose went to Santo Renfo to investigate the portal that Arak and Trenton used to get into the Upperworld. The two rogues were spotted three days away in Santo Underhill. Thankfully, Ambrose closed the portal. They won't be returning to the Upperworld in a hurry."

"Where is Ambrose?" asked Grandon.

"He's err... still at Santo Underhill."

"How long will it take to get here?"

"Six weeks."

"Six weeks?" asked Grandon with a worried expression. "Is he coming back here or meeting us at Fort Delmar?"

"We asked him to meet us here."

"But Fort Delmar is closer to Santo Underhill," noted Theran.

"Indeed."

"Then he should meet us there," ordered Theran.

"I'll send him another message."

"Tomorrow morning head for Fort Delmar directly and wait for Ambrose," Rabin said looking up at Rufus. "That will keep you out of any altercations and keep the children safe." Rufus eyed one of the maps on the wall behind the stage.

"Enroute you must pass through Kirk Heidengaard. There you'll meet an old friend, Doctor Kembereley. He was the last person I met before my capture. That evening I handed a diary to him, he will give it to you. The diary is important to me. Keep it safe, guard it with your life."

"Dr Kembereley has a lot of information regarding the whereabouts of some of our friends," added Theran. "Note it carefully please."

"Certainly," replied Rufus.

"Althea, Caleb and Jarrett will accompany you. Caleb has a few small detours to make along the way. I hope you understand."

"Certainly," said Rufus smiling at Caleb. "But is it wise to put Althea and Jarrett together on the same trip? They don't get on at the best of times and a long journey will—"

"Nothing like time together to help resolve differences hey?" replied Theran dismissively.

"One more thing," announced Rabin as they were about to walk away. "You'll understand that this must stay a secret. You mustn't discuss it with anybody, is that clear?"

"Of course," replied Rufus.

"Nobody must know about the children, nor of the detour through Kirk Heidengaard, or the route you're taking."

"Yes master."

"You're a wanted man Rufus," Theran reminded him.

"Yes, I am somewhat aware of that."

"May the druids guide your hand," said Rabin before standing up and walking slowly out of the room.

*

Glorious vibrating music filled the air when the children walked into the busy gardens. Groups of eccentric characters busied themselves talking and cajoling in small groups. A few cheery conversations filled the air and an uplifting boisterous song shot out from across the garden.

Saul, Ruby, and Henry sat quietly at the side of the garden. All the talk about war and danger had been overwhelming, and it made them more anxious to get home.

"I hear I'm travelling with you," said the voice of Althea. "I say I'm really looking forward to visiting Kirk Heidengaard again, it's been ages since I visited."

"You've been there before?" asked Ruby.

"Hmm," replied Althea. She sensed the worried moods surrounding the children. "Look, I'm not sure what I can say to make you feel better. But we will get you home safe and sound. It's only a matter of time before Ambrose Dunster catches up with us."

"He will get us home won't he?" asked Ruby anxiously.

"Yes. He knows exactly what to do, and the moment he finds out that you've entered the Netherworld, I'm sure he'll make it a priority." Althea said assuringly.

"There must be someone else that knows how to open a portal," asserted Ruby.

"I'm afraid not. It's a rare gift. He's the only sorcerer we know that can open portals. In the meantime, cheer up. Try to enjoy being here while you can. Who knows, you might even miss the Netherworld when you get back home."

Althea's naturally warm presence made them feel better.

"She's right you know," murmured Saul thoughtfully.

"What?" murmured Henry. A crowd at the entrance burst out into uproarious laughter.

"This place is marvellous, I mean it's magical and, well, if they really can get us back just before we left, then maybe we shouldn't be so gloomy."

The children realised that despite all the talk of war, they were in a wondrous dreamy paradise that they could not have conjured up in their wildest imagination. Steadily, they felt cheerier, and a little while later, they took a walk around the gardens soaking up the positivity and smiling every time huge cheers shot up around them whenever a new sorcerer or group arrived.

*

The commotion and activity around the hall continued late into the night with sporadic bursts of merry laughter resounding from some of the rooms. The corridors were brimming with busy activity as sorcerers moved around Kirby Hall, conducting absorbing discussions huddled in corners and enjoying glasses of wine, and cups of coffee and tea around the fireplace in the main dining room.

Late into the night, the children finally dragged themselves into their room. For a little while longer, they sat on the balcony looking out at the glorious night sky and the magnificent gardens.

The silence was broken by a soft knock on the door.

"Good evening children," said Caleb as he walked in closely followed by Jordan. Caleb was tall and gaunt. He had black hair, oriental features, and a kind face. The likeness between him and Jordan was remarkable.

"I hope you're feeling comfortable here. If you need anything, I'm sure Jordan will be happy to help. Pack two lots of all clothing items, no more please," Caleb placed four bags neatly on the sofa. "We need to travel lightly. If it doesn't fit in the bag, we can't take it. Pack some warm clothes, you'll find some in the cupboard."

"Warm clothes?" queried Ruby.

"Yes. There's going to be lots of snow. We leave after breakfast," he said as he walked out.

"How far is Kirk Heidengaard?" asked Saul folding up a shirt and squeezing it carefully into the bag which seemed remarkably small.

"Around five hundred miles," replied Jordan.

"Crikey! We'll be walking for days," complained Henry.

"Well, we won't be walking most of it."

"Steragon?" prompted Henry excitedly. "Please tell me we're going to be travelling in a carriage pulled by six steragon or something."

"Krays."

"A carriage pulled by krays?" asked Henry excitedly. "And anyway, what are krays?"

"No, not a carriage. Wait until the morning, you'll—"

"Is this your jumper?" Ruby walked angrily into the room waving a red jumper.

"Err."

"Henry!"

"Well, there wasn't enough space in my bag and—"

"Maybe if you'd bothered folding everything up properly you might be able to fit a few more things. Honestly, Henry do I have to do everything for you, I'm not your mother you know."

"Feels like it sometimes," muttered Henry quietly enough, he thought, for Ruby not to hear him.

"Oh really?"

"Do you travel everywhere with the council?" interjected Saul just in time.

Jordan nodded.

"Just you and your father?"

Jordan nodded again.

"And what about the rest of your family?" asked Saul guardedly.

Ruby and Henry stopped and listened expectantly.

"Well," Jordan pursed his lips together, not sure about where to begin. "My grandfather and uncles were all killed during the war."

"Killed?" asked Saul with a worried look on his face.

"Yes. There was just me, my parents, and sister left. About two years ago, my father and I were out hunting for food. My mother and sister disappeared while we were away. They were probably kidnapped. Everything's been chaotic since then," Jordan's voice trailed off as he said this.

"What do you think happened to them?" asked Ruby.

"We think they were kidnapped by Naquin gipsies, they're travelling gipsies who kidnap wanderers and sell them to Goran slave traders."

"Sell them?"

"Slave traders?" asked Henry.

"That sounds terrible," said Saul. He walked over to a table and poured a jug of water into four glasses.

"They're greedy and selfish. They'll steal anybody and anything if they can sell it. We've spent two years searching for mum and Jessy. We've been through hundreds of cities, towns and villages and left small pictures and messages behind hoping someone somewhere will recognise them. Joining the council has made it easier because they're also helping to chase leads and information. Father's convinced that mum and Jessy are still alive. But I'm not sure."

"Not sure?" asked Ruby.

"Yes. But I don't want to spoil whatever little hope he has left."

"You don't think they're still alive?" asked Ruby.

"For a while, I did and was convinced they were alive and well. But whenever we get to a dead-end, our hopes are dashed, and we become disappointed. So, I suppose it's better not to keep dreaming about it."

"When was the last time you saw them?"

"Seven years ago. I was six and don't remember it much to be honest. After they were taken, we heard lots of rumours, but the only thing we were sure about was that they were taken to the East, perhaps even over the Black Ocean to Goran."

"Your father has a tremendous will to continue searching for them," said Ruby supportively.

"Yes, it's the only thing that keeps him going."

Jordan's story cast a solemn mood and an otherwise exciting

evening became a bit gloomy, contrasting remarkably with the cheery celebration in the garden.

"Try to remain hopeful," suggested Ruby comfortingly. A cheer shot up outside the balcony.

"Yes, I shouldn't be so pessimistic. Now and again, we come across villagers or travellers claiming they saw a group of travellers that had a small blond-haired girl with them, possibly my sister Jessy. Everything seems to point towards Goran."

"Along the route, we're going to travel," guessed Saul.

Jordan nodded.

"That's why we might be making some detours along the way right?" asked Henry.

Jordan nodded.

~ 8 ~

Krays

The children walked down for breakfast and noticed that the hallway was laden with travel bags. More sorcerers had arrived overnight. During breakfast, Theran and Grandon moved between groups relaying, agreeing, and confirming plans for the journey ahead.

"Vanden Port Castle group please," requested Theran loudly.

A short chubby man stood up and hobbled towards Theran. "Ahh, yes—"

"You're leaving in half an hour." Theran ticked a name off a list.

"Now about this *no-sorcery* nonsense—"

"The Arkan Decree."

"Yes."

"Those are the rules Chadwick, I didn't make them, and you'll follow them like the rest of us. *Kinsley Morgan!*"

A thin slender long-faced lady stood up. She had dark brown skin, braided hair, and wore a collection of beads around her neck.

"Mansley and Winnie Danton are joining you."

"But… that makes thirteen of us."

"Well done, you can add up."

"Can we make it… fourteen?"

"Are you superstitious?" quizzed Theran.

"Not particularly err… superstitious. It's just that the numbers seven, fourteen and fifteen are somewhat err… how can I put it, *fortuitous,*" Kinsley replied flatly. "Now, when I got caught in Edgering, you know during the war, I was—"

"Oh, very well. Take Berto," said Theran, impatiently

scribbling changes to his list.

After breakfast, Theran ushered the children to the front garden. It was a cold foggy morning. The hills and alcoves were shrouded in a moving white mist, and the distant orange forest and Lake Kirby were barely visible.

A sudden hush came over the crowd as Rabin walked out accompanied by Doe Fester, Ryder, and Rabin's entourage of personal guards. Theran and Grandon scurried towards Rabin and engaged themselves in a busy hushed discussion.

Suddenly, a clatter of loud horn-like sounds filled the air. A moment later, a herd of osseri were led around the hall to the front. Sorcerers climbed onto the osseri and set out on their long arduous journeys. Steadily, the osseri clambered down the hill and disappeared into the fog.

The children watched this phenomenal sight and asked themselves, not for the first or last time if they were dreaming. Their thoughts were interrupted by a freakish gust of wind, accompanied by a terrible screeching sound. The children looked up and were horrified to see four huge dragon-like beasts gliding downwards out of the fog.

The creatures had two large red eyes glaring out piercingly from a huge scaly head. Two horns pointed forwards from the top of the head and a set of large teeth poked out from each side of its huge powerful jaw.

The beast's yard-long neck led down to a long body supported by four powerful legs; five long claws protruded from each foot. Two huge leathery wings stretched out from the side of the long body and a powerful thick long tail swished gently from side to side.

"D… dragons," murmured Henry deliriously.

"Don't be silly. Nobody's ever tamed a dragon. These are krays," remarked Jordan with a knowing smile before rushing off towards the krays. He approached one of them, took hold of the reins and tugged it gently towards a bucket of food, before leading the remaining three to their food.

The children watched on in horrified silence as one of the krays shook its head wildly and made a grunting sound. It seemed that at any moment the beast might take a huge bite and swallow Jordan with one gulp.

"One big feed will last them a week!" shouted Jordan, clearly not perturbed by the monsters.

A while later, Jordan walked back and stood proudly next to Saul, Ruby, and Henry and watched the krays eating.

"We're... travelling on these?" asked Saul, his jaw wide open in shock.

"Yup," replied Jordan matter of factly.

"No way!" exclaimed Saul instantly. "I'm not getting onto that… thing!"

"Those things are… I mean… *You can't be serious!"* cried Henry in disbelief.

"They're perfectly harmless if you treat them right, and as long as my father is with us, we're completely safe. Trust me." Nobody spoke a word. The children stood glued to the sight of the krays eating wildly out of the buckets.

"They're aggressive towards strangers but good towards people they recognise," said Jordan after a while.

"And do they recognise us?" quizzed Saul.

"Not yet, but they will."

The children remained to be convinced as Caleb walked to each kray and stroked its tremendous scaly jaw while talking to it quietly. Moments later, he threw a huge red leather saddle confidently over the kray and then tied two belts at the underside of the fearsome beast.

"Good morning," said a voice behind them. "Saul, Ruby, and Henry if I'm not mistaken."

A brown coated man with a round chubby bearded face put his hand out to the children. Saul recognised him instantly as the man pinned to a wall by Siraf.

"I'm Jarrett. We're travelling together."

The children shook his hand in turn.

"You're from the err—"

"Upperworld," offered Ruby.

"Ah, yes. I'll wager you haven't been on a kray before have you?" They shook their heads. "Well, this'll literally take your breath away."

A servant hoisted the travel bags onto the back of a kray's saddle. Meanwhile, Caleb stood in front of a kray, stroked the animal's jaw softly and looked straight into its eyes uttering something unintelligible. Moments later, he walked towards the children.

"Now this will feel quite disconcerting," Caleb began. He ushered them towards the krays. "Don't fear the krays. There's just one simple rule. Don't panic. The kray can sense fear and..." Caleb left the rest to their imagination.

"The most difficult bit is when we take off and land, you'll feel overwhelmed as the wind hits your face. Push your head down as far as you can towards its neck. It'll be easier once you're in the air. When you're ready Saul, climb onto the front saddle and hold the grip."

It was a daunting experience. Saul walked to the kray with an air of nervous reluctance. He stood next to it for a moment and anxiously watched its tail swishing heavily from side to side.

"Is there no other way we can travel to—"

"That's it just push your right foot into the stirrup," interrupted Caleb.

Pursing his lips together nervously, Saul waited a few moments and then put his foot firmly into the stirrup. *Don't panic, don't panic,* he said to himself. Saul launched himself onto the saddle. He had pushed too hard and nearly fell embarrassingly over the other side. Steadily he gathered himself, closed his eyes tightly and clenched the saddle grip not daring to move an inch. The kray did not seem to have even noticed. Saul could smell the leathery skin and felt the animal's lungs slowly inhaling and exhaling beneath him. The occasional grunt of the animal made him panicky and he tried his best not to show any sign of fear. A few moments later, the kray made a strange guttural sound that sounded bizarrely like the low purring of a cat.

"She likes you Saul," said Rufus climbing up behind him nonchallantly.

Somewhat encouraged by Saul not being eaten alive, Ruby walked to the kray, followed by Henry, and moments later, everyone was ready to depart.

"Hold onto your saddles!" exclaimed Caleb. He shouted something unintelligible, and suddenly, the krays leapt upwards and shot into the air. Instantly the travellers were flung backwards, their hair thrown back wildly. Saul, Ruby, and Henry clenched the saddle grip tightly and moments later, their hands began to feel numb. The force of the wind made it almost impossible to breathe properly.

"Push your head down!" shouted Jarrett. "It'll be fine once we're in the air!"

The children forced their heads down towards the leathery bodies of the kray and felt the terrible bitter gushing wind flow over their backs.

Neither of them dared to look downwards over the side of the kray. A little while later, they felt the kray slow down, the wings flapped more steadily, and soon the children could barely feel the wind. The kray was in the air now and floating gently through the sky. Now each of them ventured a glance downwards and was staggered at the sight of the huge stretch of foggy land beneath them. They marvelled at the breath-taking scenery of valleys, rivers, lakes, and forest which stretched across the horizon, and momentarily, they forgot their strange predicament.

*

The first few days of the journey passed by swiftly. Cities, towns, and villages disappeared into the distance behind them to be replaced by a vast landscape littered with jungles, forests, and hills. Glorious waterfalls and cavernous valleys decorated the beautiful landscape. Now and again, a winding road crept out beneath them carrying a lonely traveller straddling along, or a river emanating calmly into the distance to be met by a huge lake.

As dusk fell and darkness crept in, solitary lamps lit up the darkness beneath them like twinkling stars. Villages appeared now and again, lit up cosily by street and house lamps, and then disappeared to be met by a barren dark landscape.

Even now, a few days into their accidental incursion into the Netherworld, the children never tired of watching these wondrous scenes from their vantage point a few hundred feet above, and still, they continued to be mesmerised by the richness of the Netherworld.

Each evening they found a resting place, briskly set up camp and then followed their monotonous chores. Jarrett and Henry erected the tents, or rather Henry watched in continued disbelief as Jarrett guided the tarpaulin onto the poles with his hands floating in the air in front of him. Althea, Saul, and Ruby lit the fire and prepared food, and Caleb and Jordan tended to the krays.

*

On the first evening, the children sat exhaustedly around the campfire. Sitting on a kray all day was tiring. Their fingers were stiff with cramp from holding the saddle grip, and their faces felt numb from the continual beating of the wind.

Sitting around the campfire that evening was the first of many memorable moments of jovial conversation and nostalgic discovery. The children were entertained by magical stories about the days gone by, and the legends of the sorcerers, druids, and the council. Jarrett was brimming with warm sarcastic humour and rib bruising jokes, and Rufus, Jarrett or Althea were never short of magical anecdotes about the sorcerers and their history. Collectively they remembered the great days before the war, when the sorcerers were advisors to the kings of the five states, and when they enjoyed the privileges of court. Occasionally, they digressed into the dark times that befell the Netherworld, the outbreak of war and the devastation that came with it.

Soon after the purge, Jarrett had resorted to professional burglary. He stole jewels and treasures and sold his services to the highest bidder. By his own admission he was quite traitorous, and occasionally switched sides during a job because he had received a higher bid for the stolen goods. This seemed quite contrary to the sorceric code that he had pledged his allegiance to, but *they were hard times,* he proposed.

"The moons must get quite confusing," began Ruby. "I mean remembering which is which," she added looking up at the three moons that lit up the beautiful sky.

"Not really. There are three bright moons. Lunam-Rube," began Althea pointing to a reddish moon. "Lunam-Fus and Lunam-Pras," she added pointing to a very grey moon and a strange green moon that seemed the closest of the three. "We use the suns and the moons to guide our travel."

"I thought there were six moons?" asked Saul.

"There are. You won't see two of the moons for another month, and the sixth moon for another two months," explained Althea.

The fire flickered spontaneously as a soft breeze fanned the flames. Two birds tweeted in the trees, fluttered from one branch to another, and then flew away into the darkness.

"How did Rabin escape?" Saul asked impulsively as the tired travellers sipped their tea. A soft breeze filled a brief silence.

"After the war was lost," began Althea. "The noblemen set out to destroy the council. They were intent on removing every last vestige of the council. We had been a thorn in their side for decades, now they wanted their revenge. We were betrayed by many of our own friends and then persecuted by the noblemen and their henchmen, the searchers."

"The searchers?" asked Henry inquisitively.

"The searchers are a group of bounty hunters," explained Jarrett.

"Then one day we heard rumours that Rabin had been killed," continued Althea. "It was a terrible time. We were in turmoil. Everyone was confused and depressed. Time and time again we heard this rumour, often from trustworthy sources. Soon nobody doubted it, and we all believed that Rabin was indeed dead.

"Many sorcerers were killed or imprisoned, the rest of us retreated into the hills, caves, and forests. It was chaos."

"But couldn't you use your magical powers and fight your way out?" asked Ruby.

"It's not quite so straightforward," replied Rufus. "When you've been backed into a dark room with twelve soldiers surrounding you, you can't just magic your way out."

"Especially if they've bound your hands," added Jarrett. "Our power comes from our hands you see, well for most of us it does."

"Many times, during those dark days, we thought about reconnecting with our friends," continued Althea. "But each time, the comfort and safety of our homes encouraged us to stay put.

"And then one morning a few months ago, twelve years after the purge, our solitude was disturbed by a man called Lugo Hagan. He rushed to Soren Forest in search of Rothman, Belina, and Paulo, three loyal members of the council. They listened cautiously to his claims to have critical information.

"At the back of their mind lay the cynical fear that this was yet another prelude to a betrayal, a trap. You see, the Gorans had been deliberately planting rumour and conjecture and were constructing elaborate plots to destroy whatever was left of us."

"So let me get this right," interjected Saul. "Your enemies are the noblemen and the Gorans right?""Yes," Althea replied. "Oh, and the dark council that the Baron is re-forming."

"And the searchers, but we've already mentioned them I suppose," hinted Jarrett casually.

"Yes, of course, that goes without saying."

"The wizards," murmured Rufus as he bit his toast.

"Didn't we declare peace with them when the Duke of—"

"Not quite," interrupted Rufus. "We never got around to signing the peace declaration. Technically we're still at war with them."

"And don't forget the warlocks," said Rufus.

"Warlocks?" asked Henry.

"So, you're at war with just about everyone right?" asked Saul.

"That's… one way of looking at it," replied Jarrett sheepishly.

"You see, a few bad apples have caused no end of problems for the sorcerers," explained Rufus. "These powers demand huge responsibility. Aside from the druids, the sorcerers are the most powerful beings in the Netherworld. Many times, these powers have been abused leading to scuffles and big disagreements which inevitably lead to another enemy lining himself up against us."

"That's the reason why the council was formed," said Jarrett. "To keep us disciplined and *answerable.*"

"Well like I was saying," continued Althea. "Lugo turned out to be credible and trustworthy. He knew things that only important members of the council could know, and he knew where some of our friends were being held prisoner. Lugo asked Conrad to meet a man called Eisen Roth at the Cliffs of Breth Finton within two weeks, it was urgent. *Everything will be revealed,* he promised. *Does it have to be Conrad?* they asked. *Yes, it does,* he insisted.

~ 9 ~

Brixius Serum

Twilight settled in as Conrad and Caleb circled the cliffs of Breth Fenton. They descended downwards, all the while looking out for signs of danger.

"I may be a couple of hours," suggested Conrad climbing off the kray. "I saw a village at the foot of the cliff. Why don't you get some food?"

"I'll leave a kray. If this is an ambush at least you can escape," replied Caleb patting the kray softly.

Conrad pulled a sword out of his bag. The fearsome sight of the kray was normally enough to put off would-be ambushers, but he felt safer with the sword at his side.

By the afternoon, Conrad became restless and nervous. He paced around the cliff looking for signs of an approach, before sitting down at the edge of the cliff to calm his nerves. He looked out nervously across the mesmerising ocean and played with the beads on his wrist or fiddled with his three necklace charms.

Then, he squinted his eyes and looked at the distant sea. A boat carrying a single solitary figure was edging slowly towards the shore. Conrad looked back cautiously at the kray before reaching for his sword and moving it nearer.

Steadily, the boat reached the shore. A tall dark-skinned man with frizzy hair climbed out and walked steadily up the hill. He was dressed in rugged brown clothes that seemed too big for him giving Conrad the impression that he was a farmer or peasant.

"Good afternoon sir," began the man anxiously as he approached Conrad. "My apologies for the delay, the tide comes in late in the autumn you see."

"Later still in the winter," replied Conrad in response. "The views from the cliff are remarkable, don't you think?"

"Magnificent. Just magnificent my friend."

They breathed a collective sigh of relief. After years of bitter experience, the sorcerers had learned to use a code for introductions with strangers and anything other than these words signalled impending danger.

The man appeared as anxious as Conrad. He looked around at the trees behind Conrad and then back down to the beach and the hill. "Can we sit under the trees over there?" he asked nervously.

"Of course."

From under the tree, they could see out into the ocean, down the hill and around the open space in front of them.

"Excuse the approach. I'm risking my life and that of my family by coming here," he said looking around apprehensively.

"I'm Eisen Roth. I work for the King of Warin. I've been the prison cook for twenty-three years. I prepare two meals a day for the prisoners. I wash the dishes and undertake kitchen duties. Do you know Fort Warin?"

Conrad shook his head.

"Good. Nobody knows much about it. It's a maximum-security prison. Fort Warin houses some of Petonia's most important prisoners. It's two days from here at the shore of the Black Sea. Five months ago, something very strange happened. I began to receive premonitions."

"Premonitions?" Conrad asked, still playing with the beads around his wrist.

"Yes. One evening, as I walked out of the prison entrance, a strange misty symbol seemed to fill my whole vision, almost like a dream," the waves lapped wildly in the shore below and the tree above them rustled softly with the wind. "It disappeared as soon as it came."

"Did you feel anything else?"

"Huh?"

"Did you feel cold and sweaty, or maybe even dizzy?"

"Yes. I felt like I might pass out. I remember having to lean on the wall for a few moments as I walked in."

"Hmm," Conrad said thoughtfully.

"Two days later, it happened again. While I was cooking in the prison kitchen, a sequence of symbols appeared in front of me. I shook my head wildly, blinked, and they disappeared. But I remembered the symbols, clearly enough to write them down.

"Nothing happened for a few days and I tried to forget about the incident, putting it down to tiredness and fatigue. But now and again, I pulled out the piece of paper and came close to showing the symbols to a friend. One afternoon, I was passing through the old shopping quarter of Warin."

"I stopped suddenly as I walked past an antique shop. A coat of arms sat proudly in the window with one of the mysterious symbols marked along the outer edge. It was the Ancient Goric symbol for the letter *M*.

"Goric consists of letters and symbols which replace words," a sudden gust of wind rustled the trees at the side of the cliff. The wind was becoming blustery. "I brought home a book on ancient Goric. I went through it and converted the Goric symbols into Petonian."

"Malkin!" he gasped after a moment. *"The name of my son!"* Eisen paused again, seemingly as taken aback now as he was then. "I then began to think about the premonition. How did I, who have never learned ancient Goric, see my son's name in ancient Goric?

"This played heavily on my mind until one night when I had a strange dream of a bearded old man. This vision morphed into a set of steps reaching down into the dungeon of the prison. Both scenes seemed to repeat themselves a few times before I woke up with a shudder. I was breathless and sweating. After a few moments, I became convinced that this had been a premonition, not a dream.

"I became anxious. Why was I having premonitions? Was I going mad? A week later, I had another premonition. This time, the bearded man led me to my garden where my son was playing around the tree. The vision turned into a stone staircase, and I saw myself walking downwards. It was an intense experience and again I nearly passed out. However, what made it more intense was the emotional experience of seeing my son walking.

"Malkin had a strange illness, one which made him steadily weaker. Around a year ago, he began to lose the power of his muscles and as time progressed, he became bedridden. Malkin had months to live.

"I thought long and hard about the premonition. The staircase led down to a cell in the dungeon, the most secure cell in the fort. I was convinced the message came from there. But if it did, who was the prisoner in the dungeon and what was he trying to say or do? How did he do this? Was he a wizard? A warlock maybe?"

Suddenly, Conrad became very attentive and listened absorbedly to every word. "I had to go down and see him. But how to do it? The dungeon was the most secure part of the prison. Two guards constantly guarded it. We weren't allowed access. Twice a day the guards came up to the kitchen, collected food and returned an hour later with empty trays.

"One afternoon I was presented with my moment. A fight broke out outside the prison gate. A guard charged into the kitchen, handed me a set of keys, and ordered me to take the food to the prisoners. The key to the dungeon, I couldn't believe my luck!

"I walked down cautiously, careful not to fall down the dark stone staircase. I entered the dungeon. It was dark and dingy. A straw bed sat in one corner and the flickering wall lamp cast a steady shimmer of light.

"An old bearded man sat cross-legged on the floor. His hands were chained to the floor. I recognised him immediately as the man I had seen in my premonition.

"'Eisen Roth,' he murmured. 'We don't have much time. I'm going to do something for you, when it's done, you must return my generosity. Is that agreed?'

"'Who… who are you?' I asked.

"He didn't answer, instead he cited a complex recipe involving the fregrin crystal which has to be ground down with some herbs and then prepared in a complex sequence. He made me repeat the recipe three times so that I remembered it. It takes the best part of a day to complete—"

"The fregrin muscle resurgent?" interrupted Conrad. "Who was the man?"

"Yes, that's what he called it." Eisen hesitated for a moment before carrying on.

"'Wait until your son is better. When he's better, you must halve the brixius serum that you're administering in my food.'

"'I can't possibly do that, it's treason, I'd…'

"'Your family will get a safe passage, and we will protect you,' he promised. 'But you must keep your side of the bargain, is that clear?' I nodded reluctantly.

"The brixius serum was administered twice a day in this man's food to keep him in a sedated state.

"My family live in a village called Thyser in Arizmendi which is three hundred miles away. If it ever became known that I had changed the dosage, soldiers would raze my village down before I could get a message to them.

"For weeks I struggled with why I should possibly help this man.

"Who was the—?"

"Then my personal life took a dramatic turn," continued Eisen, ignoring Conrad again. "My son became very ill. I was desperate. One night, I did everything the old man asked. I prepared and administered the potion. For a few days, there was no change in Malkin's condition, I became impatient. Then, steadily, but surely, Malkin began to improve. My joy knew no bounds!

"I kept my promise and halved the serum. Three days later, I received another premonition." Eisen stopped for a moment and let the sound of waves and the rustling of the trees fill the conversation. "Rabin asked that—"

"By the beard of the druids," Conrad gasped. He reached for the sword and shot to his feet. "What cruel trickery is this?"

"Hear me out," Eisen said quickly, "Rabin asked that I reach out to you Conrad,"

Conrad was stunned by these words. He looked frozenly at Eisen Roth. "We've had no sight or sound of our master for thirteen years. We've left no stone unturned—"

"You never thought to look in Fort Warin, did you? To discover whether anybody is being held there," interrupted Eisen Roth assertively.

"Why would we? It's the most unlikely of prisons and who would think to—"

"Just the place to keep the most highly regarded prisoner in the Netherworld don't you think?"

Conrad sat in stunned silence as he absorbed this.

"Rabin suggested you wouldn't believe me," Eisen said softly. "He asked whether you can still hear the grasshoppers in the grass. Can you still hear that distant waterfall and the birds in the trees? Rabin asked if you remembered the friend that saved you on the night of the blue angels."

"The blue angels…" Conrad muttered to himself dreamily. "Why… yes…" A distant memory struck him, instantly reminding him of his childhood under the tutelage of the great sorcerer.

Conrad was quiet for a little while as he tried to come to terms with this. The story was too fantastic to be a trick. If this were a trap, he would have been caught by now.

"We have to rescue him," he announced getting to his feet.

"There's a plan," said Eisen emphatically. "Come to Warin and take lodging at the King's Chariot. It's near the southern wall of the prison, twenty yards from the prison entrance. Expect to wait some days, maybe seven. You'll receive further instructions," Conrad nodded softly. "The city is littered with soldiers. Come alone and enter as a trader, that way you'll avoid suspicion."

Conrad nodded again. Eisen Roth spent a while longer describing the city in intricate detail. He explained the route to the city and told Conrad about the Forest of Heth Warin where the kray should be kept.

The suns crept down over the horizon. The ocean had become a dark silhouette in the background, the tide had come in further and the waves lapped loudly against the hill. A soft fire lit up the darkness a few yards away as Caleb cooked for them. A comforting smell of food carried itself with the breeze.

"You've put yourself at great risk," remarked Conrad as they ate.

"Yes," replied Eisen quietly. "I've put all my trust in Rabin," he added, nervously eyeing the kray which was gorging wildly at a bucket of food.

"You don't have much time Conrad. You need to be there on the seventh moon of Lunam-Rube."

Conrad was quiet as he calculated how much time he had. "But that's just two days from now."

Eisen Roth nodded. "It is indeed. But it's not far from here, you can be there in two days," he added. "Thank you for listening my friend. May the druids guide your hand."

With these words, Eisen Roth stood up and prepared to depart. He gathered his coat from a branch on the tree, embraced Conrad and then walked down the cliff. Moments later, Conrad heard the boat paddle away slowly under the moonlit sky.

*

Within an hour of arriving in the city, the cobbler of Warin became busy selling and repairing shoes. Conrad pushed his shoe trolley through stone-cobbled lanes and alleyways. He made his way to the centre of the city and found himself facing a heavily guarded fort. Immediately, the fort adopted a shrine-like presence. For Conrad, this was a druidic temple, and he looked up at it with mesmerising awe.

While he worked, Conrad secretly eyed and studied the prison entrance. Although he was not an expert in prison breaks, he could see that Fort Warin was heavily fortified, there was likely to be a lot of security all the way down to the dungeon.

Conrad walked into his bedroom in the King's Chariot. He smiled. He was presented with a clear view of the prison entrance, lit up wonderfully by street lamps. From here, he could learn the time the prison guards left and the time the guards changed at the front.

The inn was busy that evening, there was barely enough space to move. Conrad got to know some of the *regulars* at the inn. He joined in a game of *sledgers,* a card game that kept him and his new friends occupied to the early hours of the morning. After a fortuitous sequence of conversations, Conrad discovered that one of the men around the table was a prison guard. Conrad could not believe his luck! After a few drinks, the man revealed the layout of the dungeon and even the number of guards positioned at various points in the prison.

Conrad's routine the following day and the next few days was the same. From morning until early evening, he was kept busy preparing shoes. He was continually wary of anybody approaching him, mindful that this might be the contact, the instructions, or the order he was waiting for. Nothing happened.

On the fifth afternoon, Conrad stood at the corner of a dusty street.

"Shoes! Shoes to repair!" he shouted periodically. Suddenly he saw Eisen Roth cross into an alleyway. Instinctively, he ran towards him.

"Eisen!" he cried reaching for Eisen's shoulder.

Eisen turned around sharply. "What the devil are you doing?"

"I haven't heard anything, I need to—"

"Idiot!" Eisen looked around nervously. "You're putting my life at risk! Never approach me again, do you understand?"

"But I haven't heard anything. I followed your instructions, how long—"

"You have to wait," Eisen said through gritted teeth.

"But what if—"

"You *will* be contacted," repeated Eisen firmly before turning away into another alleyway leaving Conrad in a dejected mood.

*

On the seventh night, deeply impatient and frustrated, Conrad decided to leave the city the following morning. Enough was enough, and he felt angry about having vested so much time in a wild goose chase. He lay in the bedroom, drifting in and out of sleep.

"Conrad."

Conrad jolted out of his slumber. Somebody had whispered his name. The room was lit up softly by the light from the street lamp, but he saw nothing but emptiness. He lay awake now in that strange state between a deep sleep and a dizzy awakening. He began to shiver, his body felt numb. He pulled the duvet more tightly.

"Conrad—"

It was a clear voice, seemingly coming from someone standing at the foot of the bed.

"On the third moon of Lunam Fus, when the moon is highest, you'll hear a flutter of owls and the howling of three wolves. When that happens, tear a hole through the wall on the right-hand side of the entrance."

Conrad's spine tingled. This was the unmistakable voice of Rabin, his great teacher, the leader of the council. The voice was loud and clear as if he were standing at the side of Conrad's bed. For a moment, Conrad struggled to believe his senses.

"Yes, my master," he replied dreamily.

"The flutter of owls and the howling of three wolves, do you understand?"

"Yes master." Conrad struggled to grasp his emotions.

"Bring two steragon and wait by the side of the fort closest to the Inn. Position a kray with two saddles close to the gates of the city.

"On the same day, you must save the house of Roth in the village of Thyser in Arizmendi."

"The house of Roth—"

"Transport Eisen Roth's family to Kirby Hall."

"Master," rasped Conrad, a tear rolling down the side of his face.

"Those who are still loyal to the council must gather at Kirby Hall on the twenty-third moon of Lunam Fus."

"Master, where are you, are you—"

"Do you understand?"

"Yes, but are you well?"

Silence filled the air.

"Master... are you…" Conrad tailed off. A still quiet night and the occasional hooting of an owl in the street outside filled the silence. Conrad had come out in a trembling cold sweat.

Conrad was a spirathon. He could harness the powers of telepathy and communicate through thought. He had undergone difficult tiring lessons often culminating in breathlessness and exhaustion. Nearly always he ended up in a cold sweat.

For a few moments, Conrad sat bolt upright in his bed, struggling with his emotions. He wiped a tear from his cheek and frantically packed his bag. He walked down the stairs quietly and slipped a copper coin under the door of the Innkeeper with a note that he would return within days and welcome the use of the same room.

*

Conrad returned to Warin three weeks later. Throughout the journey, his thoughts were besieged by the problem before him. He could not work out how to get through a wall that was almost a yard thick.

He was not an explosives expert and could not possibly calculate the proportion, weight and strength of explosives needed to tear the wall down. Too weak, it would alert the whole city but not penetrate the wall, too strong, and it would probably blow up the whole fort. What he would not give to have an alchemist at his side.

These thoughts hounded him for two days, and by the third night, one night before the third moon of Lunam Fus, Conrad had still not found a solution. He walked up to his room in a tired resigned mood. He entered the dark room, drew the curtains instinctively and turned on the lamp.

"Conrad," whispered a sharp voice behind him.

Conrad froze. Was he hearing Rabin again? Surely not. He had not felt the customary cold shiver seer through his body.

"My dear old friend," the voice added.

Conrad recognised the voice. "Nicholas Darby! You're a sight for sore eyes!"

"Quiet," replied Nicholas, his finger over his mouth listening out into the corridor.

The short balding man was just the person Conrad wanted to see. Nicholas Darby, the explosives expert, a spectacular burglar, and the only man who could possibly tear the perfect hole through the prison wall.

"What are you doing here?"

"Casing the joint," replied Darby perching himself into an armchair. "I've come to help you," he added noticing the bewildered look on Conrad's face.

"But how did you know—?"

"Never mind that. Listen. I've measured the width of the wall, it's a thick one, they must have some important people in there," he said as Conrad sunk into the sofa in relief. "Around a yard wide. The biggest problem is the rock they use on the walls of the fort. Agrarian Rock." Darby noticed the confused look on Conrad's face. "It's the toughest and hardest rock that you could possibly use to construct walls."

"I'm so glad you're here," said Conrad slowly.

"By the way, who are we rescuing?"

Conrad looked up and smiled. "You don't know?" The look on Nicholas' face told him. "Rabin," announced Conrad after a pause.

Nicolas' jaw dropped. "By the beard of the druids, be serious man this is no time for—"

"I'm absolutely serious."

"He's alive? Is it true?"

"Very... alive."

"And… it's not a trap?"

"No."

"How much time do we have?"

"We have to do it tomorrow," came the hesitant reply.

"What! I thought it was next Thursday?"

"No… tomorrow."

Nicholas stood up and paced around the room, speaking to himself.

"This isn't good, not good. Think! Two sacks of Cellit, a bottle of Magnerium. No. Two to be sure. Need a diversion, a fight, no, maybe another explosive…" He continued like this for a while, carefully calculating the materials needed to construct the explosive.

Anybody who knew Nicholas Darby was used to this. He had a scrupulous instinct for planning, and when he was planning, he would pace around and share his jumbled thoughts, reorganise them loudly and eventually arrive at a plan that nearly always worked.

Nicholas walked to the window and peered out into the street. "Do you know anything about the layout?"

Conrad explained the layout in as much detail as he had gathered.

"And the master is in the dungeon?"

Conrad nodded.

"How many steps lead down into it?"

"I don't know."

"Are there any windows?"

"No."

"What about the back?"

"I don't know."

"How many guards?"

"There are always two guards at the door of the cell and

another eight within a hundred yards of it," replied Conrad trying to be helpful. "There's only one entrance to the prison and it's covered by two guards," he added quickly before providing a detailed layout of the fort.

"Can we pay any of the guards?" asked Nicholas guardedly.

Conrad shook his head. "I thought of that. No. They're tough nuts."

"We need around ninety seconds to get Rabin out of there," Nicholas announced after a while. "Carefully planted controlled explosives will make a hole the right size and give us enough opportunity to get in, out, and away before the guards can act."

Conrad thought about this for a while.

"We have to distract the two guards at the entrance," continued Darby. "So, a dummy explosive around four hundred yards towards the back will keep them busy."

It took the best part of the night for Conrad and Darby to plan the operation to the scrupulous and careful detail that Darby expected. Nothing was left to chance. Minute details that Conrad did not understand were mulled over continually by Darby.

*

It was a hot stuffy day. The suns were setting slowly over Warin and an inconspicuous breeze fanned softly across the city.

Andreson stood at the prison gates fiddling lazily with his quadbow. Now and again passers-by stopped to admire the prison gates and the architectural structure of the fort before being ushered away by Andreson or his fellow guard Stillson.

An owl hooted above the prison gates.

Andreson looked frustratedly at his watch, only a few minutes had passed since he last looked. He was bored. He waited impatiently for his shift to be over, realising that three years at the gates had taken their toll, he desperately needed a new job.

"Why do you do it Stillson?" he asked.

"Hmm?"

"Why do you do it? The way you treat that old man. It's cruel."

"He's supposed to be some great sorcerer or something right?" replied Stillson with a cheeky smile.

"Yes, apparently."

"Have you ever seen magic?"

"No. Why?"

"Well, if he's so powerful maybe he should react. You know, show some magic or something."

"He's not done anything to you Stillson, leave him alone."

"But wouldn't you like to see some magic, I mean *real* magic?"

"You know very well he's not a wizard, he's just a political prisoner," snapped Andreson.

The owl hooted again. *"Damn parrot!"* Stillson cried throwing a stone at the bird.

The stone hit the wall and three owls flew away. A wolf howled in the distance. Another wolf responded followed by a third.

Suddenly, a loud bang shot out from the back of the prison. Andreson and Stillson looked at each other momentarily before tearing along the side of the prison wall towards the back, their boots clattering loudly on the stone floor.

Meanwhile, Conrad walked purposefully up to the prison gate. He stopped by the wall to the left of the gate, placed a small bag next to it and scurried away.

A second bang, much more powerful than the first, crashed through the air. Nicholas and Conrad were thrown to the floor and the ground shook as pieces of rock flew across the gates of the prison. Dust rose into the air clouding the front of the prison.

"Get the steragon. Quick!" shouted Nicholas amidst the deafening screams that filled the air.

Nicholas Darby clambered up and ran to the wall. He stopped in horrified shock. Although the outer rock had been blown to pieces, an inner wall stood as solidly as the day it was built.

Nicholas sighed, his shoulders slumped, and a disappointed scowl spread over his face. In forty years of explosive alchemy, he had never miscalculated an explosion nor failed to get through a barrier. The guards would return within moments, Nicholas and Conrad would be caught, and Rabin would be put under a stricter guard.

Then, a third explosion shook the ground. More rock and smoke filled the air, and for the second time, Nicholas Darby fell crashing to the ground. A rock hit him on the head sending a seething pain through his skull. He was bleeding.

What's going on? he thought as he pulled himself up.

"Nicholas!" cried Conrad a few yards away.

"Conrad we've failed… it's a trap, quick… have to escape…" murmured Nicholas Darby deliriously.

As he said this, Eisen Roth walked calmly out of the prison gate.

"No," replied Conrad pulling Nicholas up.

"Have to get away—"

"You haven't failed, look."

The dust settled to reveal a gaping hole where the wall had been. The hair on Conrad's back stood up and a shiver filled through Nicholas Darby as they recognised the figure emerging from the smoke.

A brown-cloaked elderly man stepped unsteadily over the pile of rubble outside the wall. A firm expression was set on his soft wrinkled face. He walked slowly and unsteadily, and it seemed that he might fall over and collapse at any moment.

"By the beards of—" began Nicholas.

"Master!" cried Conrad.

"Stop him!" ordered Stillson.

In an instant, Rabin lifted his hand, a bolt of white light stretched wildly through the air sending Stillson across the floor clutching his chest. A satisfied grimace spread over Rabin's face.

"The steragon Conrad, quick!" screamed Nicholas Darby as he walked into the rubble to meet Rabin.

Conrad tore away from the commotion and returned moments later pulling four steragon. Rabin, Conrad, Nicholas Darby, and Eisen Roth climbed up and tore out of the city. A rattle of steragon hooves filled the air as bystanders turned their heads to see the strange sight.

"You did well my friends," said Rabin as they reached the edge of the city.

"But we failed master," said Nicholas Darby regretfully.

"Far from it," replied Rabin. "I could never have blasted out of that prison. I needed you to remove the outer wall, and you did that wonderfully."

A while later they found an open spot where Caleb waited impatiently. He was momentarily dumbstruck when he saw Rabin climbing off the steragon.

Within moments, they were gliding steadily through the air. Conrad looked to his side to see his master sitting comfortably on a kray. It was a surreal experience, and a torrent of emotions filled his heart.

~ 10 ~

Kirk Heidengaard

By the evening of the third day, the travellers were feeling weary of the trip and its nauseating daily routine. The appearance of a huge waterfall or bright orange or red forest no longer overwhelmed them as it had when they set off. Even the charm of the steadily setting suns was wearing off.

Now the terrain far below them was looking wilder and sparser as the wonderful views and greenery steadily disappeared, to be replaced by an increasingly grey landscape. Soon they were passing over desolate villages and cities, long since ravaged by the war.

For the last hour of travelling on the third day, Ruby had heard the kray making a strange purring sound. The journey ended for the day, Ruby dismounted and walked away. Now the purring became louder and more pronounced. She stopped, turned around and walked back to the kray. It raised its head. Ruby stood in front of it, careful to maintain a safe distance from its head. Instinctively, she stepped forward and patted the kray softly on its bony jaw. She looked deep into the kray's red eyes for a moment, and then reached out and softly stroked its hard leathery skin.

It was a strange magical moment. The kray continued purring and moving its head up slowly before lowering it again.

Rufus edged closer. "Be careful Ruby," he urged. Everyone turned and looked nervously at Ruby and the kray. Ruby stepped away slowly.

Rufus raised his hand over a pile of firewood, it went up in flames. "It could have your arm off in a second. That's the last thing we want to add to our problems."

"Sorry I... I shouldn't have done that," replied Ruby apologetically. "But it's strange. I feel like it's been trying to talk to me all day."

"We have a lot of distance to cover tomorrow," announced Caleb from a few yards away. "It'll take a day to cross the Mongollon range."

The wind tore across suddenly, causing the flames to flicker wildly.

"We leave before the sun rises. There are no stops in the day, be sure to have a hearty breakfast," Caleb ordered pulling out the poles for the tents.

Despite feeling tired and exhausted, Saul could not get to sleep. He lay awake tossing and turning before giving in and looking in tired boredom at the side of his tent as it moved gently with the wind.

A little while later, finally feeling quite dreamy, Saul was annoyed when a gust of wind rattled the tent. *That was a kray,* he thought before falling asleep.

The following morning, the children packed their beds wearily and dragged themselves out to be greeted by the welcome sight of a campfire and breakfast. Suddenly, the guttural roar of a kray filled the air. A moment later, Caleb climbed off. "We leave in five minutes," he announced.

*

The wind picked up as the morning progressed, and by midday, it was tearing and lashing against their faces.

"The Mongollan range!" cried Caleb against the wind. "We'll be reaching Windcross soon. Hold tight!"

A vast mountainous terrain filled the horizon as far as the eye could see. Steep snow-covered mountains climbed up towards the sky and merged into the white clouds.

Steering through the Mongollan range was a tortuous frightening experience that made the travellers feel dizzy and sick. The wind bit their cheeks and shrieked past their ears with a deafening rattle. The turbulence pushed and shoved the kray helplessly and knocked them off their trajectory.

Eventually, they crossed the peaks of the mountain. The krays settled into a steady pace, the wind became calmer, and the travellers breathed more freely.

"Now you know why it's called Windcross!" shouted Rufus to Saul who was still holding onto the saddle grip for dear life. "We've just climbed the peak of Mount Lamus. About two miles down there's a gulf between the summit of Lamus and Richdale, the wind tears through it at treacherous speeds. If you think this is harsh…" Rufus let Saul guess the rest.

"Couldn't we have gone around it?" asked Saul stretching his right hand to relieve the cramp.

"No, it would have added two days of travel, we can't afford that!"

"I can hear explosions," said Henry above the noise.

Far behind them, they could still hear a series of distinct loud bangs echoing through the mountainous valleys.

"The wind charges in from the North West and North East and collides violently at the gulf between the mountains!" replied Rufus. "The summits of Lamus and Richdale are named after two warring brother kings who in mythical history lived in a continual battle with each other. Today the districts of Lamus and Richdale still argue, bicker, and contrive against each other, and there is a local legend that the wind is a continuation of the lifelong battle between Lamus and Richdale!"

This had been the most arduous day so far. The travellers had not eaten all day and had held perilously to their saddle grip.

That evening they sat lazily around the fire, thoroughly exhausted by the day's trials.

"Get used to the weather," said Rufus taking a bite out of a toast. "It rarely stops snowing in Kirk Heidengaard and it often comes down handsomely."

"I heard you can see a blizzard coming from a mile away," suggested Caleb. "During the winter it becomes a ghost town. It snows for weeks and very few people leave their homes."

They all smiled as two owls on either side of the camp hooted in turn.

*

"You seem happy about something," muttered Henry as they lay down to sleep. "Not that you shouldn't be of course," he added, realising how rude he must have sounded.

"Yes, I've been meaning to tell you all day. We've had some good news," began Jordan excitedly. "Well, we don't know whether it's good news, but it gives us a lot of hope."

"Go on," prompted Ruby encouragingly. The tent rattled softly as a gust of wind hit it.

"Last night my father was out following some leads. He discovered that around two months ago a group of slave traders passed the Mongollan range. The traders held thirteen or fourteen slaves and one of them matched the description of my mother. There weren't any children with them though." Saul sat up in his bed and all three of them listened attentively.

"The traders stopped at an inn in the Valley of Mongollan. The brave innkeeper crept out secretly and fed the slaves. One of the women gave the Innkeeper a small pouch and named my father. She said he would come searching for her."

Saul, Ruby, and Henry raised their eyebrows.

"The bag contained a bangle, a hair ribbon and a necklace. My mother's necklace and Jessy's bangle and hair ribbon!"

"What?" exclaimed Henry.

"That's marvellous!" cried Ruby.

"It is, but we're trying not to get too enthusiastic."

"Not get too what?" asked Ruby annoyedly.

"Why on earth wouldn't you get excited about that?" added Saul.

"Well, I'm not sure if—"

"Listen," urged Saul. "If you don't get enthusiastic about this you won't get enthusiastic about anything."

"Well, our hopes have been dashed too many—"

"Look. You're getting closer and closer to finding your mum and sister. Start being a bit more eager."

"I think you're so used to disappointment that you're scared to face what might be a real opening in your long search," said Ruby.

They spent the night going over the news a few times. Jordan was hard work, and it seemed that every possible happy emotion had been sucked out of him at some point. It was difficult sparking some enthusiasm out of him and getting him to feel happy about the direction their search was taking.

Before they fell asleep however, Ruby was sure she heard a tinge of excitement in Jordan's tone. Now and again, his voice rose in excitement, and numerous times he laughed and giggled at one of Henry's jokes.

*

The following afternoon, the white frozen wastelands of Argel Crustic and Kessel Fermin appeared in the distance. The temperature dropped, and soon they were caught in a shiver and breathing out puffs of misty air. Later, a steady flurry of snow began falling around them, and by the late afternoon, the weather worsened to give way to intermittent blizzards.

"You'll have to resume on foot now," announced Caleb that evening as he pulled the bags off the saddles. "The krays aren't used to this weather." During the day, the krays were panting harder and seemed to have slowed quite notably. "Kirk Heidengaard is a day on foot."

"We'll need to stay in Kirk Heidengaard for three days," added Jarrett. "And then it's another three days from there to our rendezvous point in Crow Claw."

"We won't wait longer than that Rufus," added Caleb sternly.

They spent a while planning the journey to Kirk Heidengaard and the three-day journey to Crow Claw. It was carefully crafted, with every possibility accounted for and nothing left to chance. Caleb explained the route. He drew a map with landmarks clearly marked out including the point in Crow Claw where they would meet.

Four tents were erected close together around the fire, kept alight in turn by Rufus, Jarrett, Althea, and Caleb. The inside of the tent was terribly cold as the children tucked into their sheets and huddled closer together.

"We'll be going different ways tomorrow," announced Jordan as they snuggled under the sheets. "We'll be gone before you get up."

"You're not coming with us?" asked Ruby.

"No. I have to stay with the krays," replied Jordan. "It's only a few days. We'll be waiting for you at Crow Claw."

*

"Let's get a move on," said Jarrett peeking his head into the tent. Saul, Ruby, and Henry felt cosy underneath the bed sheets. A chill brushed their face whenever they peeked out from beneath the sheets. Nobody wanted to get out.

Although not having to climb nauseous frozen heights on a kray was relieving, they felt strangely deserted without the kray and lonely without Jordan.

Late that afternoon, Solarius set quickly across the distant white horizon. A bitterly cold wind struck relentlessly against their faces. Their feet froze, and their chests trembled.

"Sowren," announced Jarrett suddenly.

In the distance, a herd of white savage-looking furry beasts trenched towards them, their heavy paws landing wildly in the snow and their tails swinging softly behind them. The sowren was covered in long fur. Two curved horns protruded out of a short-necked head and a large jaw revealed a set of sharp teeth.

"Are they tame?" asked Ruby anxiously.

"Very," replied Jarrett almost shivering. "We'll be travelling on one before long."

"We're travelling on those?"

"Unless you fancy walking for a couple of days?"

"Henry we've travelled on krays," helped Ruby. "Travelling on a sowren can't be more daunting."

"Be thankful it's not an amaruk," suggested Althea.

"Anarak?" queried Henry.

"Amaruk," corrected Althea rubbing her cold hands together. "The amaruk is a brown sowren like creature which, although from the same family as the sowren, is a strong fierce hunter. They're kept by slave traders and prison owners to chase down escapees. The beast can tear through forests, up hills and down into deep valleys tossing aside anything that dares to venture in its path. Once it has the scent of its prey, there's little in the Netherworld to stop it."

"If you see one, run first and ask questions later," smiled Jarrett.

The herd came closer, and now the travellers stopped momentarily as the sowren passed within touching distance. They felt tremors under their feet as the herd walked past.

"If my bearings are correct, that's the white forest," Jarrett announced gesturing towards a huge stretch of trees that filled the landscape to their right. It was a strange sight particularly because it seemed to blend invisibly into the snowy horizon. "We're close now. If we walk alongside it, we'll be at Kirk Heidengaard in no time." It was a good thing they did. A while later, the snow came down heavily, quickly turning into a relentless blizzard.

"Aha. Here we are," announced Jarrett suddenly with a beaming smile.

Jarrett led them out to a beautiful white valley. On one side, two of the moons were rising lazily over the distant horizon, and on the other side, they were welcomed by a warm glow emanating from the beautiful city of Kirk Heidengaard. It was a breath-taking wonderfully picturesque scene, reminiscent of a Christmas card.

Saul, Ruby, and Henry's first impressions of Kirk Heidengaard surpassed the steep expectations they had built over the long journey. They were enthralled by the huge steeples of the University which climbed up into the horizon. Lamps lined the edges of the walled city casting a warm glow over the city gate.

A few yards away from the gate, a group of old men sat huddled around a fire smoking pipes and jovially joking, cajoling, and reminiscing. One side of the gate was lined with stalls, each one busy with groups of people buying something or talking busily.

Suddenly they heard a familiar grunting sound. They turned around to see a herd of sowren walking towards the city gates. Two or three people sat comfortably on the back of the great beast, there was even space for a couple of luggage cases. The passengers disembarked carefully outside the gate and trotted off purposefully into the city.

Two travellers turned their heads as they passed. They smiled and gave a customary greeting by dropping their head and touching their hats.

"Wait here I won't be long," Jarrett said before following the sowren's worn path towards the top of a hill.

"Where's he off to?" queried Henry.

"The stables. We need sowren for our journey out," replied Rufus.

Rufus and Althea led the children through the gates and then up a long street into the city square. On one side of the square stood the glorious stone-pillared parliament building of Kirk Heidengaard. A set of steps led up to the grand entrance, a group of statues of famous citizens of Kirk Heidengaard stood proudly outside the great building.

The children had forgotten how close it was to Christmas until they arrived at the city square. A huge Christmas tree glowed spectacularly from the centre of the square. Parents and their children stopped for a moment to look up in admiration as they passed by. At one side of the square, carol singers sang to their heart's content.

Innumerable wooden stalls, warmly decorated with holly, lights and decorations, were dotted around the square. The stalls were brimming with activity as hundreds of people moved between them carrying bags of Christmas shopping and occasionally stopping to greet friends.

School had finished for a month, and children trotted through the streets jovially, shouting, cheering, and hauling snowballs at each other before being reprimanded by parents, street traders or wandering pedlars.

The travellers helped themselves to hot chocolate and sweets at a stall before resting on a bench in the square. They admired the busy activity whilst guzzling down their drinks which felt like a luxury compared to the tasteless tea they had become used to.

"Ah this brings back memories," said Althea after a while.

"Yes, university life hey?" replied Rufus dreamily.

A loud group of university students aptly dressed in their robes trudged past singing loudly, their robes flowing and flapping wildly behind them.

"There seem to be a lot of students around," observed Henry.

"Yes, Kirk Heidengaard is a University city. Most of us were educated here," replied Althea looking to the children.

"You learnt sorcery here?"

"Yes."

"But do sorcerers need to be taught sorcery? Aren't you born with sorceric powers?"

"We are," replied Rufus. "But we have to learn sorceric discipline, particularly how to rein and control our powers. Unfortunately, sorcery was banned in Petonia a long time ago," added Rufus disapprovingly.

"The alchemists have taken over the universities and have plotted with the noblemen to dumb down the curriculum and replace sorcery with rubbish like alchemy or the philosophy of druidic teachings," Rufus added sarcastically.

"Why would they ban sorcery?" asked Ruby.

"It's all part of the fallout from the purge," began Rufus. "The noblemen wanted to rid Petonia of the sorcerers, so they started by banning sorcery in the universities. Then they banned the use of sorcery across the whole state. Whenever they heard even the rumour of a sorcerer using his or her powers, a small regiment was sent to arrest the sorcerer."

"That's why you don't use your powers in public right?" guessed Saul. Rufus nodded.

A little while later Jarrett walked back down the hill.

"Took a bit longer than I'd hoped," he puffed breathlessly. "We've got four sowren for the journey out of the city, and I've secured rooms at the Cobbler's Inn, I've stayed there many times."

*

"Another hour and it'll be a blizzard again," said the bellboy as Rufus handed him some coins. "You'd better stay indoors unless you want to inconvenience the search team." The snow had turned into a heavy downfall as they walked around the University, through busy bazaars, shopping precincts and extraordinarily tight alleyways to the Cobbler's Inn.

That evening they had their first proper meal in weeks. They sat in the busy restaurant at the Cobbler's Inn and helped themselves to three fully laden courses one after another before perusing the chocolate drinks menu that stretched down into a busy list of tempting varieties of caramel hotchox, hazelnut hotchox, almond coldchox and skinny and fat hotchox.

During dinner, Rufus, Jarrett, and Althea carefully planned the events of the following day. Althea and the children would explore the city, while Jarrett and Rufus would find Candlewick Inn where Rufus was due to meet Doctor Kembereley.

*

The following evening, Saul, Ruby, and Henry sat in the bedroom in front of the fire drinking hotchox and listening to Althea's stories about the history of Kirk Heidengaard. Suddenly, Jarrett and Rufus walked in and closed the door loudly behind them.

"There's a problem," muttered Jarrett. He walked to the window carrying a worried expression.

It was snowing hard again, and they could just about see a wagon that had arrived moments earlier. A group of men climbed out. They wore long black coats, carried a bag of arrows around their shoulder and a sword at their belt.

One of the men unloaded the bags, another pulled out a set of crossbows from inside the wagon while another two spoke hurriedly with two passers-by.

"Searchers!" exclaimed Althea.

Jarrett sighed. Rufus and the children joined them and looked on anxiously.

"Do you think they were sent by Winfred, Stergo, and Kayla?" asked Althea.

"No. I think they're independent," replied Jarret. "If they were sent by the rulers, there would have been many more."

"How could they possibly know I'm here in Kirk Heidengaard?" said Rufus worriedly. "Nobody knew of our plans at Kirby Hall, Rabin insisted that the mission stay a secret."

"Maybe they're not looking for you," suggested Jarrett. "Maybe they're after that Hermish translator that Harper Jones was on about."

"You heard the rector in the Chapel," replied Rufus. "They've heard rumours I'm heading this way."

"The sooner we meet the doctor and get out the better," said Althea.

"Are we safe?" asked Ruby.

"Probably not," began Jarrett. "The searchers are immoral, greedy, and opportunistic. They'd kill their own mothers if there was money to be made," Rufus added grimly.

"I recognise some of them. That one there," said Rufus pointing at a stocky tall man.

"Bonecrusher Jones," replied Jarrett worriedly. Saul raised his eyebrows.

"Yes, he and his cronies spent thirteen months hunting down the Barber of Kettlemon. They burnt two villages down in their efforts," said Rufus sternly.

"No that was Headsmasher Johnson."

"There's Nailsplicer Smith," announced Jarrett.

Nailsplicer Smith? Saul mimed to Ruby and Henry worriedly.

"The man with the scar look," Jarrett replied pointing out a brawny looking man carrying a scar etched deep into the left side of his face.

"We have to plan our movements carefully," Rufus murmured after a long silence.

For the rest of the evening Jarrett, Rufus, and Althea planned the short journey to Candlewick Inn. It was no longer as simple as walking there and back. Jarrett planned two separate escape routes in case things went wrong.

"If we get separated—"

"Separated?" asked Althea quickly.

"Yes. If we get separated, we'll meet at 'Crow Claw'," explained Jarrett before explaining the route in meticulous but confusing detail, continually referring to the suns and moons.

"Saul will go in with you to Candlewick Inn. We'll be in a restaurant opposite looking out for you."

"Why don't we just stay here, isn't it safer?" asked Althea.

"If there's an err… incident, at least we can all escape together. I'm sure it'll be perfectly fine though," he added unconvincingly.

The thought that the searchers might tear down the bedroom door at any moment made for an anxious restless night. Rufus and Jarrett took turns to sit with a book in the hotel lobby, watching out for anyone acting suspiciously. Now and again, they walked around casually through the hotel corridors and occasionally into the snowy street.

By midnight, Ruby and Henry were sleeping peacefully, but Saul was a restless bundle of nerves. He was a light sleeper at the best of times, and the present predicament had him tossing and turning worriedly all night. The slightest noise had him wide awake listening in frozen anticipation for footsteps or voices.

The night passed without incident, and the following day, a very tired Saul and equally sleep-deprived Rufus left for Candlewick Inn. They walked through the tight shopping alleyways and bazaar, stopping occasionally to buy supplies for the onward journey out of Kirk Heidengaard and mingling in busy crowds of shoppers who went about their daily business, notwithstanding the intrepid weather conditions.

The shopkeepers of Kirk Heidengaard were renowned for their welcoming spirit. Almost every shopkeeper offered them hot milk, hotchox, or chocotea and made them feel welcome. Saul determined resolutely that, despite the arrival of the searchers, Kirk Heidengaard was the most wonderful place in the Netherworld.

Candlewick Inn was tucked away to one side of the University library. It was a busy place attracting the students and professors of the University, and like the rest of Kirk Heidengaard, radiated friendliness and joviality.

Rufus and Saul seated themselves in a quiet spot overlooking the main street. Jarrett, Althea, Ruby, and Henry walked into a restaurant opposite them and seated themselves by the window.

"Two manrin juices please," ordered Rufus handing over some coins.

The walls of the Inn were lined with paintings of the city and its history. One wall carried portraits of celebrated University professors, who had once been regulars at the Inn.

A student sat playing a piano in the corner. Students sat huddled in small groups laughing and cajoling about the events of the day and celebrating the eccentricity of some of their renowned professors. Every time another student entered the Inn, there was uproarious sarcastic rejoicing that another *Heidengaardite* had managed a timely escape from what must have been a *terribly invigorating, motivating, and inspiring lecture.*

For the first time since meeting him, Saul noticed that Rufus looked nervous. He looked surreptitiously around whenever the door opened and glanced suspiciously at passers-by in the street. Now and again, Rufus asked Saul to keep an eye on *the man in the far corner by the door* or the *two men who've just walked in.*

A while later, a smart gaunt handsome man, whose tidy and well-kept appearance fell against the grain of the clientele that seemed to visit the place, walked up to their table.

"Doctor Samuel Rufus?" he asked quietly.

"Maybe," replied Rufus looking up.

The man seated himself directly in front of Rufus.

"Allow me to introduce myself, Doctor Kembereley," he extended his hand. "I'm an old friend of Rabin," Rufus shook his hand hesitantly. "You seem to be... in a lot of demand."

"It would seem so," replied Rufus quietly.

Saul stopped sipping at the manrin juice and listened attentively. He glanced out into the street. Three men had accompanied the doctor and were waiting in the street.

"Let's get some formalities out of the way," suggested Rufus.

Doctor Kembereley looked around before pulling out a beautifully decorated square box and placing it into Rufus' hand.

"I was expecting a diary," said Rufus.

"That is, apparently a diary."

Rufus raised his eyebrows. He turned the box around a few times and ran his finger across the sides noticing that it did not have an opening. He handed the box to Saul and pointed at Saul's bag.

"I've never met you before, how do I know you're Doctor Kembereley?"

The waiter arrived with a beer for Doctor Kembereley.

"If I'd wanted to set a trap, I would have captured you before you walked into the Inn. Maybe yesterday when you and Jarrett were gallivanting around the city. We could easily have picked off your friends in the square," he added.

"There's probably not much I can say to convince you," began Doctor Kembereley taking a swig of his beer. "I'm the one that sent the soldiers to rescue you during the Battle of Wicker."

Rufus thought about this for a few moments and felt embarrassed for mistrusting Doctor Kembereley.

"I've known Rabin long before you took your vows. I owe my life and livelihood to him. I was the last person he met before his capture that fateful night," continued Doctor Kembereley, "and he certainly trusted me enough to give me that box."

"I'm sorry, I hope you understand my… anxiety," said Rufus quietly. "Rabin said you have some information for me." Rufus pulled out a notebook and pen.

"I was asked to locate some of your friends. It's taken a lot of work, but we have some information." Doctor Kembereley took a swig of his beer. "Somer Johnson, Charles Shackle, Caulene Falden are at Vanden Port Castle. Lorraine Calvert and Frederick Roffman are at the Amberlight Mine, that's a deep mine, be careful there. Cleo Lane, Cesar Bowden, Colin Roffman and Botha Enssad are at the Sarbasto Ice Mine in the far North of Goran."

"They're mining in the ice mines?"

"Hmm. Green diamonds apparently."

"That's cruel."

"Many sorcerers were sent to the mining ships. Abraham Herman is on a slave ship between North Goran and the Catellan mines, Darnell Harper's on the mining ship between Catellan and East Goran," continued Doctor Kembereley taking another swig of his beer.

He continued for a while, naming sorcerer after sorcerer while Rufus scribbled frantically in his notebook. By the time Doctor Kembereley had finished he had named forty-eight sorcerers in seventeen places making the task of rescuing them seem daunting.

"I'm sure you'll find sorcerers that I haven't mentioned once you get into some of those prisons. There are also many more prisons, castles, forts, mines, and ships that will have sorcerers that we don't know about. But it's a start."

Rufus read back some of the names and places to make sure he had written them right.

"Why hasn't the Baron killed them all, why keep them prisoner?"

"The Baron's building an army of sorcerers," began Doctor Kembereley. "Most of the Goran sorcerers have refused to join him, so he wants Petonian sorcerers to join the army. The best way to break their will is to make them work hard."

"Why won't the Goran sorcerers join him?"

"There's a lot of animosity between them and the Baron. They're still holding on, but it's only a matter of time before they turn."

"An army of sorcerers," Rufus muttered quietly.

"Can't they just use their powers to escape?" asked Saul naively.

"Good question young man," smiled Doctor Kembereley. "The Baron discovered a dark secret which eliminates their power and makes them behave like mortals. I don't know what it is. Maybe it's something in the air they breathe or something they eat. You must discover it," he said turning to Rufus, " if you're to get far in the war that is brewing."

"Rabin was drugged with the brixius serum," noted Rufus.

Doctor Kembereley raised his eyebrows. "Ah, that makes sense."

"You said that most hadn't joined him, does that mean some have?"

Doctor Kembereley was quiet for a few moments.

"Be careful of the friends you keep, many Petonian sorcerers have turned to the Baron willingly," he took a slow sip of his beer. "Dorothea Verrill, Fiona Hawksworth, Tom Forrell, Rabina Ziccard..." He read out a series of names.

"A roll call of traitors," sighed Rufus when Doctor Kembereley had finished. "I didn't think Rabina would ever turn, and Tom… he was one of my best friends. Listen, we believe there's a traitor amongst us."

"Of course. Why are the searchers here right?"

Rufus nodded. "If I give you some names, can you tell me if you recognise any?"

Doctor Kembereley shook his head when Rufus had finished announcing the names of sorcerers, many of whom Saul, Ruby, and Henry had met in the last few weeks.

"I can't say that any of those people are traitors, they don't sound familiar, but there *is* a traitor in your group."

The sound of broken glass followed closely by a tremendous *"yay!"* made all three of them turn suddenly.

"There's one more thing," continued Doctor Kembereley. "Two men came here four weeks ago claiming to be on a special assignment from the Baron. They were looking for Joseph Lockwood, a professor at the University. He had gone home for a break. He didn't return and they set off to find him. They're still searching for him.

"A week ago, the Baron put out a reward for his capture. He really wants the professor, more desperately than he wants you," Doctor Kembereley stressed this last part and smiled.

"Why?"

"We aren't sure," said Doctor Kembereley. "The professor is a specialist in *cryptic Hermish*, a coded version of the ancient druidic script. Valak's been looking for cryptic Hermish translators for a year now. I thought you should know this." He sipped his beer.

"Time to leave I think," urged Doctor Kembereley. Three searchers were at the door of the inn. "That list is very important, look after it. And please pass my wishes to Rabin. There's a door at the back of the Inn, it'll take you to the side of the Inn. Can you see it?"

Rufus stood up. "Stay with me," he ordered Saul.

They walked out of the Inn into an alleyway. As they sped back to the Cobbler's Inn, Rufus looked behind sporadically to see if they were being followed.

"They're on our trail. We need to leave straight away," urged Althea as she, Jarrett, Ruby, and Henry walked through the door.

"We can't go anywhere until that clears," said Jarrett pointing at the window. A heavy downpour of snow had caught up with them, and the street outside the windows had become a white blur.

"People travel through the snow all the time here," urged Althea. "We can't risk staying here it's—"

"We are safer here," interrupted Jarrett. "If we get lost in the snow, there's a greater chance we'll get caught."

"And if we stay here, we've got nowhere to hide," asserted Rufus.

"We just need to hang on a few hours. Let it clear a bit."

The snow continued relentlessly, and in the end, after continued protracted discussions about the merits of staying, Rufus and Althea reluctantly agreed to stay the night and leave at dawn.

~ 11 ~

Escape!

Late in the night, Saul, Ruby, and Henry were jostled awake. For a moment, they were horrified by a silhouetted figure which turned out to be Rufus standing over them with a finger over his mouth.

"Pack your bags and get ready quick! You've got two minutes," he announced in an urgent tone.

"What's up?" asked Henry dreamily.

"They're scouring the Inns and hotels. We have to leave right now."

"They?" queried Ruby jumping out of the bed sleepily.

"The searchers," came Jarrett's frantic reply. "They're heading for the Inn. Be quick!" Jarrett whispered loudly, peering through the window towards the entrance.

Althea walked into the room shoulder bag in hand. She frantically tidied up the beds and then walked up to the balcony.

"Up to the roof and across to the opposite side of the block! Head for the city gates," ordered Rufus. He ushered the children towards the balcony. "Up you go."

One by one, Henry, Ruby and then Althea followed Jarrett up a cold slippery drainpipe.

"Climb to the roof and wait for me, don't try to catch up with the others," ordered Rufus as Saul climbed up after them. "They've probably moved on. We have to stick together."

It was a good thing the searchers had not positioned someone in the street, thought Saul watching flutters of snow fall onto the pavement. He reached the top of the roof and waited impatiently for Rufus.

Rufus jumped onto the balcony as a clatter of footsteps and shouting filled the corridor. Rufus climbed up quickly and smiled at Saul.

"No time to lose," whispered Rufus assertively. "They'll be in the street in moments." The door of the bedroom crashed down.

Rufus and Saul ran across the roof, slipping and sliding uncontrollably. They crossed several rooftops, climbed down another drainpipe and sped down an alleyway.

The snow was coming down heavily now and it was difficult to see more than a few yards ahead. But they could see just enough to spot the vague blurry outlines of Althea, Jarrett, Ruby, and Henry cutting through an alleyway ahead of them. They followed them through a maze of tiny alleyways, lined with dark bricked terraced houses. The doors were set a foot into the walls of the houses and every house seemed to be identical.

Suddenly a whizzing sound shot past their heads. Four arrows tore into a door in front of them with a solid clattering thud! The searchers had caught up!

The twists and turns through monotonous alleys, each one seemingly identical, made them feel they were going around in circles and that at any moment they would run straight into their assailants.

Then, an arrow shot past and skimmed Saul's right shoulder. He felt an excruciating pain and threw his left hand over the shoulder. Blood! His coat was torn at the arm and there was a cold wet feeling underneath.

"Rufus! They've hit me! I'm bleeding!" he shouted. Why doesn't he stop and wait?

The cold air bit into his face and chilled his lungs. He tried desperately to keep up, but began to fall behind as he slipped and scraped whenever he turned a corner.

Suddenly, a wall appeared from behind the snow. He skidded uncontrollably and his right shoulder crashed into the wall sending a piercing seething pain through his body.

"Oww!" he cried landing flat on his face.

Saul pulled himself up slowly. He spat snow out of his mouth and clasped his shoulder firmly.

Which way had they gone? Was it the alleyway ahead of him, or the one he had just passed? Then, he heard a familiar voice in an alley to his left. He sped off quickly towards it. It was hopeless, the blizzard was coming down fiercely and Saul could not see anything or anybody ahead of him!

Saul spent a moment gathering his thoughts. The city gates, they'll be waiting there for me.

Saul set off through the snow-ridden alleyways, turning and wandering through alleyway after alleyway feeling increasingly lost and confused with a nightmarish feeling of déjà vu as he entered each alleyway.

To his right, an alley opened into the city square. Saul recognised the lone monument of the beautifully decorated Christmas tree and the bench they had sat on when they arrived. Now Saul recalled the way out of the city. Thanking his lucky stars, Saul charged through the square towards the gates.

The gates were deserted, his friends were nowhere to be seen. With a knotted brow and a pounding heart, Saul ran wildly first one way and

then the other, his gaze moving sporadically from side to side and then far into the distance.

"Rufus! Althea, Jarrett!" A whistling wind drowned out his voice. *"Ruby! Henry!"*

Saul stood frozen to the spot for a moment. Now he edged towards a tree some yards away from the city gates. He sat down and tried to comprehend his predicament.

~ 12 ~

Sowren

Saul's attention was disturbed by two voices and the grunting and chuffing of a sowren. It came from inside the gates. The searchers had caught up! Almost at the same time, a lone sowren emerged in the distance, trotting slowly towards the city. Saul's face lit up. Someone was perched on top. He jumped up and waved his arms wildly.

"Jarrett!" he screamed.

Saul was sure Jarrett had looked up, but at the same moment, a carriage emerged from the city gates pulled by two sowren. Saul recognised two of the searchers that had walked into the Cobbler's Inn. Both looked grumpy, miserable, and angry. The rest were probably in the carriage.

Then a horrible thought struck him. Jarrett had to be warned, if he continued walking towards the gates, he and the searchers would cross! The sowren trotted closer and closer to the city and the searchers moved further and further away from the city gates.

Suddenly, Jarrett turned and headed away from the city. He must have seen the searchers. He was getting away! Saul sighed in relief before dragging back his enthusiasm. The carriage picked up the pace and was heading away in the same direction as Jarrett.

They're after him! thought Saul miserably. *I have to warn him.* Saul immediately discarded the idea, he could never catch up without a sowren.

The best thing to do was to wait near the gates. Someone would be back for him soon. He settled down by a snowy tree, took a deep breath and looked out into the distance. Now and again, he stood up excitedly whenever he saw the commotion of a traveller coming in or out of the city gates. Time passed. Nobody returned.

A horrible feeling sat in the pit of his stomach convincing Saul that his companions were not going to return. Jarrett had probably been caught, and Rufus, Althea, Ruby, and Henry had either also been caught or had left without him.

What now? Should he find Doctor Kembereley? He would know what to do. Saul toyed with this idea before discarding it. He did not know where the doctor lived and would raise suspicion by going around asking for him.

Slowly and carefully, Saul unravelled the problem. He determined that he had to make his way to Crow Claw, which was the immediate meeting point. But what if he arrived there and everyone else had already left?

We're meeting at Port Newton, remembered Saul. *In five weeks.* The port was two weeks travel from Kirk Heidengaard, he had to get there in time to meet them. Saul had three weeks in hand, that was plenty of time. Which direction was Port Newton? How would he get there? It was two weeks on a sowren or kray but not by foot.

I could… borrow a sowren, he resolved, remembering that the sowren were kept in the city stables. Saul headed towards the stables. Ten minutes later, Saul could smell the sowren, and now he heard an occasional grunting and chuffing sound.

Four wooden stables lined the top of the hill behind a thick set of trees. A stone building sat to one side. Saul crept up behind the trees. Five or six sowren were lying asleep in each of the stables. A collection of saddles hung on the wall above a line of huge empty food buckets.

"Have Gilliam's sowren ready in half an hour!" shouted a voice that made Saul jump.

A stable boy walked into the stable and emptied what seemed like grain or muesli from a wooden chest into a bucket. He poured two jugs of water in and mixed it vigorously before putting the bucket in front of one of the sowren. He made a clucking sound with his mouth. The huge beast clambered onto its huge paws and overshadowed the boy.

The sowren ate hungrily. Meanwhile, the stable boy brushed the sowren's fur, whistling busily as he did so. Next, the boy pulled down a saddle from the wall, placed a small step ladder next to the sowren and then climbed up and threw the saddle over the great beast, securing it solidly underneath. He waited for the sowren to finish eating before unlocking the chain around the sowren's neck and leading the sowren out into the distance.

How difficult can it be? Thought Saul. He crept into the stable and removed a saddle from the wall.

Having worked out the machinations of the saddle, Saul pulled over an empty bucket. He mixed some grain and water before placing the bucket in the middle of the stable. Saul wandered over to a sowren that lay quietly watching his antics.

"Here boy," whispered Saul as if the huge animal were a small puppy. It did not move. "Come on boy," he muttered more loudly.

Still, it did not move. Saul kicked himself for not paying more attention. What did the stable boy do to get it up? Then he remembered. He clucked a few times. Instantly the sowren raised its head. Saul waved the bucket around enticingly, the sowren clambered onto its feet, plodded over to the bucket, and began eating hungrily.

The sowren was a huge creature, about the size of an elephant thought Saul. The sowren's saggy fur hung down off its body and its huge paws were the size of tree stumps.

"There, there," muttered Saul stroking the grunting animal.

Next, Saul pulled up a stepladder and climbed up steadily, the huge saddle hanging out of one hand. He raised the saddle over the sowren and balanced it carefully on the animal's back. Saul climbed off the ladder, reached underneath the sowren and secured two of the buckles underneath it before pulling the third buckle under the neck and securing it tightly. Again, Saul looked nervously through the opening of the stable towards the stable boy's quarters. *So far so good.*

Saul's brain worked frantically. He took a box of grain from the back of the stable and an empty bucket up the ladder and tied it securely to the saddle.

Now the reins, he thought. Saul's mind was engrossed in a thousand thoughts, and he did not realise he had climbed off the ladder too quickly. He slipped and fell onto his right arm. A foaming pain hit his arm! In all the anxiety of getting the sowren ready, he had taken his mind off the wound, and for a few moments, Saul lay on the stable floor holding his shoulder.

He got up a few precious moments later. A light turned on in the building in the snowy distance.

Where were the reins? Saul stood rooted to the spot, turning his head one way and then another. Maybe he could ride the sowren without a set of reins he thought, before immediately discarding the idea. How would he guide and direct it?

Saul charged out and ran past the stables looking frantically into each one. To his relief, he saw a collection of reins hanging on the wall of one of the stables.

Saul charged in and immediately jumped backwards as a sowren shot to its feet, growled, and lunged forward! The huge fearsome face of the sowren hung threateningly within a foot of Saul. Through the corner of his eye, Saul saw that the metal chain was pulled to its limit.

Saul's heart pounded in his throat as he stood frozen to the spot looking frightfully into the eyes of the sowren.

"There, there," he muttered in a poor attempt to mimic Ruby's calm approach to the kray.

The sowren continued growling quietly. Saul stepped steadily backwards towards the wall of the stable, not daring to turn his eyes away from the sowren. He felt around blindly behind him for the reins, still not moving his eyes away from the sowren. Suddenly, the pile crashed onto a set of metal buckets. Another sowren awoke in a stable nearby and began to growl loudly.

Everything was going wrong! He had to abandon the plan, but the reins were at his feet, the sowren was almost ready to go and Saul just needed a few more carefully executed moments.

Another light turned on in the house, someone was shouting. Saul clutched a rein and charged back to the first stable. He threw the reins over the sowren and tied them to the third buckle. He was ready to move.

"Sam! Someone's in the stable!"

Two stable boys ran out of the stone building carrying a lamp in one hand and a stick in the other. Saul was angry with himself; the clambering and growling were enough to awaken the dead. He climbed up the ladder and tugged the reins violently. The sowren jerked forward and then stopped to a sudden, sharp, crashing standstill, nearly throwing Saul off.

Saul had not released the chain! He jumped off angrily, moved the ladder next to the sowren's neck, climbed up and was relieved to see a simple release mechanism. He pushed the latch down, the chain crashed to the floor.

The stable boys were yards from the stable. Saul climbed back onto the saddle, kicked the ladder away and pulled the reins for the second time. He nearly fell back as the sowren charged out of the stable.

The sowren tore through the opening out into the snow, the two stable boys jumped backwards landing on their backs.

"A sowren!" screamed the second boy. "Get a sowren, quick!"

Saul held on frantically as the sowren charged away from the stables. It was a rough and uncomfortable ride made worse by Saul's inability to guide the animal. Steadily, Saul came to grips with the reins and soon he was guiding the sowren in a straight line towards the white forest.

*

Saul had a small head start, made easier by a fierce blizzard that had settled in. Soon, the footprints of the sowren would disappear making it impossible for his assailants to track him.

Saul kept his head down to shield his face from the oncoming snow. Now and again, he looked up to see ahead of him, and some moments later, he was relieved to see the white forest emerging from behind the snow. A few yards into the forest, Saul brought the sowren to a stop.

Saul waited there for a while, pondering, and calculating his next move. He would be hopelessly lost in this strange world without knowing clearly how to get to Port Newton, but which direction should he take? Then he recalled a conversation about following one of the moons for the entire journey. But which moon? Was it the largest, Lunam-Rube or the smallest, Lunam-Fus, or was it Lunam-Pras? *Why can't they stick to maps?* thought Saul angrily.

Saul looked up into the sky through the sketchy forest openings. It was the large moon, Lunam-Rube! The conversation became clearer. They had to follow Lunam-Rube at night and Solarius in the day, this would eventually lead to Port Newton.

Saul led the sowren out of the white forest and spent a moment inspecting the sky. All three moons were struggling through the snow clouds. To the right was the sobering view of Lunam-Rube. Saul took a deep breath, smacked the reins, and set off.

*

Saul was drifting asleep. Once or twice he nearly fell off the sowren. He tried to force his eyes wide open, but it was hopeless. He had to rest.

Saul dismounted by a thicket of trees. He removed the box of grain, then the saddle and reins, before sitting down in the cold snow. The sowren shook itself wildly, showering Saul with snow. It brought its rear legs down and settled onto the snow. Within moments, the sowren was asleep.

Saul shook off the snow and smacked his clothes frustratedly. As he pulled the tent out of his bag, two objects landed softly in the snow.

The notebook and Rabin's diary! Rufus needed the notebook desperately, so desperately, he had read out the names of the prisoners and their locations carefully to be sure he had them right.

And then there was the diary, the very reason they had travelled to Kirk Heidengaard. The *diary* was a wooden box, beautifully decorated with patterns of flowers, leaves and animals marked around the edges. Saul turned it over in his cold hands wondering what could be inside it that was of such importance to Rabin. Maybe he should open it and see. He turned it over a few times, there was no opening. He sighed and placed it into the bag.

Saul stamped down an area of snow, placed a blanket on the snowy floor and set up the tent.

Somewhere in the back of Saul's mind rested the anxiety that the stable boys might creep up on the tent during the night. But he was too tired to move on, he just had to chance it. With these thoughts permeating through his head, Saul slowly and steadily fell into a deep sleep.

Saul was awoken by a rumbling sound. He sat up dreamily and listened intently. The sound became a low guttural growl. After a few nervous moments, Saul crawled to the opening and listened more carefully. The shadowy figure of the sowren was standing up tall against the night sky as still as a statue. The sowren's head was focussed and its back legs were crouched down as if preparing to jump. It was growling at someone or something.

Saul stepped out into the still night and gazed anxiously at the object of the sowren's concern, a white snowy thicket of bushes. It was still and lifeless. A few moments passed, the sowren settled, and whatever the threat was, seemed to have disappeared.

"There, there," muttered Saul quietly. He reached up and stroked the jaw of the sowren. A distinctive black mark on its chin gave the gargantuan a strange sense of character. The brute of an animal was looking out for Saul, and this made him feel safe.

Saul sneezed and quickly stepped back into the tent into what now felt like a very warm and comfortable bed.

When Saul woke up, the sun was lighting up the inside of the tent. He clambered up, pulled the tent together, and saw the huge figure of the sowren still in a deep sleep.

Saul placed three handfuls of grain into the bucket and realised quickly that there was no water. Saul nearly kicked himself, he was surrounded by it! He threw a few handfuls of snow into the bucket and swished it around with his hand. A while later, the mixture thickened up, and he placed the bucket in front of the sowren.

"Up boy," he murmured, waving the bucket under the sowren's nose, and making a clucking noise.

Watching the sowren eat made Saul feel hungry. He looked around the barren white wilderness wondering where he might find food. Then an idea struck him. Saul lifted the empty bucket. The leftovers looked like muesli mixed with granola. Instinctively, Saul dipped his finger into the grain and licked it with a contorted look on his face. It tasted sweet, quite nice in fact. Saul sighed. He had transport, food and seemed to know where he was going, perhaps things were not as bad as they seemed.

Soon, Saul was ready to leave. The tent was packed, the saddle was strapped meticulously on the sowren's back and the food was secured firmly on top.

Saul paused and then trotted over to the thicket of bushes that had caused the sowren so much consternation. He looked around carefully for footprints or signs of someone having been there overnight. It had been a still night with no snowfall, if someone had been there, there should have been footprints. There was nothing, no footprints, and no sign of anybody having been there.

*

By the second afternoon, the journey felt monotonous. The snow became soft, and by the following day, the air was warmer, and the snow became slushy. The Sowren was struggling and panting more heavily. He was not used to the warmer temperature, thought Saul.

In the afternoon, Saul saw a green valley in the distance and realised that he had to begin walking and let the sowren loose. Maybe it had a homing instinct.

Saul climbed off the sowren and prepared one last meal. He watched the sowren eating it, and strangely, Saul began feeling sentimental. The sowren had become his friend. Saul had started talking to it, and now and again, the sowren had grunted what seemed like a response.

When it had finished eating, Saul looked into the sowren's eyes and stroked its neck. "You've been a wonderful friend," he said. "But it's time to let you go."

The sowren grunted and raised its head. Spontaneously, Saul reached up, pulled its head down, and hugged the animal. The warm fur felt comforting. The sowren responded with a purring sound almost as if it knew that it was time to part separate ways.

Moments later, Saul threw his bag over his shoulder and walked towards the distant valley. He had hardly walked a few yards when he heard a loud high-pitched growl. Not the threatening defensive growl of the night before, but a friendly one. Saul turned, he looked at the sowren. It was standing at the same spot. Instinctively Saul waved at it and walked away, this time promising himself not to look back.

~ 13 ~

A Carriage to Nowhere

Henry was panting for breath. He slipped and dashed across the snow trying woefully to keep up. Rufus, Jarrett, Althea, and Ruby were stretching further ahead. *They're still in sight*, he thought consolingly, *just have to keep up.*

"Slow down!" The howling biting wind tore through the narrow alleyways and drowned out his voice. Keeping up was difficult. He was continually wiping his snow-covered glasses, leaving a watery smear that only made it worse.

I should wait, he thought quickly. Saul was somewhere behind, he was sure of it. Together they would find their way and navigate through the maze of alleyways. But what if he was wrong, what if Saul had passed through another alleyway and was already in front? The tiniest delay was dangerous.

Henry stopped and looked behind and then ahead of him, he took his wet glasses off, squinted and looked again. It all looked the same, a huge smeary blurry white mess!

What now? He could not just run aimlessly, he might run straight into the clutches of the searchers. After a moment, Henry convinced himself that Saul was still catching up. He had to wait, together they would find a way out. Directly in front of him, Henry saw the door to a house. Like most of the house doors in the Kirk Heidengaard alleyways, it was set two feet into the wall. With the snow coming down like a thick curtain, the door would provide good cover.

"Come on, come on," Henry muttered as he stood pasted against the door looking out intently for Saul to pass.

Suddenly, a brown cloaked figure shot past! Henry froze with fear, his heart pounding wildly. Was he seen? Had the searcher seen the footprints? Perhaps he was walking back towards Henry. Should Henry run in the opposite direction?

Henry wanted to peek out, but his wiser self convinced him to stay hidden until he was sure the searcher was well out of reach.

After a while, Henry came away from the door. He looked around cautiously. Comfortable that the searcher had passed by, he walked along aimlessly for a while. Of one thing he was sure, he had to get out of the city and reach the gates. His last hope was that everybody was waiting there for him. Drowned in these thoughts, Henry walked along slowly and gloomily.

Suddenly, a hand reached out behind him and wrapped itself over his mouth! An arm came around the other side and pulled him into the air. Before he knew it, Henry was being carried through the alleyway. He pulled, kicked, writhed, jerked, and struggled to break free.

To his horror, Henry saw a wooden carriage standing ahead of him. It was pulled by a huge sowren which puffed and grunted into the air sporadically.

"Rankin!" cried a rough voice behind Henry's ear. *"I've got one!"*

A burly heavy man dressed in the tell-tale brown cloak of a searcher emerged from the front of the carriage. He dropped his hood to reveal a deep scar that ran down from the eyebrow to the bottom of his cheek. Henry gasped. Nailspicer Smith!

"Where are the others Edgerton?" he rasped.

"They're probably ahead."

Rankin reached down and took hold of Henry's legs. Together they threw him into the back of the carriage. Henry shot to his feet and charged at the door. Rankin jumped into the carriage, tied Henry's legs and arms, and threw a tight rope around his mouth. Henry wriggled desperately as Rankin walked out and locked the door shut.

A moment later, Henry felt the carriage moving away slowly. It turned twice. After a third turn, it came to a stop. Henry heard three voices. He threw his feet down against the carriage floor. It was in vain. The voices ignored him and continued talking. A moment later, the carriage was on its way again.

It was too much to bear. Henry lay helpless on the cold floor of the carriage and began crying uncontrollably, wishing he could be back home with his parents in their wonderful warm living room. With every moment that the carriage rolled away, Henry became further convinced that he would never see his family again.

~ 14 ~

The Ballards

It was a cloudy day. The landscape was gradually becoming greener and it felt warmer. Suddenly, Saul came to the horrible realisation that he was lost. He had forgotten to calibrate his journey with Solarius, and even if he had tried, the day had been so downcast he would not have seen any of the suns through the dark sky. To make matters worse, Saul could not recall how long he had been wandering aimlessly.

What now, he thought? It was unwise to move on unless he knew which way to travel. Saul underwent a tirade of confusion and panic before sitting down against a tree. He felt deeply alone, depressed, and saddened at his prospects. Saul clenched his teeth and pursed his lips tightly, trying hard not to cry.

A while passed before Saul heard a clattering sound. He turned his head and was met by an elderly man and a girl sitting on a cart. The cart was pulled by a strange black ox-like creature with three curved horns protruding from its head and two huge front legs which seemed to dwarf the rear legs. The back of the cart was laden with a pile of hay that stooped way above the man and girl.

"Good afternoon young sir," said the man touching his straw hat.

Saul returned the greeting and touched his forehead.

"Are you lost?"

"Err, yes."

"I thought as much. We don't often get travellers in these parts."

Saul did not know how to respond. Should he engage in casual conversation or dive straight into the problem at hand?

"Sir, do you know the way to Port Newton?" he asked.

The man eyed Saul suspiciously from his shoes right up to his hair, wondering it seemed, why a lone boy needed to get to Port Newton.

"You're many days from there," remarked the man guardedly. He had sharp grey round eyes, a pointed nose and a small pointed beard which he infrequently scratched. He looked kind and gentle.

The girl smiled at Saul, and in return, Saul looked away, embarrassed at having stared at her. She was pretty. Her beautiful black hair was tied up in a ponytail. She was very pale and had blue eyes.

"But if you must, it's two days from here," continued the man after a pause. He proceeded to give detailed directions. "Of course, if it were a clear day," he said looking up noticing how downcast it was, "it would be easier to travel."

Saul tried to remember and repeat back as much of the instructions as he could, keen not to get lost again.

"You'll pass Beezel Mount, cut across the side of the mount. Stay clear of the mount. Don't enter it or go near it."

"Beezel Mount, cut across, don't enter," repeated Saul.

"I'm only mentioning it as a reference point."

Saul nodded and repeated the instructions.

"What's your name?"

"Saul."

"You're travelling alone?"

Saul nodded.

"You're not part of a err... group?"

Saul shook his head.

"It's a long walk," the old man began in a more commanding tone. "You should rest before you continue your journey. There are long stretches with nowhere to stop. Get some food and drink, maybe stock up your supplies. Why don't you rest a few hours with us? We aren't far from here."

The girl shot a frowned expression at the old man.

"I shouldn't, I need to move on."

"Grandfather you said we wouldn't take guests again after—"

"I insist," the old man scowled at the girl. "It's rude to turn hospitality down in these parts. We could lend you a nark, you'll get there in no time."

Perhaps that wasn't such a bad idea thought Saul. He assumed that the strange beast pulling the cart was a nark. The man seemed friendly, and Saul could do with proper food.

"I suppose an hour out of my journey won't make much difference," replied Saul.

"That's the spirit," smiled the man. "I'm Christoff Ballard, this is my granddaughter, Shari."

Christoff shuffled to the side of the cart, Shari moved uncomfortably to the middle and made space for Saul. He sat down to an unwelcoming flat look on Shari's face. Her frozen demeanour made Saul feel uncomfortable.

The cart made its way through flowery hills surrounded by the busy sights and sounds of birds tweeting merrily in the trees and grasshoppers chirping sporadically.

Eventually, they approached Roba Simms. Along the way, Christoff pointed out the home of the sheriff, the village hall, and a five-acre plot of land owned by Christoff's brother.

Saul was feeling happier now and began to enjoy and appreciate the beautiful, flowery, and picturesque village. He felt optimistic about his predicament. Part of the problem, he conjectured, was that he had not had any company for a few days. Caring companionship and friendship seemed to make the whole experience of the Netherworld more bearable.

Narks grazed lazily around cottages, and now and again, a villager looked up inquisitively from the front of his cottage as the cart clambered through.

"Don't mind them," said Christoff apologetically. "We rarely get visitors in these parts."

Eventually, the cart pulled up outside a cottage at the farthest outskirts of the village. Christoff, Shari, and Saul were greeted at the door by an older boy who Saul presumed to be Shari's brother. Saul followed him through into the kitchen which sat snugly at the back of the cottage. A few candles and a roaring fire cast a wonderful welcoming light in the room.

"Where you from?" asked the boy gruffly.

"Err… near Kirby Hall," replied Saul thinking quickly and not realising the hesitancy in his reply.

"Ernea Kirby Hall? I didn't know there was a place called *Ernea Kirby Hall*," muttered the boy sarcastically.

"Stop bothering him Joffrey! Who cares where he's from?" interjected Christoff. "He's our guest. His name is Saul, and he has a long journey ahead of him."

Shari placed some bread, butter, and a knife onto the table, and then a plate in front of Saul and Christoff.

"You should leave," she whispered blankly before walking away.

Saul raised his eyebrows. He found her attitude confusing and did not understand what had annoyed her.

"Eat, drink," invited Christoff as Shari returned with soup. "You may stay here as long as you wish. In fact, you should be our guest for a few nights," he added with a twinkly smile as he bit into his bread. "You must have travelled for a long time, maybe you're tired. You did say you were alone, didn't you?"

Saul nodded.

Christoff's mood changed suddenly. "Did you bring some bread Joffrey? How many times do I have to tell you?"

"I'm sorry to have imposed like this," said Saul.

"It's not a problem," insisted Christoff.

Christoff Ballard was a kind and hospitable host. Remarkably different to Shari and Joffrey whose coldness was irritating.

The Ballards were a peaceful family. The three of them lived together in the cottage. They whiled away their days toiling in their small farm trying, with great difficulty, to grow enough to feed themselves. Like so many families in the Netherworld, they were victims of the centiwar, Christoff's wife, the eldest son, and his wife, had been kidnapped many years ago never to return. Joffrey and Shari were his grandchildren.

Saul became captivated by the inviting pleasant manner of Christoff who, after Saul had eaten to his heart's content, flowed into exciting stories about the colourful history of Roba Simms.

Saul was so enthralled by the tales of wonder and enchantment he had not realised it had become dark outside. Shari was sitting quietly in the corner of the kitchen. Joffrey had returned and had perched himself in an armchair by the window looking out from time to time with an air of quiet inquisition. The fireplace announced itself proudly around a heavy glowing fire.

The pressure of getting to Port Newton weighed heavily on Saul's mind and continually nagged him. "I must go," he announced finally.

"One night won't affect your plans, we can lend you a nark, you'll be at Port Newton by sunset tomorrow," said Christoff tersely. "Joffrey you'll accompany Saul tomorrow. Make sure he gets there safely," he ordered looking firmly at Joffrey.

"Yes, but you promised never to take guests."

"Don't be so rude you insolent child," said Christoff sternly. "We had a bad experience with a guest once," explained Christoff turning to Saul.

Saul weighed this carefully before agreeing reluctantly. He could not afford to get lost, particularly with such little time to get to Port Newton.

Time passed by in the candlelit kitchen with Christoff churning out more exciting stories.

"And that was when Etheridge Ballard my great great great great, err no, my great great great great great grandfather moved to Roba Simms. Now in the year that—" there was a knock at the door.

A nervous silence filled the room, nobody seemed to want to open the door. Saul wondered, frightfully, whether the searchers had tracked him down.

Eventually, Joffrey opened the door. Heavy footsteps and the thud of a stiff walking stick filled the corridor. A tall man walked into the kitchen. He wore a tall hat and an extravagant black cloak. He had dark black eyes and his face carried a serious flat expression. The man walked in and passed his hat and walking stick to Shari.

"The chill's picking up," he said walking up to the table and pulling a chair.

"Get Sir Roker a drink," ordered Christoff. "Thank you for coming so quickly."

"Always on the lookout."

Saul felt relieved as Christoff and Roker continued talking for a while about the upcoming elections, the parties, and the scandals.

"So, this is the boy," said Roker suddenly.

"Yes."

Suddenly, Saul's arms were grabbed from behind and tied tightly to the chair. A hand came over his mouth, and in an instant, his mouth was tied with a rope. Saul kicked and gesticulated wildly but he could not move or make a noise.

"A fine specimen don't you agree?" asked Christoff coming around in front of Saul.

"Hmm. Seems quite useless for work. I'm not sure how useful he'd be."

"No, you're not serious!" rasped Christoff. "He's twice as strong as that peasant you took in the winter, look at him!" he squeezed Saul's arms. "A good worker I tell you, he'll serve you well."

Saul tried to shout through the ropes.

"Your peasant lasted a week in the mines," scowled Sir Roker. "This one won't last much longer."

Saul was horrified to learn he was being sold to a slave trader by a family he'd naively trusted. The room around him became a blur. He felt dizzy.

"A genuine mistake I assure you, we weren't sure of his err... dubious background," pleaded Christoff. "But this boy… well look at him, he's as fit as a fiddle and as strong as a nark. He'll serve you well."

Sir Roker eyed Saul with apparent disappointment. He did not seem impressed notwithstanding Christoff's enthusiasm.

"What do you bid?" asked Christoff enthusiastically. "Come on, come on. You didn't come all this way for the tea did you?"

"Grandfather we shouldn't," pleaded Shari. *"You said you wouldn't! You promised that—"*

"Shut up!" Christoff struck Shari with the back of his hand.

"Three gold coins," replied Sir Roker cautiously.

"Three gold coins! What the…? Three gold coins? After all the trouble we've been through. You won't get a finer worker, he'll serve you in the mines for years. The going rate is seven, that's what they sell for in Ember's Tavern."

"If there are slave traders who'll offer you seven, then take your scoundrel to them. With your reputation I'm sure they'll be queuing up," replied Sir Roker with his customary scowl. "Three gold coins."

Saul kicked the table wildly.

"His legs, Joffrey, his legs," muttered Sir Roker quietly. "I won't be able to sell... damaged goods."

Sell him? Thought Saul. Was he to be sold further?

"Loosen the rope around his wrists as well, I don't want him marked or scarred."

The room was quiet. Sir Roker looked over Saul carefully.

"Six?" proposed Christoff. Sir Roker did not reply. "You drive a hard bargain," conceded Christoff, banging his fist on the table.

"You've given him a look over?" Asked Sir Roker.

"Yes," lied Christoff.

"He's not injured, scarred or marked?"

"No."

"He's not an escapee?"

Christoff shook his head.

"There are no tattoos or numbers on him?"

"Why of course not, what do you take me for?"

Sir Roker was quiet for a moment as he eyed Saul from foot to head.

"Have him ready first thing in the morning" Sir Roker stood up. "And err… did any of the villagers see you bringing him in?"

"Mmm, maybe a couple."

"A couple? The whole village saw you!" cried Shari incredulously.

"How many times do I have to tell you to *shut up*!" Christoff's hand was clenched in a fist.

"That can't be helped now," said Sir Roker consolingly. "But you have to be more cautious," he added turning to the door.

"And our debt is cleared?"

"Yes."

"And a err… small… shall we say holding on the boy?" asked Christoff sheepishly.

Sir Roker took Christoff by the collar, lifted him off his feet and pinned him against the kitchen wall.

"You're in no position to bargain, peasant!" he growled. "Quite frankly it's a wonder I don't take the boy as compensation," he added pushing Christoff so hard he fell flat on his face.

"First thing in the morning," Sir Roker muttered as he walked out of the cottage.

As the door closed, Christoff ran into the kitchen, paused for a moment before erupting into a celebration.

"A drink," he proposed to himself. He charged to a cupboard and pulled down a canister.

Shari stood trembling in the background not daring to move or say anything. Her unpleasant demeanour made sense. Saul had not taken the hint.

Sometime later, Christoff stood up and walked towards Saul with an inquiring glance. Saul's gagged mouth was in excruciating pain, his arms and legs felt paralysed.

"What's up with your arm?" Disappointment filled Christoff's face as he pulled down Saul's shirt top to reveal the wound left by the arrow in Kirk Heidengaard. "Just… my… luck," he said disappointedly.

Saul noticed a look of anticipation on Shari's face in the corner.

"Does it hurt boy?"

Saul nodded vigorously, hoping this would put Christoff off delivering him to Sir Roker.

"It doesn't look serious to me, maybe just a scratch," Christoff scratched his chin. "It'll heal by the time you get to the mines."

*

It was a tormenting night. Saul was beset by a flood of emotions, occasionally shaking his head while trying to pull his wrists apart. Pain flooded through his wrists, and he could feel blood trickling down.

"Cut it out!" shouted Christoff drunkenly from his bed a few times.

It was the middle of the night. Saul was drifting in and out of sleep. Suddenly, he felt a cold hand come tightly over his mouth. Saul panicked and wriggled violently. Saul was no good to Sir Roker, and Christoff had no use for him!

"Quiet," whispered the voice of Shari. "You have to be quiet. I'll set you free, but you mustn't make a sound, do you understand?"

Saul nodded.

Christoff snored loudly sending a shiver through Saul and Shari.

Shari loosened the rope around Saul's wrist, his mouth and then his ankles. Saul was free, in a lot of pain, but free.

Shari led Saul through the kitchen, into the corridor and to the front door which she opened with meticulous care and patience, careful not to let it creak.

"Do you remember the way?"

"I think so."

"The path that led you down here," Shari said pointing out into the village. "Go back up that path, then follow Lunam Pras towards Beezel Mount," Saul looked up, relieved that it was a clear night.

"Don't enter the mount. Just keep moving. They'll give chase as soon as they find out. You have a head start but it isn't much against narks. Christoff will be angry that you've escaped," she said quietly. "A few months ago, one of his slave deals went badly, you were the plan to redeem himself with Sir Roker. You'll probably have both Christoff and Sir Roker after you.""Thank you," said Saul taking Shari's hand. "Come with me."

"I can't."

"But they'll—"

"Don't worry about me, I'll be fine," replied Shari letting go of the hand.

Saul paused for a moment. Surely, he could not leave Shari. Christoff would work out that she had betrayed him. Christoff snored suddenly before Saul waved goodbye and walked out of the door still in two minds about leaving without Shari.

~ 15 ~

Beezel Mount

Saul limped, stumbled, and clambered through the dark village lane before arriving at the fateful spot where he had met Christoff. He looked to the sky and carefully marked the direction of travel.

The wound on his shoulder was sore and his ankles hurt with each step. But the fear of what lay behind propelled Saul forward. By the time Christoff awoke to discover his prisoner had escaped, he would be miles away. He would run, jog, trot, and limp right through the night if necessary.

But an hour later, Saul's spirited trot became a tiring walk. Two hours later, Saul stopped suddenly. He heard the sound of water, maybe a river. But where could it be? Ahead of him lay a dark thicket of trees and there was nothing else around him. He edged through the trees. A while later, they opened to reveal a deep desolate valley. In the middle of the valley, surrounded by a moat, sat a castle nestling firmly on a hill.

Beezel Mount!

To one side, not far from Saul, a stone bridge led into the castle. The valley was packed with conifers stretching upwards into the sky. The moat splashed and gurgled softly and glistened now and again to the reflection of the moons.

Momentarily, Saul forgot the warnings that Shari and even Christoff had given. He should have walked away, but was too tired and hungry. Saul stood at another crossroads in his abysmal journey. He could run as fast and as far as his already diminished energy allowed, or he could hide in the mount, with all its unknown dangers, and wait for his assailants to pass by. *I just need to hide until the morning.*

Saul walked towards the stone bridge, and as he did so, noticed something move in the moat. Suddenly, he caught the vague outline of a huge extraordinarily long slimy snake-like creature as it swam past. This *thing* was much bigger than a kherk, and, judging by its macabre looks, was probably dangerous.

In the distance behind the thicket, he heard someone shouting. Without thinking, Saul ran along the side of the moat until he reached the bridge. At the far end, the bridge stopped at a wide stone archway which led into a lonely darkness.

A screech filled the air and made Saul jump. He looked up at the moonlit sky and caught the outline of several huge birds encircling the mount. Deirons! He remembered, with relief, that deirons were scavengers. They would not hurt him, but what were they scavenging on?

Saul took a deep breath and stepped onto the bridge. He walked across slowly and nervously. It was a long bridge that seemed longer with the anticipation of a serpent swimming through underneath. At the other end, Saul stepped tentatively into a dark courtyard. A set of outbuildings and verandas were barely visible under the moonlight. At the far end sat the silhouetted shape of the castle. On the ground floor, a tiny light shone out from a window. Saul paused and wondered if someone actually lived here. He walked towards it anxiously, now and again looking back at the entrance and planning a rapid escape.

As Saul walked through the courtyard, he saw the source of the stench that filled the air and the reason why so many deirons were encircling the mount. Dozens of dead animals, some stripped to the bone, others seemingly quite fresh, lay scattered around the courtyard. Saul reached into his bag, pulled out a cloth and placed it firmly against his mouth.

Something moved. Saul stopped still and turned his head. Two red dots sat in the deathly darkness. Was his mind playing tricks? A pair of red dots moved to his left. Eyes! Far behind him, he heard a gnawing sound. Whatever it was, was eating one of the carcasses! Now Saul noticed seven or eight pairs of red eyes all around the dark courtyard.

He had to get out! But then he heard a rustling sound near the bridge accompanied by a faint voice. All the red eyes disappeared suddenly, and a shifting scattering sound moved towards the bridge. There was nothing to it, he had to go towards the castle.

A large wooden doorway led into the castle. Saul stepped into a lobby lit up by a set of wall lamps. A stone staircase led upwards into darkness. Someone lived here, and the question on Saul's mind was whether that 'someone' could possibly be worse than whoever was in pursuit.

To the left, a light shone out from under a door. Saul reached for the doorknob and pushed the door slowly. He was stunned momentarily by the smell of strong chemicals, reminding him of the science laboratory at school.

"Hello?" Saul said quietly. "Is… is anybody here?" Silence filled the air.

A candle flickered gently on a window ledge. On one side of the room, test tubes, a Bunsen burner, basins, and an array of small bottles of liquid and powder littered a dusty table. Whoever lived here was an alchemist and Saul recalled that the alchemists and the council did not get on.

An armchair, a table, and a footstool sat in the corner of the room. On the opposite side, a sink and stove were tucked against the wall. Saul walked in and gazed around intriguingly.

"I've been expecting you Saul Anan," said a hoarse voice behind him. Saul jumped in shock and turned sharply. A tall thin bald man stood at the door. He had a wrinkled forehead and was holding a walking stick. The candlelight flickered off his small round glasses giving him an eerie ghostly look. He carried a sarcastic smile.

"Expecting me?" asked Saul worriedly.

The man did not answer. He pointed his walking stick to the footstool. Saul stood looking nervously at the man.

"You have nothing to fear Saul. Take a seat."

Saul thought about this for a moment before walking to the stool. The bald man walked to the sink and filled a kettle with water. He lit the stove and placed the kettle on it.

"I'm Saul Smith," announced Saul nervously correcting the man. "Not Saul Anan."

"You're from the Upperworld?"

Saul nodded. How could he know that?

"My name is Darius Algar."

"Sorry to have come into your… house, I… won't stay long, I promise, just an hour, I'm a bit lost you see," said Saul quickly.

"Stay as long as you wish."

Saul was not keen to stay. The last time he had been invited to stay as a guest, he was sold to a slave trader.

"Tea?" asked Darius. It seemed impolite to refuse.

"Err yes sir," replied Saul firmly eyeing the door. He could jump over the bed and head out of the door, and assuming Darius lived alone in this desolate place and given that he walked with a walking stick, Saul could be away within moments. But that was assuming Darius lived alone, what if someone else was here?

"You can leave whenever you want Saul," said Darius with his back to Saul. "I'm not going to stop you. I'm not sure you'll get far through that courtyard though." His walking stick tapped across the floor as he walked over with a glass of water and a mug of tea. Saul wondered why he had not heard Darius creeping in. Darius lit a lamp and sat down in the armchair. The room lit up and did not feel as unfriendly.

"Are you… an alchemist?" asked Saul nervously.

Darius was quiet for a moment. "It's what I've resorted to I suppose. What brings you here Saul?"

"It's a long story," muttered Saul quietly. *Where have I seen him before?* Saul thought with intrigue. There was something remarkably familiar about him, but Saul could not quite put his finger on it.

"Look I'll be straight with you," began Saul after a few moments. "I've had a terrible time and it couldn't possibly get any worse. You don't have to believe me, but I was nearly sold as a slave. There are these people after me you see, Christoff Ballard and his friends. I shouldn't have gone with him to his house, but I did, I know it was a mistake—"

"Slow down Saul," said Darius soothingly. He leant forward and put his hand on Saul's. "Start from the beginning and talk slowly. You're safe here." Something magical about Darius' touch made Saul feel calm and relaxed.

"We accidentally entered this world because we were, well, we were being nosy."

"By *we* do you mean you, Ruby and Henry?"

"How did you know—"

Darius raised his hand. "That doesn't matter right now. Continue."

Slowly and more composedly, Saul explained the circumstances that had befallen him, Ruby, and Henry in the last few weeks. Darius sat back listening intently, raising his eyebrow now and again.

"So, they finally discovered that Rabin is alive," Darius mumbled to himself rhetorically when Saul had finished.

"Do you know Rabin?"

"Yes."

"Is he a friend?"

"Was," he paused, "a friend."

"And you know the council?"

"They're the reason I'm here."

"Why are you here? I mean why would you want to live in a place like this. It's terrible, I can't imagine—"

"I don't *choose* to live here Saul, this is a prison," scowled Darius.

Saul raised his eyebrows. "A prison?"

"Yes. Beezel mount is a prison."

"It doesn't seem to be much of a prison. Why can't you just walk out? I mean I walked in. There wasn't a lock on the gate. Sure, there were these strange creatures—"

"Leariks."

"Leariks," repeated Saul slowly. "But they didn't do anything as I walked in, maybe you could just run out when they're off guard or something," continued Saul naively. He realised immediately that like so many things in the Netherworld, it was not as easy as that.

"My dear Saul, I have three problems. The leariks, the walvark, and dark magic," Saul looked at Darius quizzically. "The leariks," continued Darius after a while. "Are dangerous evil creatures whose staple diet, when they can find it, is human flesh," he continued smiling. His words sent a chill through Saul's spine.

"But you needn't worry, they're adequately fed thanks to the villagers of Welgar Thorton. They visit every week with my supplies and meat for the leariks. The local villages can't risk the leariks running havoc in the countryside you see, there'd be nothing and nobody left. I suppose you could probably walk in and out for another day without being troubled.

"They were brought here from the Valleys of Andrus Roda to keep me penned in. The learik is a dangerous hunter. Once it is primed with a target, the beast will spend weeks, months, even years, hunting down its target with relentless obsession.

"I'm primed," continued Darius. "I automatically become their target the moment I reach the gate. They'll have me down, dead and devoured within moments of crossing that gate, and if I do manage to get through, they'll hunt me down" Darius said this with the now-familiar smile. It was a friendly welcoming smile, and Saul was warming to it.

"Then there's the walvark in the moat."

"The kherk-like serpent?"

"Yes. But it's not very *kherk-like*. The kherk is a magical, friendly creature. The walvark, on the other hand, is a vicious beast. Unfortunately, the only way out is over the bridge. The walvark will pounce on me the moment I get near the bridge.

"And if that isn't enough to keep me in, and even if I could get around these *minor* problems, there's the overriding dark magic that binds me here and saps my sorceric powers.

"I've tried a few times. As I said, I have the undignified embarrassment of resorting to alchemy," he gestured towards the lab of Bunsen burners. "A few families in Welgar Thorton owe me favours. Whenever it's their turn to feed the learik, they bring a few chemicals for my experiments."

"The learik isn't really a problem. I can knock them out with a carefully crafted *noxious* gas, I've done it a few times just to test it. But when I approach that entrance, my strength deteriorates, I can't breathe, my legs collapse," he said bitterly. "The boundus curse," he added quietly.

Silence filled the room, disturbed now and again by the soft crawking of a bird outside the window.

"What did you do to deserve such punishment?"

Darius sank back into the chair. The candle flickered softly, and the shadows in the room danced sporadically against the wall. "You're the first company I've had in three years, I suppose I should make the most of it."

"Don't the people from that village stop and—?"

"No," interrupted Darius. "They leave their supplies at the gate. Now and again, we exchange a few words but that's it.

"As a child, I discovered I could talk to animals. I don't know how I did it. People don't take well to that kind of thing where I'm from. To me, it felt like I was speaking normally like I am to you. The animal chirped, barked, or growled back and somehow, I understood what it was saying. I soon realised that I had sorceric powers. Then I discovered I could move things without touching them, I could do things that normal Netherish people could not.

"My parents sent me to the best place to develop my talents, to the greatest minds and powers in the state, the University of Kirk Heidengaard."

Darius smiled. "I still remember the first day I entered those magnificent gates. The splendid corridors and halls, the great library, and the lodgings where we whiled away many long nights. How I miss Candlewick Inn, exploring the great city, and those late nights in the city square. What a glorious time it was for all the students." Given his recent experiences in Kirk Heidengaard, Saul struggled to understand the fond sentiment Darius attached towards the city.

"I spent my days developing my sorceric powers under the guidance of some of the greatest sorceric minds of the time, the great Garza Wells, Marie Rio-Stinson the brave and the magnificent Gunter Schwartz.

"At Kirk Heidengaard I made two great friends, Joseph Lockwood and Nathan Haran."

Saul's ears pricked up when he heard the first name, instantly remembering the conversation with Dr Kembereley.

"We were inseparable. We worked together, lived together, and spent most of our evenings together. We went our separate ways after we finished University. Lockwood and Haran became professors of sorcery, dedicated to studying and researching sorcery. I joined the Order of Justice.

"I was a reliable, conscientious apprentice. Soon, I became a trusted member of the council.

"Then war yielded its ugly head, and the two states became anxious about the threat of war. Both the Goran Senate and Petonian Council spent months negotiating peace between the two states. But there were powerful forces at play. The wealthy noblemen stood to gain tremendously, and they desperately wanted war. They were already profiting handsomely in the weapon factories, the mines, and the banks, all propped up to support the war economy. They couldn't allow for peace to settle.

"When war broke out, the Goran Senate and Petonian Council worked together to end the war and bring peace, but steadily, even they were dragged to the periphery of war. Soon, much to the bitter remonstrations of the Council elders, the Senate and the Council were facing each other on the battlefield.

"Have you heard of Elden the great?"

"No," replied Saul.

"The Dark Senate?"

"No."

"The Dark Senate are a breakaway group of powerful Goric sorcerers. They fought in the war for Goran. While the Goran Senate and Petonian Council were pushing for peace, the Dark Senate was doing everything not to let it happen. They were led by Elden the great, one of the most powerful sorcerers alive. He's the reason I am here," he sighed and let these words fill the room.

"We received a distress call when the Mines of Atalan were invaded by a Goric army. We arrived and disposed of the soldiers easily.

"Then we entered the mines and faced up to pitch battles with the Dark Senate. Slowly and steadily, we cleared them out. We were winning. We made our way out of the mines, confident we'd finished the job. And that's when I clashed with Elden the Great, the scum of all scum.

"A terrible battle followed in which I discovered the full extent of his renowned powers. He shot bolt after bolt at me, I was thrown from wall to ceiling to floor, unable to respond to his powerful assault. By the time he finished, I lay barely conscious, battered, bruised, and wounded on the floor. Elden left me for dead and walked away. In a moment of madness, I clambered to my feet and fired two fatal lightning bolts. I showed no mercy, no solace," an angry scowl spread across Darius' face. He paused and composed himself. "My biggest weakness is my short temper, and on that day, it got the better of me.

"The Order of Justice were horrified to see Elden lying dead on the floor. They knew this meant serious trouble for them and especially me.

"The Dark Senate wanted vengeance, and days later, they led a huge army into Petonia. Village after village, town after town was plundered in their search for justice. They refused to leave until the perpetrator was identified and executed.

"What to do? I pleaded and begged with the Council. I argued self-defence, but the Council were already divided. Some had become corrupted by the noblemen, others wanted to see me gone. The rest wouldn't and couldn't tolerate open war. So they reached an agreement with the Dark Senate, to disclose my identity on condition that I was not executed, but banished for life.

"Maybe I should be glad I wasn't executed," Darius remarked. The window rattled quietly against the wind.

"But that was a long time ago, things have changed. Surely the Council will free you now," suggested Saul enthusiastically.

"Lifelong banishment," began Darius, "means lifelong banishment. It's a *matter of principle* thing that the Council likes clinging onto. As the years have progressed, I've started feeling increasingly bitter about the whole experience. If they'd wanted to, the Council could have protected me, they could have fought the Dark Senate and dealt them a huge blow. But they didn't stand up for me, they could have—"

Darius stopped sharply. He was distracted by a loud fluttering at the window followed by a steady croaking noise. A blackbird was tapping its beak on the window sill and croaking infrequently. Darius looked up with a concentrating glint in his eyes. His expression changed. He stood up sharply.

"You have to leave," he said in an urgent tone.

"Leave?"

"Your *friends* in Roba Simms are in pursuit."

Saul raised his eyebrows in surprise. "Yes, I think I was followed, they must have tracked me!" Saul got up frantically.

"They're half a day away but can catch up very quickly. They've got searchers with them and they'll come into the mount if they must. I won't be able to protect you and—"

"I thought you said this was safe—"

"Normally nobody dares to come into the mount. But these people will do whatever it takes, even come into the mount. Let's get you on your way," Darius stood up and walked towards the cupboards.

Saul wondered how Darius could possibly know all this before recollecting Darius' story and realising that the bird in the window had probably spoken to him.

Saul collected his bag and winced quietly as he threw the bag over his shoulder.

"What's that?" Darius asked in a stern tone.

"Oh, just a scratch."

"You've injured your ankles," returned Darius. "And your shoulder. Let me have a look."

"It's nothing, really," said Saul dropping his bag. He pulled down the top of his shirt to reveal a purple wound. He had not paid much attention to it until now and realised embarrassingly that the wound had become a yellowy purple and the edges had turned a horrible dark purple.

"We must see to that," said Darius. He walked over purposefully to his array of Bunsen burners, tubes, and canters.

Darius was busy around the table for a few moments as he mixed strong-smelling powders and liquids. A while later, he returned with a small bowl with white cream inside it. He applied the cream to Saul's shoulder. A chilling dizzying feeling ran through Saul's body. Finally, Darius applied it to Saul's ankles.

"Twice a day for a week," ordered Darius. "It's a good thing we've dealt with it, you won't get far carrying wounds and angry slave traders on your back."

"Thank you," Saul said embarrassingly.

Darius placed some bread onto a cloth and pulled out some cakes from under the sink. Next, he pulled out a metal flask and filled it with water. He placed these into a cloth bag before adding some fruit. He poured the rest of the white ointment into a small metal box. From one of the draws, he pulled out a bag of coins and handed these and the food to Saul.

"This will keep you going for four days, by then you should be reunited."

Darius' generosity left Saul lost for words. "This is too kind, I—"

"Nonsense," interrupted Darius, "I do not need the money and the food is being replenished tomorrow morning. Besides, one day, I'm sure you'll have the chance to repay this small gesture."

Darius led Saul out of the room. "Do you know the way to Port Newton?"

Saul repeated the directions given by Christoff and Shari.

"Well you can ignore all of that," returned Darius sternly. "You'll save half a day if you go through the Forest of Lost Souls.

It's a diversion, but I don't think the searchers will pursue you through the forest, especially if they're travelling on narks."

"It's just a historic name," he added noticing the worried look on Saul's face. "There aren't any *lost souls* left in the forest."

Darius and Saul walked out into the courtyard. There was a jostling sound as a group of red eyes came together on either side.

"See those five stars coming together like a cross?" Saul nodded. "That's the Shyan constellation. Follow that. You'll pass by two villages, Hille Minturn and Tanem. Don't stop, just pass by." Saul nodded. The Roba Simms experience had put him off Petonian villages.

"The forest is too dense, once inside you won't see the moons or constellations. Follow the deiron to the outer edge of the forest." Darius gestured towards a deiron sitting on a building in the courtyard. "Once at the edge, you follow the Shyan constellation. Do *not* divert from the path, you can't afford to lose time," Saul nodded nervously before repeating the instructions back to Darius, carefully noting the order of the two villages, Hille Minturn first and then Tanem.

Saul sped out of the courtyard. The red eyes followed him, shuffling along now and again. He reached the stone bridge and slowed down in relief. He walked over the bridge carrying a heartfelt feeling that he had not heard the last of Darius Algar, that somehow Saul's destiny in the Netherworld was more connected with Darius than he could imagine. This had been by far the strangest encounter in the Netherworld. The kindness shown by the rogue sorcerer was remarkable, and without it, Saul would have suffered any number of unpleasant fates.

The splashing of the water became louder as he walked along. Then suddenly, through the corner of his eye, Saul saw the water rising to his left. He turned his head in horror, stopped dead in his tracks, and gasped.

~ 16 ~

The Rickety Old House

The carriage moved along slowly. Now and again, Henry heard Rankin and Edgerton talking casually. Occasionally, the carriage stopped, there was a brief exchange of words with a third or fourth voice, and then it moved on.

Later, the carriage came to a jerking stop. The door opened. Edgerton climbed in, released the rope from Henry's mouth and threw a small piece of bread on the floor in front of him.

"Eat!" he grunted before stepping out.

"Please!" cried Henry as the lock on the carriage door closed with a grating sound. "Please, let me go," he whimpered, realising the hopelessness of pleading with the two men.

Food was the last thing on Henry's mind, and for a while, he lay on the floor wondering what he could do to help himself out of his feeble situation. Ideas were hard to come by. His hands and feet were numb with pain and his mind was a confused emotional mess. Later, Henry pushed himself across the carriage floor and took a few bites of the bread as it lay on the floor. If he was going to have any hope of escaping, he had to keep his energy up.

Henry bit into the bread and wondered what fate awaited him. Jarrett's words resonated in his head: *the searchers are cutthroats; they'll murder their own mothers if there's money to be made.*

After what seemed an eternity, the carriage eventually stopped. The door was unlocked, and Henry was dragged out. It was a cold still night. Two owls hooted sporadically, one of them was so close it must have been perched on top of the carriage.

"Into the house and don't try anything stupid," snapped Rankin, undoing the ropes around Henry's legs.

Henry shuddered at the sight of a dark ghostly house sitting against the moonlit sky. He guessed that they had travelled many miles from Kirk Heidengaard. Although there was a strong chill in the air, the snow had gone and the sowren had been replaced by two narks.

Henry was jostled through a long corridor. The floorboards creaked with each step and there was a dank stale smell in the air giving an impression the house was abandoned. Rankin grabbed a wall lamp and cast a flickery light around the corridor.

"Down the steps," he ordered.

Henry walked steadily downwards into a cold dark cellar. A strong damp smell pervaded the room. The floor was cold, the atmosphere felt humid.

Rankin placed the lamp into a holder on the wall. He pushed Henry onto a chair, loosened his hands, and tied them securely to the back of the chair. Finally, he tied both of Henry's legs to the chair before walking out.

The silence was broken by a quiet murmuring upstairs. It turned into a conversation and then a loud argument.

"What do you mean you lost him?" shrieked a loud timbered voice. "You've come all this way with this insolent brat to tell me you lost Rufus?"

"Master we had no—"

"What good is the boy? You should have got rid of him you idiots. It's Rufus we need."

"We did think about that," began Ranking. "But—"

"We have a plan," said Edgerton excitedly. "Let's hold him ransom."

"The council want the boy, right?" Rankin continued. "And we want Rufus. Let's organise an exchange."

The sound of boots walking around the room filled the silence.

"Hmm, well, maybe that's not such a bad idea. I'll give you a few days. In the meantime, get as much information as you can from the brat."

Heavy boots walked along the creaky corridor down the stairs and into the cellar. Edgerton stepped in, stopped in front of

Henry for a moment and then walked around the chair a few times.

"Where's Rufus going?" he asked, the sound of his boots thudded annoyingly across the cellar floor.

What do I say? Thought Henry frantically. His safety depended on cooperating, but if he revealed anything, he would probably put Saul and Ruby in danger.

"Are you deaf, boy? Where's Rufus going, which city?" asked Edgerton again.

"I don't know."

"He must have said something?"

"I wasn't paying attention to where we were—"

"What's your name?"

"Henry." The thudding of Edgerton's boots around the chair was distracting.

"Where's the box that Kembereley gave to Rufus?" asked Edgerton.

"What box?" asked Henry wondering how they knew about the box.

The questioning went on for quite a while. Edgerton walked around the chair asking questions and Henry remained resolutely stubborn and refused to reveal anything useful.

Eventually, Edgerton loosened Henry's ropes and threw him to the ground before leaving the room. The cellar was left shrouded in darkness save for the slightest hint of light peering through the keyhole.

Henry wondered when and how this terrible ordeal would end. He began to cry, tears trickled slowly down the side of his face.

*

An hour passed by, maybe two. A sharp pain cut into Henry's wrists whenever he tried to wriggle free. Upstairs, murmuring conversations were interspersed with the sounds of boots moving between rooms.

Later, Edgerton appeared at the door and resumed his monotonous line of questioning. *Where was Rufus? Where was the box? Where were the other two children?* The interrogation went on, with Edgerton determined to get the answers and Henry stubbornly determined to stay quiet.

Henry could never work out how long he had been in the dark cellar. He never saw the sunlight and could not tell the time of day. Now and again, he heard the barely audible sound of birds tweeting outside, suggesting it must be daytime. Later, he would hear an owl or two.

On the third or fourth night, Edgerton walked to a dark corner of the cell and pulled over a small table. A rope was tied to the table, the surface was covered with dry blood.

"Do you know why they call me Nailsplicer Smith?"

The blood on the tray answered the question.

Edgerton untied Henry's hand and tied it to the table laying his palm flat on top of it.

"No!" screamed Henry.

"*Fingersplicer Smith* is a more accurate nickname." Henry jerked frightfully as Edgerton pulled up a sharp chopping knife and stabbed it into the table.

"No please!"

"Now speak up!" screamed Edgerton. "You know where the box is. Does Rufus have it?"

It was too much for Henry to bear. The feeling of fright quickly changed into a strange sensation of rage which surged through Henry from head to toe. His blood was boiling, and his head was pounding.

"Well then?"

Pure anger gushed through Henry's veins. He had never felt this way before. For a moment, Henry felt he had the strength to rip off the ropes and strangle Edgerton.Edgerton raised the knife.

"NO!" screamed Henry. And then everything happened in a blurry instant. *"NO!"* he screamed again.

The knife did not land on the table and Henry did not remember what happened next. He thought he had lost consciousness, but now and again he caught a glimpse of Edgerton lying on the floor holding his hands tightly against his head screaming: *"Stop! Stop!"*

Somewhere in the back of his consciousness, Henry knew that he had done that to Edgerton. But how? Surely a mere scream could not have floored Edgerton.

The combined noise of Henry's shouting and Edgerton's screaming brought Rankin charging down the steps. He stood momentarily at the door looking suspiciously at Edgerton.

"What the devil is up with you, you cretin," he said tersely as he pulled Edgerton up. "What have you done to the boy, idiot?"

Henry was sitting in the chair, his head bent to one side in a stupor.

"I… don't know," murmured Edgerton rubbing his head. "Is he alright?"

Rankin moved closer to Henry. "He's breathing. That's a good sign I suppose. Lay off him for a while. We'll attend to him in the morning." The door closed behind them as they left. Henry heard the lock turning shut.

Quite perturbed by the whole experience, Henry lay on the floor looking at the tiny light that shone through the keyhole. Once again, he pondered the abysmal fate that awaited him.

Time and again, he saw the alleyways of Kirk Heidengaard appearing like a distant blurry maze, and he concluded that he had got lost because he could not see ahead of him. And he could not see ahead of him because of his stupid glasses. If they had not kept getting covered in snow, maybe he might have seen more clearly, maybe he could have escaped with the rest of them.

That night, Henry lay on the floor in a terrible agonised state. Over and over he hoped for a miracle, for some help, for some strange intervention. As the tears trickled down his cheek, he kept muttering *help me, please help me* repeatedly before falling asleep.

~ 17 ~

The Forest of Lost Souls

Saul stood frozen in shocked, horrified silence; his whole body paralysed with fear.

The water in the moat bubbled wildly revealing the horrific figure of the walvark. Its huge head rose steadily, propped up by a long thick scaly serpentine-like body. Two dark eyes gleaned out from its head, and long hair drooped off the sides of a gaping sharp-toothed mouth, big enough to swallow Saul whole.

"Keep walking, you idiot!" shouted the muffled voice of Darius Algar.

Saul could not walk. He stood rooted to the bridge waiting for the inevitable fatal strike of the walvark. He felt stuck in a nightmarish dream, frozen, unable to move despite his best intentions.

I'll wake up any moment, I'll wake up any moment, he kept thinking. But he did not.

Then, as if in slow motion, the walvark brought its head down towards Saul. Saul saw the reflection of his tiny figure in the eyes of the walvark. This was it, thought Saul, the terrible, terrifying end.

"You fool!" screamed Darius in the distance. "Do as you're told and run!"

The walvark did not move, instead, it stood poised, its glistening head swaying softly from side to side peering down at Saul. A set of hard scaly fins stood up from the top of its head, reached down its back and disappeared into the moat. Water slid down its face and body. The scales on its body and the teeth in its open mouth twinkled in the moonlight as water dripped slowly off them.

What was the serpent waiting for? With one short sharp swoop, it could swallow him whole, instead, the beast stood frozen in a tantalising frightening pose.

Saul stepped sideways. Suddenly the serpent jerked its' head closer to Saul.

Saul realised immediately that the walvark, like some of the dinosaurs he had learned about at school, probably only saw moving objects. Saul froze, and again the walvark stood still looking ahead at Saul but never seeming to realise that he was standing yards away.

Suddenly there was a huge splashing sound behind the walvark. Instantaneously the beast jerked its huge head backwards.

"Run you fool!" came the panic-stricken voice of Darius Algar muffled by the water splashing against the side of the mount.

Steadily, Saul stepped sideways until he found himself at the edge of the bridge. Now he tore away from the bridge and fell to the ground some distance away, panting for breath and trembling with fear. His thighs were aching in pain and the blisters on his feet were throbbing. He lay on the floor looking at the moat and watching the serpent arch back down into the water.

Before he had time to think about the remarkable sequence of events, Saul's concentration was disturbed by the fluttering of a deiron's wings as it swooped over his head. Saul sighed, gathered his thoughts, and then sped off in the direction of the Shyan constellation.

*

Sometime later, Saul saw the outline of the forest appearing ahead of him. He entered the forest and realised why the deiron had to guide him through. The Forest of Lost Souls was a dark shadowy forest, too dense for Saul to see the constellation. Ahead of him, Saul heard the comforting fluttering of wings, and as he walked along, navigating his way through bushes and around thickly formed trees.

The news that his enemies were onto him continually played on his mind. Now and again, Saul looked back suddenly with the disconcerting feeling that he was being followed. But whenever he turned around, he was met with nothing more than leaves rustling in the soft wind or the stirring of a bush.

Soon, tiredness caught up with Saul. His legs felt weary, his bruised ankles were aching and the blisters on his feet were terribly uncomfortable. Saul decided to rest in an open space lit up eerily by one of the moons. He put up the tent, moments later he landed on a pillow made of his bag and coat.

*

It did not seem long when Saul was awoken out of a deep sleep by a shuffling sound. Someone or something was walking around the tent. Saul listened very carefully. It was gone, leaving Saul wondering if it had been a dream.

When Saul finally began to nod off, his sleep was broken once more by a sound outside the tent, a distinct and clear rustling sound that began near his pillow and carried itself around the tent towards the opening.

Saul shuddered and did not dare to breathe as he waited in frozen anticipation for someone or something to enter the tent. Nothing happened. The forest went quiet.

Suddenly, a flash of light lit up outside the tent! There was a wild commotion, a shuffling sound and then the whimper of a man's voice.

"Away!" cried another deep and booming voice, distinctly different from the first.

Saul heard two or three people running away from the tent.

What was going on? Saul's heart pounded wildly as he sat frozen with fear expecting someone to walk into the tent.

A deathly calm was filled sporadically with the hooting of an owl or the wind rustling through the leaves. *Now I know why it's called the Forest of Lost Souls,* he thought.

After a while, Saul crept out and was greeted by the soft quiet light of one of the moons. He made his way nervously around the tent. Saul sighed heavily, satisfied that there was no immediate danger, he stepped back into the tent, determined to pack his bags, and leave.

A shiny object caught his attention. A long heavy sword lay at the foot of the entrance. It had probably been dropped in all the commotion.

Saul picked it up and took it into the tent. He landed exhaustedly on the sheets and spent a few moments questioning his sanity. Eventually, yawning and struggling to keep his eyes open, Saul forced himself up, packed the tent, and looked up for the deiron.

*

Saul had walked around an hour before coming to a sudden standstill. Ahead of him, a light glimmered unsteadily through a clump of bushes. This could be a fellow traveller, or quite possibly one of his assailants stopping for a rest. Saul edged closer, tiptoeing carefully over and around tree trunks and bushes.

A bearded man, who would have passed off for a tramp in Saul's world, sat on a short wooden stool. He was toasting bread on the end of a stick against a campfire. He wore a woollen hat and a loose jacket. There was a kind look on his face, but given Saul's last experience of a kind looking bearded man, he was reluctant to charge forward and introduce himself.

The man sat in front of a small tent. Next to him lay two travel bags and various food utensils. Quite strangely, a large black dog and a small black cat lay asleep at his feet. A wooden staff lay across a brown sack on the floor. *I wonder if he's a sorcerer,* thought Saul excitedly.

The light from the campfire cast strange shadows over the bag, giving the impression it was moving now and again.

Saul's attention was drawn suddenly by a rustling some yards away. Slowly, he removed his bag, untied the heavy sword, and with great care, removed the sword from the hilt. Saul stood in silence for a few moments listening out carefully.

Saul had been so engrossed with the rustling sound he didn't notice the man's dog standing yards away from Saul. The dog growled softly, instinctively, Saul stepped out of the thicket.

"Kind sir," he began.

The man looked up in alarm. The cat woke out of its slumber and perked its head up.

"Child," replied the man. The light of the fire reflected mesmerizingly in his eyes. Saul lowered his right arm, realising how threatening he must have looked with the sword in his hand.

"I need help. I've been separated from my friends. Could I... could I pitch my tent near you?"

"Yes. Of course," replied the man in a slow kind voice.

Saul edged towards the fire and put his bag down. In the back of his mind rested a paranoid thought that the man might be a bounty hunter or searcher prowling through the forest to look for Saul and claim a reward. Other than the staff, there did not seem to be any weapons near him.

The dog began to sniff Saul and the cat sunk into its paws before steadily dozing off. Meanwhile, the man began toasting a second bread.

"So, where are you headed?" he asked after a while.

"Port Newton sir."

"That's half a day from here," Saul nodded, hiding his excitement, it was much closer than he thought. "Archibald Krayden at your service," announced the tramp offering his hand.

"Saul at yours," came the reply.

Archibald finished cooking his supper and placed a pan of water on the fire for his tea. Meanwhile, Saul opened his bag and pulled out a piece of bread.

Archibald passed a plate with a toast and slice of fish to Saul. "Save that Saul, you'll need it for the journey."

"That's very kind but I don't want to impose."

"You aren't imposing, there's more than enough here for the four of us," he threw a slice of fish at the cat.

Suddenly, the dog shot to its feet again and ran towards the thicket. Something was causing a stir. But why didn't his assailants show themselves? They were more than a match for Saul, a tramp and his two pets.

"Are you from these parts?" asked Saul, one eye on the bushes.

"No."

Archibald Krayden continued eating quietly, now and again stoking the fire beneath the pan. Saul smiled at the cat as it bit and chewed at the fish.

The silence was broken by a rustling sound from behind him. The dog growled softly, and the cat perked her head up.

"I have something to say sir," began Saul anxiously. "I… I was followed here. Two people came up to my tent. They're very dangerous people and..." Saul's voice trailed off quietly. His eyes were focussed on the thicket.

Archibald carried on eating, seemingly unnerved by this. There were a few more moments of uncomfortable silence as Archibald Krayden looked searchingly into the forest. He turned his head and then squinted his eyes as if he could see something. "Don't be scared of what's following you Saul," he said quietly.

"You don't understand," began Saul quickly. "I haven't told you the full story, one of my friends is on the run, not for anything wrong I have to say, and these people are chasing him, they're called *searchers*."

The fire flickered gently, and the cat sunk her head again, rolled over, stretched her front legs, and then dozed off again.

"Don't be afraid of what's following you." Archibald bit his toast and looked deep into the fire. Saul looked curiously at his bright glassy eyes.

"I can leave if you want," suggested Saul quietly. "I've probably put your life in danger as well."

"No. You're welcome to stay the night with me," insisted Archibald, still looking fixedly at the fire. "You'll be safe here."

The bag moved for the second time. Now Saul was convinced it was not a trick of the light. He watched the bag fixedly, just to be sure. Suddenly it protruded upwards before falling flat again.

Maybe Archibald Krayden was a cat thief. Saul remembered his father telling him about the gipsies, tramps, and vagrants who wandered the forests and woods of some of the Eastern European countries. Apparently, they stole cats and ate them or fed them to wolves. Archibald glanced casually at the bag before continuing with his toast. A moment later, it moved again.

"Sir, your... your bag is moving."

"Very restless tonight aren't we?" Archibald said quietly to himself, looking crossly at the bag. He lifted the staff and placed it back on the bag, flattening it out. This was strange, thought Saul, the bag looked empty now.

"If you don't mind me asking," began Saul nervously, "what's in the bag?"

"I don't mind you asking," began Archibald, "but you really don't want to know."

"Well I've seen some very strange things recently, and I don't think anything could surprise me now."

There was a brief silence. "There's a pretty nasty ghost in that bag."

Saul's opened his eyes in shock. "A ghost?"

"Yes. A ghost."

"W... why would there be a ghost in the bag?" asked Saul, his gaze fixated on the bag.

"Because I'm a ghost whisperer."

"A g… ghost whisperer?"

"Yes, a ghost whisperer."

"What's a ghost whisperer?"

"Someone who can speak to ghosts."

"Speak to ghosts?"

"Yes. In fact, I do a bit more than that. I catch them."

"Catch them?" asked Saul. This was too much for his brain to absorb in one night.

"Yes, but only the really nasty evil ones," Archibald said, a smiley glint in his eyes. "The ones that make life a misery for people."

"You catch ghosts and put them in that bag?" asked Saul raising his eyebrows as he struggled to come to terms with what Archibald had just said.

"Yes," replied Archibald frankly. "I can show you if you like."

"No thanks," replied Saul quickly. "Is it safe?"

"Yes. The bag's tied."

"I know but can't the ghost just… well, walk through it?"

"No. I've spelled it."

"Spelled it?"

"Yes. I've put a spell on it."

"You've put a spell over the ghost?"

"Yes. I can spell ghosts."

"So, you're a sorcerer?"

"No, not quite a sorcerer. Ghost whisperers aren't considered to be sorcerers.

"I get called by families who are being haunted by annoying and sometimes dangerous ghosts, I catch them and well… just *deal* with them," he looked at the bag as he said the last part.

The flames flickered as a soft breeze passed by. Neither Archibald nor Saul spoke for a while. The bag moved again, softly enough for it to seem like a trick of the light.

"How did you become a *ghost whisperer*? Did you have to learn it, or be apprenticed or something?"

Archibald smiled at Saul. The smile wrinkles on his eyes showed up welcomingly in the light of the fire.

"Well, yes and no," he began. "It's a, err, gift."

The dog stretched its legs lazily. The fire flickered and its shadows played tricks over the bag again.

"Saul," Archibald said in a serious tone. "There's a good spirit following you."

"Good spirit?" gasped Saul under his breath.

"Yes. He frightened off your assailants this evening and wants to see you get a safe passage to Port Newton."

A shiver flooded through Saul's body as Archibald said this. He looked back at the forest spontaneously.

"He… sorry, *it* followed you to Beezel Mount and waited while you met Darius Algar. It distracted the walvark when it was ready to pounce. The spirit gave you that sword. It's your sword."

Saul was taken aback by these revelations. He became convinced that Archibald Krayden was not a stark raving mad tramp. He must have had a remarkable magical insight to know about Beezel Mount, Darius Algar, and how he got the sword.

"The spirit says it will leave you alone after tonight. Hopefully, by tomorrow night, you'll be at Port Newton," he added looking into the forest.

"Why is the ghost—"

"Spirit," interrupted Archibald. Saul wondered momentarily about the difference between a ghost and a spirit.

"Why is the *spirit* looking out for me?"

"Why are you following him?" asked Archibald looking fixedly at the thicket of trees.

"The spirit says it's better you don't know... for now." Saul looked to the forest as Archibald said this. He wanted to ask why a spirit should look out for Saul and why it had given him a sword. But Saul thought better of it for now, there were enough burdens on his mind right now.

"Take a rest child," suggested Archibald. "You needn't put up a tent, take mine. I have a feeling I'll be up all night watching over Beelzebub here," he smacked the bag down again. "We can't risk him escaping."

*

Although the night passed without incident, Saul woke up feeling he had slept inadequately. A moment or two after waking up, Saul was thankful at the smell of cooked sausages.

"Morning," remarked Archibald as Saul emerged tiredly from the tent.

"Good morning," yawned Saul, quickly moving to get the plates ready.

Archibald's dog followed Saul around the campfire excitedly, his tail wagging wildly.

"I have some food," announced Saul reaching into his bag quickly.

"s'not a problem," Archibald said putting his hand up. "I'll pick something up in the next town. Folks are always happy to give food and money to ghost whisperers."

After breakfast, Archibald sat Saul down and carefully explained the route out of the forest towards Port Newton.

"It's half a day away," explained Archibald. "As long as you come out of the forest at the right place, you'll be there by early afternoon." The deiron fluttered between trees now and again as Archibald spoke.

Finally, Archibald extended a warm hand to Saul and wished him a safe journey. In return, Saul repeatedly thanked Archibald for his generosity and expressed a hope that their paths would cross again.

Saul set off feeling a lot better and confident. He did not hear the rustling sound again, and he wondered whether it would remain a mystery forever. There was something macabre about a personal ghost, or *spirit* as Archibald had put it, and Saul could not wait to share these anecdotes with Ruby and Henry when he finally met them at Port Newton.

*

Late that afternoon, having passed the villages of Hille Minturn and Tanem, as Archibald and Darius had described, Saul finally saw the welcome outline of a city. Port Newton at last. His feet were hurting, his shoulder was sore, and his legs could bear no more travel.

Port Newton was a beautiful hilly city known for its cobbled streets and lanes winding up and around the steady gradients. As Saul got closer to the port, he was met by the busy activity of the port. Soon he was walking through a wave of people. For a little while, Saul walked around and admired the great sights of the city, riding on the relief of being in what seemed like a civilised part of the Netherworld.

Three times during the journey, Saul had calculated the number of days he had been travelling. He concluded that he had arrived a day early. There was probably no point finding Fort Delmar until the morning. Instead, thought Saul, he should find a room to rest.

As he turned into a busy street, he was presented with the *Travellers Chest* which welcomed him at the end of a small conspicuous lane.

"One bronze," said the bored-looking man mundanely at the reception.

Saul was led to a small dark room, nowhere near as grand as the room in Kirby Hall, but it was cosy, warm, and seemed safe. Weeks of sleeping rough in a tent had taken their toll, and never in his life had a bed seemed more welcoming than at this moment. Saul closed the door, threw his bag onto an armchair, lay down, and fell into a deep sleep within moments.

*

Saul awoke early in the evening. It took a few moments to gather his senses and decide that he needed to find Fort Delmar.

Across the seafront, as far as the eye could see, there stretched a line of shops beautifully illuminated with bright lights glowing warmly out onto the pathways. The waterfront and the pier were lined with bright lanterns shining spectacularly against the dark sea.

Powerful waves lashed fiercely against the port, occasionally throwing a spray of water over the sea-front. Saul wandered around for an hour through busy stalls and shops before resting on a bench and watching the hustle and bustle of the port.

Boats pulled in and out of the port. Fishermen unloaded their catches and then clambered onto smaller boats before rowing off home. Soon, lines of fishing boats decorated one side of the waterfront. Occasionally, larger ships drifted in from the sea and Saul watched these fixedly. Saul became intrigued by the families disembarking excitedly carrying bags and containers.

Saul noticed that huge metal spikes bore down from the sides of the ship into the sea. At the front and rear of the ship, the spikes ended in mid-air, while the spikes at the sides fell into the sea. It was an extraordinary sight, and Saul spent a few moments trying to understand this.

I really must find Fort Delmar, he thought guiltily. Saul wandered further down the seafront and planned to ask someone for directions.

"A small chocotea please," requested Saul walking over to a stall.

"Two tin-nickels," replied the bearded haggardly stall keeper. His appearance and rough voice suggested he was probably a retired sailor.

Tin nickels? thought Saul confusedly. He reached into his pocket and pulled out two of the lightest coins, presuming them to be tin-nickels.

"Not from these parts are ye?" asked the man.

"I'm from... err near Kirby Hall," mumbled Saul thinking quickly.

"Arr! That be many days away," said the man handing over a mug of warm chocotea. He reached out for a warm chocolate cake to go with it.

"It's on the house," insisted the stall-keeper, as Saul reached back into his pocket, feeling unnecessarily compelled to part with more money. "My mam was from your parts, and anybody from mam's district is a friend of mine."

"Excuse me sir," began Saul curiously, hoping to strike up some cheap conversation before asking for directions to the fort. "Why do those ships have spikes on the sides?"

Saul moved to one side as a short stout man in a brown hat squeezed up to the stall with his two rowdy children.

"That there be the Black Sea," began the stall-keeper.

"It doesn't look very black from here."

"Aye it don't, but two days out and it's as black as a North winter's night," continued the stall-keeper serving three more chocoteas to the short man. "Two more days in and the waters is infested with Gargarin," he added before noticing the confused look on Saul's face.

"Gargarin are the most ferocious sea monsters in the Netherworld," added the short man in a high-pitched voice. "Oh, and a couple of chocolate buns please," he added, turning to the stall-keeper.

"They're twice the size of a ship and they leap up out of the water. The spikes on the ends give the ship some protection. Nothing frightens a gargarin more than cuts and scrapes."

"We were nearly attacked," interjected the short man. "Terrifying. Thought we were gone. We saw the gargarin creeping towards the ship from the distance. Caused a terrible panic it did! But one scrape against the ship and the gargarin fled away faster than a black beel."

"Arrr," responded the stall-keeper, his eyebrows raised in awe.

"Sir where's Fort Delmar?" asked Saul. The stall-keeper spent a moment directing Saul. Port Newton was the friendliest place thought Saul, forgetting his earlier sentiments about Kirk Heidengaard. There was a strangely calming aura about the port, and for the first time in days, Saul was feeling relieved, relaxed, and comfortable.

Saul walked down towards the sea. Dozens of families lined the pier and sat enjoying the breath-taking view of the sea. Saul reached a lonely spot, sat down, and ate the cake the stall-keeper had given him while looking out deep into the black sea and quietly admiring the busy port. The sound of the sea crashing against the edge of the pier had a curious calming therapeutic effect and helped soothe the nerves that had received such a battering in the last few days.

*

All four sides of the Fort were lined with dozens of stalls and street pedlars. Dozens of tourists walked up to its imposing gates and stopped momentarily to marvel at the architecture.

The entrance to the fort was marked by a huge sign carrying the words:

The Academic Apprentice Union Conference

Underneath the sign, a smaller notice declared:

Union members only, no entrance without identity papers

I'm at the wrong place! Saul thought worriedly before moving to a conspicuous vantage point. From there he saw a long queue of ordinary-looking people waiting to get inside.

Saul panicked. He was either at the wrong place or was too late. He counted and recounted the days he had travelled from Kirk Heidengaard and concluded that he was in the wrong place at the right time. Could the council be meeting somewhere else in Port Newton? Had the plans changed?

Then his heart jumped. Above the crowd, he spotted a familiar shock of white hair standing next to a man in a green coat. He had seen them before, but where? Were they on the pier last night or was it in the dining room during breakfast? Suddenly it hit him. The man in green was Doe Festers, the eccentric quiet man who set up the tents! And the white-haired man was the *mad professor,* as everyone seemed to refer to him. Of course, the conference was a front to the real business. Excitedly, Saul trotted over and joined the back of the queue.

Saul noticed that everyone was producing a set of papers when they got to the front of the queue. Two burly giants, their heads and shoulders towering four feet over the crowd, were checking the papers before letting people through.

"Your papers!" boomed the giant when Saul reached the front. The giant now seemed to fill the whole sky above Saul.

Instinctively, Saul searched and fumbled through his pockets and bag with an air of *the papers are here I just need to find them.*

"Err… these were the identity papers, right?" he asked, still fumbling.

"No, the letter wot invited you here," the giant blurted rudely.

"Maybe if you'd bovered to read it youd've knowed that," said the second giant.

Giants were rude people decided Saul. "Err… I seem to have mislaid the letter," he said still fumbling through the bag. "Sorry."

The giant looked down stubbornly, his arms crossed, and his lips pursed together. He had a huge face and looked very intimidating.

"No papers, no entry. Move on," the giant mumbled dismissively.

"Darn tourists always trying to get a free peek," muttered the second giant rudely. "If I've said it once I've—"

"No, you don't understand," urged Saul. "I had them with me, I've mislaid them, you have to let me in."

"Where's his manners Jadrod? That's wot I wants knowing," said the second giant.

"I don't think you understands," began the first giant bending a long way down to look down into Saul's anxious face. "No papers, No—"

"Thomas!" cried a familiar voice.

Saul had never been happier to see a friend than he was to see Althea Gimble trotting out of the Fort.

"Alth—"

"You're always lagging, I hope you've led the steragon to a decent stable, not like last time when you—"

"If he's with you maybe you oughta tell him about stickin' to procedure," said the first giant loudly.

"And the manners," added the second giant. "He needs to know manners. We've got better things to do than—"

"Yes, yes, I know," dismissed Althea.

"You don't know how glad I am to see you," began Althea quietly as they walked through the entrance. "We were so worried and hadn't imagined where you were."

"What's with all this stuff about papers?" complained Saul. "I mean it was difficult enough getting here without facing an interrogation at the gate."

Althea updated Saul as they walked along. Fort Delmar was a secret meeting place. The council had enacted precautions to stop tourists and city authorities from nosing around. In the last week, a letter of invitation had been issued. They had missed Saul of course, so Althea had waited impatiently around the entrance for his arrival.

"You won't believe how much I've missed Henry and Ruby, I've got so much to tell them," said Saul excitedly as they walked through a forecourt packed with sorcerers greeting each other jovially. "Not that I haven't looked forward to meeting you but… Althea?"

Althea had stopped dead in her tracks. A horrified expression sat on her face. "Henry's not with you?"

"Of course not," replied Saul lowering his brow. "I'm on my own and—"

"Where the devil is Henry?"

"How should I know, I thought that—"

"I suppose, if he's not with you then… then he's probably lost," Althea said in a frozen tone.

"Lost?"

There was a long silence. Saul's face carried a drained look, a horrible knotted feeling filled his stomach.

"Let's get you to your quarters and try to work out what's happened."

"Where's Ruby?" asked Saul assertively.

"Ruby's with us," replied Althea to Saul's relief.

*

The fort was deceptively large. Althea and Saul were walking through a walled village set at the top of a hill. Wooden huts were spread across lush green fields busied by a plethora of activities.

At the top of a hill in the distance, archers were firing arrows at a target, and on another hill, Saul saw a group of sorcerers racing a wild immense four-horned rhino-like creature. A quinoceros, Althea told him. On another side, Saul saw a group of krays rising into the air. As always, the sight of these fearsome creatures raised the hairs on his back.

"You'll have noticed," began Althea trotting back to Saul, "That we are preparing for battle. Come on, we have to move on."

Saul and Althea walked to the centre of the fort towards a magnificent stone castle marked at each of its four corners by tall towers rising high into the sky overlooking the port and the sea. A wide archway led them into a huge busy square at the centre of the castle. A huge sign was nailed to a wooden post by the entrance reading:

No military training or sorcery inside the castle area

The square was surrounded by rooms decorated with leaded windows and black oak doors. Groups of sorcerers, giants, and vampires gathered around the square absorbed in engaging discussions. Saul recognised a few of the faces, particularly Siraf who stood at the centre of a small crowd. He raised a tentative hand and smiled at Saul sending a chill through his spine. No matter how many times anybody told Saul that Siraf was on their side, the sight of the pale sharp-toothed Nordic vampire always made him nervous.

Althea and Saul walked into a building, announcing itself to be the *meeting house*. "We've become delayed here a bit longer than we'd planned so we'll be staying here for a while," announced Althea as they walked through the lobby. "At least until we've firmed up our plans."

"What's the delay?"

"The two states have gathered at the palace of Petonia to negotiate a settlement to end the threat of war," explained Althea. "Hopefully, any moment now, peace will be declared, and all the prisoners will be released. The outcome of this will determine our next move, so it makes sense to wait a little while."

"But what does that mean for us, I mean when do we get home?" asked Saul nervously.

"Oh, don't worry about that," replied Althea dismissively. "Ambrose's probably on his way here and—"

"Probably?" Saul interrupted. "He was supposed to be here, that was—"

"Come along now," said Althea ushering Saul up a magnificent wide staircase. "There'll be plenty of time to talk later."

If the news of Henry's *disappearance* was not enough to dampen the excitement of reaching Fort Delmar, this news made Saul truly miserable.

"Saul!" Saul's heart jumped as he turned to see Ruby running up the stairs behind him, her black hair flying in the air and her arms outstretched.

"It's so good to see you!" she shrieked, throwing her arms around his neck. "Where were you?""I—"

"We've been so worried Saul. What happened?"

"Well—"

"How did you get here? Where's Henry?"

"He's—"

"This way," interrupted Althea gesturing towards the corridor. "There'll be plenty of time for that later."

Althea stopped at a door along the corridor, opened it and led Saul in.

"Listen," began Saul as soon as Althea had left. "Henry's not with me."

"Not with you?" asked Ruby with a horrified expression.

"No."

"But where else could he be? He was with you when—"

"I don't know," began Saul. "But he's not with me. Henry's lost and—"

There was a loud knock on the door. Jarrett, Junus, and Rufus walked in cheerily, closely followed by Jordan who charged in and practically jumped on Saul in joy. Like Althea and Ruby, they were distraught that Henry was not with Saul. In recent days, an underlying assumption had embedded itself that Saul and Henry were together.

"Now tell us exactly how you got here," asked Junus.

Steadily, Saul recollected the sequence of events that had befallen him since the mishap in Kirk Heidengaard. He was careful not to disclose details of the encounter with Archibald Krayden or Darius Algar, he did not want to be known as the friend of a rogue sorcerer.

"When did you last see Henry?" Junus asked in an uncharacteristically calm tone.

"At Kirk Heidengaard. He was in front of me and I thought he was with you," Saul said softly. The room went quiet for a moment. Jarrett and Rufus looked at each other uncomfortably. "We've lost Henry, haven't we?"

He knew the answer but dreaded the reply.

"Not quite *lost*," replied Jarrett quietly. The room was silent for a few moments. "But we'll be delaying our movements until he's found," he added unconvincingly.

"The master won't abandon Henry," interjected Rufus. "We *will* find him."

There was another silence.

"That's enough," announced Rufus. "We need to speak to Grandon and Caleb. They've been searching for you. Take a rest, we'll see you at dinner."

"You're not staying with us?" asked Saul as Jordan got up to leave.

"Dad's brought in a lot more krays," replied Jordan. "There's way too many for him to handle alone. So, I'm staying in the stable house. You must come and have a look, it's wonderful."

"Saul let's pop over tomorrow and help Jordan in the stables," suggested Ruby excitedly.

"Err, yes," mumbled Saul with an unintended lack of enthusiasm. "Jordan," he continued. "How was your trip. I think you went to follow some leads right?"

"Yes," replied Jordan thoughtfully. "A bit of a wild goose chase I'm afraid," he added pursing his lips together.

"Sorry to hear that," said Saul after a moment.

"We're quite used to it to be honest," Jordan said as he left the room.

"There's a bit more to what I just told everyone," announced Saul as the door closed.

Ruby looked at him quizzically. "What do you mean?"

Saul sighed quietly before repeating the adventures and misadventures of the last week. He unfolded the extraordinary meeting with Darius Algar, the terrifying night in the forest of souls and the strange encounter with Archibald Krayden.

Ruby was aghast with astonishment when Saul revealed these remarkable events. Her jaw dropped when he repeated the episode with the Ballards, and her eyes were wide open in horror when he narrated the sequence of events that had taken place in the Forest of Lost Souls.

"So, what happened to you at Kirk Heidengaard?" asked Saul.

~ 18 ~

To Crow Claw

Rufus, Jarrett, Althea, and Ruby tore through a torrential snowfall, desperately determined to get to the gates. After what seemed an eternity, they saw the snowy outline of the gates. Jarrett let out a shrieky whistle. Three men shot up from around a fire, ran towards Jarrett, and took all the bags. A fourth man led three sowren by their reins. Jarrett, Althea, Rufus, and Ruby threw their bags onto the sowren and climbed on.

"Onward!" shouted Jarrett.

The sowren lunged forward, gathering pace rapidly through the bitter blizzard. Now and again, Jarrett looked behind. Their assailants were nowhere to be seen.

"We'll be fine now," sighed Jarrett as the white forest emerged ahead of them.

They dismounted at the outskirts of the forest and edged in.

"We've left Saul and Henry behind!" Everyone turned to Ruby before being struck by the horrible realisation that Saul and Henry had either got lost in the journey between the city gates and the white forest or, worse still, were still in the city.

"How can we have been so stupid!" retorted Rufus. "Who saw them last?"

"They were in front of me at Antiques Lane, well Saul was," recalled Althea. "And I remember helping Henry through two alleys after that."

"I'm sure Saul was behind me when we approached the city gates," said Jarrett.

They carefully recounted their steps from climbing onto the roof, through the city square, and then into the maze of alleys. Although they clearly remembered the arrows flying past their ears and the desperate rush to get to the city gates, nobody was clear about what happened after that.

"No wonder the searchers slowed down," said Rufus. "I'm going back."

"Don't be stupid," asserted Jarrett. "It's exactly what they want us to do. They've found the bait and want us to go back. They'll be scouring the streets now."

"It's unlikely the searchers have got them out of the city so quickly," said Rufus. "If we go back right now, we'll find them near the gates. There's still time. But we must go back right now."

"I won't allow it."

"What do you mean you won't allow it?" argued Althea. "Since when did you—"

"Take charge of this mission? The moment Rabin put me in charge of it! Our priority is to get to Crow Claw."

"I'm not leaving them!" sobbed Ruby. Her voice drowned out in the wild blizzard. "If you don't want to go, then I'll go on my own."

The howling blizzard stung their faces, that coupled with the realisation that they had lost Saul and Henry, made them feel terribly numb.

"Fine," sighed Jarrett. "I'll go back. I'll search the city and meet you here on Sunday evening that gives me two days to find them. We'll make up lost time by travelling through the night."

"I'll come with you," said Ruby.

"Oh no you won't," said Rufus sternly. "We're not losing another one. I'll go."

"No that's too risky. You're the one they want," argued Althea.

"She's right," sighed Jarrett. "I can manage this on my own."

"We can't wait beyond Sunday," asserted Althea.

Jarrett nodded before climbing onto the sowren and heading off into the snowy horizon.

*

By the following afternoon, Rufus, Althea, and Ruby were very restless. Throughout the day, one or the other had walked to the edge of the forest to see if Jarrett, Saul, and Henry were on their way back, only to be disappointed. In the back of their mind lay the sordid thought that Jarrett had also been caught.

By the evening, Ruby returned to the edge of the forest and held a stubborn vigil looking out into the snowy moonlit landscape. Now and again, a rodent, wolf, or a herd of sowren walked across the landscape.

Ruby jumped suddenly. Something was moving in the snowy distance. She narrowed her eyes and focused intently. Her pursed lips turned into a frown as she realised that the object of her intrigue was the single lonely figure of Jarrett perched on a sowren. Ruby's heart sank. She felt numb and finally felt the cold wind biting her cheeks.

"I looked everywhere," Jarrett murmured as he climbed off the sowren. "I searched endlessly for two days. The searchers are gone, I saw them leaving," he said glancing at Rufus.

"Were Saul and Henry with them?" asked Rufus.

"No."

"You're sure?"

"Of course."

"You searched the markets?"

"Yes."

"The Inn and the University?"

"Yes." Jarrett's gaze was transfixed zombie-like into the fire.

Ruby raised her eyebrows, "maybe if we all went back, we—"

"No," interrupted Jarrett. "We have nothing to gain and precious time to lose. The boys have probably moved on."

"He's right. We can't go back," added Althea firmly.

The group sat in solemn disappointment, each one trying to reason with the terrible predicament. They could not decide whether to leave for Crow Claw or stay in Kirk Heidengaard and continue looking for Saul and Henry. It was a horribly difficult decision, and in the end, they determined that waiting here was futile. Whichever way they looked at it, the boys were either heading for Crow Claw, or as painful as it seemed, were somewhere completely beyond the reaches of Rufus, Althea, and Jarrett.

*

The weather changed remarkably during the journey between Kirk Heidengaard and Crow Claw. The snow turned into steady rain and then cleared to leave a soft tolerable chill. By the afternoon of the second day, they continued the journey on foot.

Crow Claw was a barren forest, Ruby now saw why it had such a strange name. Three, sometimes four strong branches arched down to the ground resembling the shape of a claw. The forest became green for two months every three years, and when that happened, Crow Claw was one of the most beautiful places in the Netherworld. But during the long autumn, the forest looked strange and spooky.

They spent an hour scouting the forest, anticipating that Caleb, Jordan, Saul, and Henry were tucked away behind a clutch of bushes somewhere.

"Let's rest an hour," proposed Althea.

"Yes. We need to plan the rest of the journey," added Jarrett.

Time dragged on. Rufus, Althea, and Jarrett sat around the fire, presiding over a map, and carefully fine-tuning the route.

"It's difficult terrain," murmured Jarrett who had a habit of thinking out aloud now and again. "On the one hand, we have to avoid the canyon at Balson Mees and—"

"The canyon at Balson Mees?" asked Rufus raising his eyebrows.

"Yes."

"That's the Valley of the Krays."

"Yes."

"We can't go through the valley. It's a nesting ground for mothering krays. They lay their eggs there and nest the hatchlings, it's—"

Jarrett raised a hand. "We're not going *through* the valley. We're going *over* it. There's a bridge crossing over it… ah-ha here it is," he smacked his finger on the map. "That'll save a day, we won't have to walk around the valley." Despite everyone crowding around the map, Jarrett was in a world of his own talking to himself, seemingly oblivious of their presence. Finally, Jarrett's plan was set, and they left in earnest, continually looking into the sky for signs of Caleb and krays.

*

Hours into the darkness with only a hint of moonlight creeping through the cloudy night sky and Rufus' lonely lantern lighting the way, Jarrett announced that they were at the outskirts of Balson Mees

"Look out for a narrow thicket of bushes running along the edge of the canyon," he said as they walked carefully along the side of a deep dark valley. Now and again, a chilling screech shot up causing one or the other to gasp in terror.

"Bring that lantern over here," muttered Jarrett after a while. "I don't understand, we should have reached a bridge by now," he added looking worriedly at the map.

He stopped and ran his finger across the map in one direction and then lifted the lantern up above their heads and surveyed the area around him.

"This way!" he exclaimed with relief.

Half an hour later, Jarrett slowed down, stopped, shook his head, and scrutinised the map with renewed interest.

"This is no good. Wait here" he muttered before turning around and surveying the path they had followed. Jarrett returned a while later scratching his head.

"I don't understand. The map's out of date. There should be a bridge connecting this ridge with the ridge on the opposite side."

"What type of bridge?" asked Ruby excitedly.

"A rope bridge."

Without a word, Ruby rushed back along the path. *"Over here!"* Ruby's voice echoed through the valley.

Ruby was standing next to two stumps in the ground at the edge of the ridge. A rope hung down from each stump. There was no bridge.

"It's been taken down!" cried Jarrett angrily. There was a long silence.

Ideas were scarce. The only feasible option involved a long walk around the ridge which added more than a day onto the journey.

"I think… I think I can see a way down," announced Ruby looking over the ridge into the darkness. A makeshift path led down into the valley. Rufus took a few tentative steps down, disappeared into the darkness and then reappeared a few moments later.

"I think it goes all the way down."

"What about the nesting grounds?" asked Althea.

Jarrett pulled the map out again.

"The bridge runs parallel to a river. Mothering krays never nest near rivers. They risk losing their eggs or the newly hatched younglings. We'll be fine as long as we follow the line of the bridge in a straight line."

"Turn the lantern off," ordered Jarrett. "It'll attract the krays."

Rufus smacked his staff down, a strong light illuminated the space around them.

"No lights," insisted Jarrett. "The light will bother the krays. They're vicious enough as it is, but a nesting kray is not to be crossed."

Rufus sighed and smacked the staff down again. They were shrouded in darkness. They followed Rufus down a steep, dark, and narrow path. Now and again, one or the other of them slipped or stumbled as they tried to follow the faint silhouette of the person in front. Occasionally, the screech of a kray echoed through the valley beneath them sending a shudder through their spines.

"That… that was quite far away," said Jarrett consolingly as one of the screeches made Ruby twitch.

At the foot of the path, they were met with a strong stable-like smell which became stronger with each step through the valley. There was still no sign of the river.

"I can't see anything," complained Ruby nervously. The sky had steadily clouded over, and they were walking in near darkness.

"Hold my cloak if it helps," proposed Rufus. "Nothing to worry about. I think we're nearly at the other end." His nervous voice did not radiate confidence.

Then to their left, they heard a rustling sound followed by a familiar soft croaky sound.

"A err... herix," suggested Jarrett nervously. "Balson Mees is brimming with them, it's one of the reasons the krays nest here," he added unconvincingly.

"That… was not a herix," asserted Althea quietly, "the herix has a sharper higher-pitched croak and it's quite—" Two screeches tore through the air

"Krays!" announced Rufus quietly. "By the beard of the druids."

Another rustling sound was accompanied by a high-pitched screech a few yards away. They froze. Nobody dared to move.

Jarrett fumbled with the lantern and lit it. Rufus smacked his staff down, a bubble of light filled the space around them and revealed the terrible predicament they had walked into. Dozens of huge krays crowded them on each side.

Two krays stood up and fixed their menacing gaze at the four travellers. A kray standing five yards away let out a piercing deafening shriek, a second kray responded, and moments later, many more were lifting their huge heads and screeching into the air.

"Listen," began Jarrett in a panic. "The nesting female kray won't harm you, they won't step out of the nest. It's the mates we need to worry about, and—"

A terrifying roar, distinctly different to the shriek of the female kray, rained down from the sky. A second roar filled the air and before they knew it, a continuous wave of deafening cacophonous roars filled the air.

"The mates!" cried Jarrett. "They must have been nesting close by!"

Rufus, Althea, Jarrett, and Ruby were dumbstruck. They stood frozen to the ground, nobody daring to move.

After what felt like an eternity, Rufus stepped forward slowly, with Jarrett, Althea and Ruby following close by. They stepped steadily and carefully around huge three-foot-high nests. Now and again, a kray shrieked loudly whenever the three travellers got too close to the nest.

The male krays were swooping closer and closer. Now they could feel the breeze of the huge wings.

Suddenly, Jarrett tripped, fell over, and landed in a crashing sprawl onto the edge of a nest. A mother kray shot instinctively onto its hind legs, its huge jaw crashed down, missing him by a whisker. A kray near Rufus jabbed at his arm, and another kray flew down at Ruby, missing her diving body by an inch. All around them now, krays were striking and jabbing at them. They began to crouch downwards into a protective huddle.

Suddenly, Jarrett screamed as a kray swooped down, lifted him by his arm and threw him a few yards away from the rest of the group. Jarrett crashed into an agonised heap on the floor as more krays came closer and closer.

"Stop!" Ruby cried in a frightened panic. She stood up, frightened out of her skin, her hands in the air as if warding someone off. She was shaking gently. *"Stop! Stop!"*

What happened next was remarkable.

Slowly but steadily the screeching and roaring quietened down. Two krays stepped backwards, and another three lifted their heads away. A piercing tension filled the air as Ruby stood upright with her hands in the air. Steadily, the krays backed down.

A few moments passed, and now the mates began to circle higher in the sky, the screeching and roaring became more sporadic.

"There, there," muttered Ruby as she reached up to stroke a mother kray standing in its nest an arm's length away. The kray moved its head closer and let out a quiet purr.

"Get back Ruby!" screamed Althea.

"I know what I'm doing," muttered Ruby with gritted teeth.

The shrieking slowly turned into a steady purr as the krays steadily retreated into their nests.

"Follow me," Ruby ushered after a while. She stepped back from the kray and started walking away, all the while muttering *"there there"*.

Nobody said anything until they reached the safety of the opposite end of the valley. It took a while to find the corresponding path up the ridge, and once at the top, Jarrett set up a fire and joined Rufus and Althea in busy conversational murmurs.

"In all my years," Ruby heard Althea say quietly. "I've never seen anything like what that girl does with the kray. It's uncanny. It can't be a… gift can it?"

"Of course not. She's from the Upperworld," replied Jarrett. "But I don't know how she does it. Maybe it's just a bit of strange luck."

Ruby sat alone at the edge of the cliff looking sullenly into the deep cavernous darkness. She breathed in deep slow sighs. She was tired, exhausted, and upset. The incident had tested her wits to their limits. She missed her parents and desperately wanted to go home.

~ 19 ~

Ghosts, Spirits, and Henry

Saul sat back and reflected on Ruby's remarkable adventure. His own eventful journey seemed to pale into insignificance as he tried to imagine walking through the Valley of the Krays.

"How do you… well, you know, talk to the krays?"

"To be honest, I haven't a clue," began Ruby hesitantly. "I suppose it's a bit like I'm talking to a pet dog or something. I can't understand all that screeching or roaring, but somehow the kray knows what I'm saying."

Saul raised his eyebrows with a bewildered look. "You know in this world it's considered kind of… *weird* if you can talk to animals or ghosts."

"Well, I can't really talk to animals, it's just krays," explained Ruby. "Listen, are you going to tell Rufus and Rabin about Darius Algar?"

"No way," replied Saul swiftly. "Darius is some kind of *rogue sorcerer*, and terribly unpopular amongst the Gorans, the Petonians, and even the council. Imagine how they'd react if I told them that he tended to my blisters, fixed my shoes, gave me some ointment for my wounds, a bag of coins and set me on my way," he continued in a dancy tone.

"So who do you think your friendly ghost is?" asked Ruby jokingly.

"No idea. But it's weird, isn't it? This… *thing* followed me the moment I left Kirk Heidengaard, all the way to Beezel Mount and the Forest of Lost Souls. I hardly know anybody enough in the Netherworld to attract such attention."

"You're sure something was following you?"

"Yes."

"It wasn't just the wind making a rustling sound? I mean

people say they can *hear the wind talking* and all that."

"It wasn't the wind Ruby," asserted Saul. "Archibald accidentally said that the ghost was a *he*, and I trust his judgement."

"He said it was a ghost?" asked Ruby.

"Yes. I mean no. I mean he said it was a *spirit*."

"Spirit? What's the difference between a spirit and a ghost?"

"I don't know."

"Shouldn't you have asked?"

"Yes. No. Who cares? I mean does it even matter?"

The room went quiet as Saul and Ruby thought about the conversation with Archibald.

"Do you think that…"

Ruby stopped abruptly, the room went quiet and grim as the same stomach-churning thought crossed both their minds. There could only be one person in the Netherworld looking out for Saul.

"Could it…?" Ruby struggled to hold back a tear.

"No," replied Saul dismissively. "It wasn't Henry, I mean it wasn't Henry's ghost."

"But it all adds up Saul," said Ruby in a quiet weepy voice. "We don't know anybody in this world. Who could possibly be looking over you?"

"Look if it's Henry's ghost, it would mean he's…" Saul did not finish the sentence.

Neither of them wanted to accept that the strange ghost in the Forest of Lost Souls was Henry. But the more they sat thinking out this terrible possibility, the more convinced they became.

"We *have* to speak to Rufus," Ruby urged. "This is too serious not to."

"We can't. If Henry isn't dead but we go on about *the ghost of Henry,* they might call off the search. We can't let that happen." Saul had a point and they both wanted to cling onto the unlikely but desperate hope that Henry was still out there somewhere. "I mean at least they might find his body," he added with tears in his eyes.

*

The afternoon settled into the evening, and the courtyard lamps spread a warm glow through the bedroom. Saul and Ruby sat quietly in the room feeling sullen and numb, neither of them wanting to say or do anything.

Although Saul and Ruby were feeling miserable as they walked down for dinner that evening, the mood at Fort Delmar was jovial. Small groups continued pouring in through the great gates and it seemed that hundreds of sorcerers had been freed in the raids that took place over the last few weeks.

Now there was not one, but a group of vampires and giants who stood out tall and gaunt above the crowds. A gathering of small grumpy dwarves stood huddled together, keeping themselves to themselves. Perhaps the most intriguing group were the four druids, a group of long-haired bearded sorcerers who looked more like the sorcerers and wizards that Saul and Ruby had read about at school.

Despite the joviality, a terrible sinking and churning feeling ate through Saul and Ruby. Nothing could excite or interest them as they conducted themselves in a sedated manner. While neither of them dared to admit it, they could not help feeling that the ghost that seemed so interested in Saul's progress from Kirk Heidengaard to Port Newton was the ghost of Henry and that their beloved friend was dead.

Saul kicked himself for not being more inquisitive about the noises in the bushes, the intercalation outside the tent, and the rustling sound near Archibald Krayden's tent. Did Henry's ghost divert the walvark's attention?

The following morning, there was still no news. Countless times a tear had trickled down Saul's cheek when he thought about Henry, and many times that day, Ruby disappeared quietly somewhere to have a good cry.

By the afternoon, they decided to visit the meeting room in the main square and speak to Rufus about Henry's ghost. They walked up to the open door, peered through, and saw a busy room full of sorcerers. Rabin sat at the end of a long table, Conrad to his left, and Jarrett, his arm heavily bandaged, to the right. The sight of Rabin sitting at the head of the meeting table made Saul and Ruby quiver with nerves, and for a moment, they had second thoughts about approaching anybody.

"So, it's agreed," said Rabin. "The battleships can be cloaked and are exempted from the bilateral agreement restricting the use of sorcery." There was a shout of *"aaay!"*

"It is also agreed that the mission itself is not exempt from the agreement and that the use of sorcery is strictly forbidden and not exempted from the bilateral agreement." There was another, less enthusiastic *"aaay"*.

"Then my friends I call this meeting to an end. May the ancient druids guide our hand and grant success." There followed a loud shuffling and murmuring as the sorcerers exited the room.

"Ahh, just the people I need to see," said Rufus as he walked out.

"We need to speak to you," urged Saul. "We're worried that Henry is probably dead, well I saw his ghost, at least I think it was his ghost, actually it was a *spirit*, it was in the Forest of Lost Souls when I was travelling here," everything came out jumbled and Saul regretted not thinking it through.

"Saul saw a ghost in the forest of souls, and we reckon it was Henry," explained Ruby more composedly.

Rufus looked at them with squinted enquiring eyes as he climbed the staircase to the living quarters. "Get a grip," he said patronisingly. "People hear voices and think they've seen things all the time in the forest of souls, that's why it's called *the Forest of Lost Souls*."

"This ghost also saved me from a walvark by distracting—"

"Listen. I was looking for you earlier. We have some good news. Do you know Grandon Smith?"

Saul and Ruby nodded. "He's the best we have, and now the prison break is dealt with, Rabin has asked him to find Henry," a tremendous sense of relief filled Saul and Ruby. "This morning we received some promising news. We think Henry's been seen two hundred miles away in the Valley of Rondor. Grandon and Caleb left immediately to chase it up."

"Two hundred miles away?" queried Saul.

"Yes. How he ever got there we'll never know," Rufus put his hands on Ruby and Saul's shoulders "Cheer up, he'll be here soon," he added enthusiastically, leaving Saul and Ruby stunned in the corridor.

"That's brilliant!" cried Ruby as they walked through the square.

"Two... hundred... miles away," said Saul, his eyebrows raised in surprise. "How on earth did he end up so far away?"

"How long do you think it'll take Grandon and Caleb to get to him?"

"Around a day I reckon."

"A day?"

"Yes. Well, do you remember when we stopped for lunch on that first day when we left Kirby Hall?"

"Hmm," replied Ruby eyeing a group of dwarves standing at the corner of the central square.

"Caleb said we'd covered two hundred and fifty miles, right?"

"Err... right," Ruby replied trying to remember their first day of travel.

"Well, I might not be in the top set for maths but even I can work out that the krays covered fifty miles an hour."

*

The afternoon drew on. Saul and Ruby lay lazily on their beds. The wind blew cautiously through the open window and the steady murmuring and excited talk from the courtyard down below drifted into the room. Neither of them felt the urgency to go down to dinner, but steadily they made their way down the stairs.

"Three escapees from the mines of Catellan arrived yesterday," Jordan said enthusiastically as he trotted over to Saul and Ruby in the dining room.

"The mines of cata-what?" queried Saul.

"Catellan," Jordan repeated. "Nobody has ever escaped from Catellan, but these three dervishes escaped a week ago and—"

"Dervishes?" interrupted Saul.

"Dervishes," began Ruby. "Are wise old sorcerers from the deep South of Petonia, and stop interrupting."

"They said Jessy and mum are in the mines," continued Jordan. "They've been there for months."

"The mines?" gasped Ruby. "What must they be going through?"

"Whatever it is, it won't be for much longer," continued Jordan excitedly. "Rabin wants Grandon to prepare a rescue plan."

"That's wonderful news Jordan," smiled Ruby.

Jordan's excitement was infectious, and Saul and Ruby were delighted to share in his enthusiasm.

"Grandon Smith used to be a scentia you know," said Jordan putting his napkin on his lap.

"Scentia?" queried Saul with a confused look on his face

"A scentia is a searcher who hunts people." Saul and Ruby looked even more confused. "Basically, he can follow signs, scents, and clues that you and I can't see or understand. He can hunt people down and find them. He single-handedly masterminded the prison breaks. The man's a genius."

*

After dinner, Saul and Ruby sought the solitude of one of the tall towers overlooking Port Newton into the Black Sea. They sat looking far into the Black Sea conjecturing how Henry had ended up two hundred miles away in the Valley of Rondor.

The evening was drawing in. Lights began twinkling across the port and the pier.

"Do you think we'll ever miss the Netherworld?" asked Saul dreamily. A loud cheer shot up from the square below, instantly followed by laughter and cheery conversation.

Ruby thought about this for a moment, raising her eyebrows. "Well, it *is* a wonderful magical place isn't it?" She replied looking out over the distant hills. "I think I will."

"I can't wait to go home. And I hope I never return. It's been nothing but trouble and—"

A shrill crowing sound filled the air. In the distance, a swarm of black crows flew wildly from side to side. The crowing became deafeningly louder as the swarm reached the fort, and now, they became steadily clearer. The crowd in the square down below stopped to look up with intrigue at the remarkable scene.

Saul and Ruby gasped. The swarm was attacking an eagle that flew at the head of the swarm. Hundreds of birds tore after the eagle, pecking and attacking it wildly. It was a horrific sight.

The swarm was getting closer to the tower. Now the swarm was within yards of flying over the tower. Suddenly, the eagle swooped downwards through an opening, into the tower and straight through the other side. This confused the crows, and they scattered in many directions.

Saul and Ruby ducked for cover as the eagle shot through. They jumped up to see the eagle tearing away from the swarm with a newly found reserve of energy. It tore further and further away from the hapless swarm before disappearing into the distance.

"That was weird," said Ruby.

"And so's this," replied Saul. A piece of paper rolled up and tied neatly with a string lay on the floor. Saul picked it up and opened it.

The Forest of Maydor, no time to lose

It took a moment for Saul and Ruby to digest the words.

"Forest of Maydor?" quizzed Saul with a knotted brow.

"What does it mean?"

"I don't know," replied Saul looking just as confused as Ruby. "I'd like to ignore it, but the eagle went to a lot of trouble to get the note to us," he added looking out of the window.

"Maybe…" began Ruby slowly. "Maybe it's a message about Henry. That he's in the Forest of Maydor?"

"But that doesn't make sense. How did Henry get an eagle to deliver this message? Besides, Grandon and Caleb have found him in the Valley of Rondor."

"They *think* Henry was seen in the Valley of Rondor, but they don't seem sure. What if they're wrong?" They thought about this for a while. "Do you think," continued Ruby, "that it could have been sent by Darius? He can speak to animals, right?"

"Hmm," agreed Saul. "On the other hand, it could be a trap by the searchers to entice Rufus into the forest," Saul and Ruby thought about this for a few moments. "They might even have Henry captive. He must have told them we're meeting here."

"Yes, but if it's Rufus they want, they would've sent a message to the council to hand over Rufus in return for Henry," proposed Ruby.

They walked down the stone stairs pondering and considering all the possibilities and reasons for the note.

As they passed the stables, Ruby stopped suddenly. She wandered in looking carefully at a kray lying in slumber. Then she walked over to it, crouched down, and began to stroke its jaw.

"Careful young lady," grunted a passing giant. "I might be big, but I can't hold a kray off."

"Stop doing that," muttered Saul with gritted teeth as passers-by turned their heads anxiously.

Somewhat embarrassed by the attention she was attracting, Ruby stood up and walked away before stopping dead in her tracks. She turned around and eyed the kray again for a few moments.

"What's up?" asked Saul curiously. "Hey, Ruby, you're acting really weird."

"Shush," she murmured dismissively.

Ruby often went into a trance-like state when she was thinking hard. She did this often at school, occasionally wandering into an extended silence until she solved the problem at hand. Although Saul was quite used to this, at this very point in time, he found it annoying.

"Hey Ruby," said Saul a bit louder almost as if he was waking her up.

"Follow me!" Ruby ran from the stable into the central courtyard towards the meeting rooms. Saul followed her through the hallway into the empty *war* room. Ruby placed herself determinedly in front of a huge map that lay sprawled across one of the walls. It was so big that the council had placed small step-ladders around it so they could reach the top.

"Become fond of reading maps?" asked Saul cheekily.

"Can't you just shut up for two minutes?" hissed Ruby. "Make yourself useful and help me find the Forest of Maydor and the Valley of Rondor," she added keeping her eyes focused on the map. "Forest areas are marked with tree signs."

Saul climbed up a stepladder and joined in curiously. The map presented the eastern coast of Petonia. Next to Petonia lay the vast expanse of the Black Sea. Long thick lines marked the many powerful rivers that tore down into the sea. Wild mountainous ranges lay scattered across the North, and five or six forests were dotted around the map.

Kirk Heidengaard sat on the far left and Saul saw the distance he had covered to get here. Balson Mees and Port Newton were tucked away along the route.

"Here!" she exclaimed, pointing at an area of the map marked with the words *Maydor.*

"Calm down," urged Saul looking worriedly to the door. "We're not supposed to be here. And here's the Valley of Rondor," he added proudly pointing his finger at an area of the map. "Now will you tell me what's up?"

"Rufus said they're searching the Valley of Rondor which is Northeast of here right?" Saul nodded. "Here." Ruby pointed to where Saul had his finger. "But Maydor is Southwest of here." Ruby smacked her finger at another point on the map.

A worried expression spread across Saul's face.

"If they spend all their time searching in the Valley of Rondor," began Ruby. "And if our mysterious informer is right that Henry is in Maydor—"

"Then we've already lost lots of time," said Saul sharply.

"Thank you," said Ruby sarcastically. "You and I have to go to the Forest of Maydor. Whichever way we look at it, whether the message was sent by Darius or the searchers, we can't just sit here and do nothing."

Saul raised an eyebrow. "And how do you propose we get from here," Saul pointed at Port Newton, "to here? I crossed a fraction of that distance and it took me days."

"We can ride a kray better than almost anyone else here can't we? And Caleb won't be back until tomorrow afternoon, so none of the krays will be missed, will they?"

"Are you mad? If we got caught, we'd be skinned alive."

"*If* we get caught. Who'll care if we bring Henry home?" Ruby replied swiftly. "Saul, we can't take the chance that Grandon and Caleb are looking in the wrong place. We have to follow this lead."

"There are too many *ifs* in all of this," Saul complained. "*If* Henry is somewhere in the forest *if* we can even find him *if* we can find the forest. If the forest is anything like anywhere else in this world, it'll take days to search it. This could be a massive wild goose chase."

"Do you have any better ideas?" Ruby asked pursing her lips.

Saul sighed. He spent a moment rationalising the flight of the golden eagle and the message it had delivered to them. Someone, most likely Darius, had tried very hard to get the message to them, the searchers had no reason to entrap Saul and Ruby.

"If we leave early in the morning, we'll be back before lunch. We won't be missed," insisted Ruby.

"Hmmm," murmured Saul momentarily. "First thing's first, we need to copy the map."

Ruby smiled in relief. She ran across the room and returned with a pencil and paper and quickly scribbled a map together. "How's this?"

Saul looked carefully at the paper, the map on the wall and then back again a few times. He took the pencil and made some adjustments. "We need the three suns to guide us."

"How far is the forest?" asked Ruby.

Saul looked around the room and found a long ruler in a drawer. He placed it carefully on the map, measuring the distance from Port Newton across to the Forest of Souls and then compared that with the distance to the Forest of Maydor.

"Maybe a couple of hours on the kray," he suggested looking nervously at the vast space covered by the forest. "Just a guess though."

They stood considering this for a few more moments.

"We have to leave well before dawn, around five o'clock, to get there around seven," said Ruby.

"How long do we search?"

"Two hours, until nine," replied Ruby. "If we don't find anything, we'll just have to come back. The difficulty will be not knowing what to look for, I mean what do we look for, a house, a village or an opening, or—"

A trickle of voices entered the building. Saul slipped the map into his pocket and followed Ruby out of the room.

For the next half hour, they continued planning their journey in meticulous detail.

"What do we do about Jordan?" asked Saul.

Ruby was quiet for a moment. They had not thought about Jordan.

"We don't tell him."

"We have to tell him. He'll feel betrayed if we took a kray without telling him," said Saul. "He's in charge when Caleb isn't around. If he notices a missing kray he'll raise an alarm."

"It's a catch twenty-two," the puzzled look on Saul's face prompted Ruby to carry on. "If we tell him, he'll probably stop us. But if we return with Henry, everyone's a winner, right?"

Saul thought about this for a moment.

"What time does he attend to the krays?"

"Around eleven I think he said."

"We could be back by then I reckon."

~ 20 ~

The Cottage

Late into the night, Henry was awoken out of his cold slumber by a scratching noise. He looked around deliriously before realising he was still tied up in a dark cellar, and that the vivid experiences still playing agonisingly on his mind were not a dream. A small glow crept into the dingy cellar from under the door casting a shadowy glare on the floorboards.

Henry heard the scratching sound again. A moment later, a faint squeaking noise came from near the door. Something was gnawing at the door! A shiver spread through Henry's body. He felt his heart pounding in his throat.

Rats! Henry hated rats, and this downtrodden abandoned neglected house was probably infested with them!

There was a heavy rattling sound. Henry looked up to see the light shine through a hole in the door where the lock should have been. It had fallen off. Something had eaten through the door around the lock and it had fallen off!

The door crept forward. Soft light spread through the cellar.

Suddenly, Henry felt a strange scurrying sensation around his ankles. Dozens of rats were running wildly around the floor and over him! He tried to wriggle around and discourage the pests, but every move sent a seething pain through his wrists and ankles.

Henry was terrified. His face was affixed in a firm awkward grimace. He closed his eyes tightly as one of the pests climbed up his ankle. He tried in vain to shake it off.

Then, against the glow of light shining in through the door, Henry saw one of these strange creatures standing on its hind legs. It was not a rat, but something much worse and much bigger. A peculiar furry eight-legged creature, about the size of a small cat, stood on its four hind legs rubbing two of its tiny front legs against its face with the other two legs bouncing in mid-air as it did so.

Vermin! Thought Henry turning his head in disdain.

The creatures carried on scurrying around and over him. A few of them seemed busy around his feet. At any moment, thought Henry, he would feel a sharp bite.

Then as he tried to twist his foot more determinedly, his legs pulled away. It took a moment for Henry to realise what had happened. The creatures had eaten through the ropes and were now scampering up towards his hands. Strangely, these rat-like creatures had come to free him.

Henry felt a strange tickling sensation around his arms and wrists. He clamped his eyes shut as this went on. Soon the ropes around his wrists were also free. Their work was done, and now the animals scurried away through the door, disappearing into the dark wilderness that had sent them here.

After a macabre turn of events, Henry had been freed. He lay on the floor for a moment trying to reason with what had just happened before realising that he was wasting time on these thoughts. Henry pulled himself up but went crashing into the floorboards with a thud. His legs had gone to sleep. It took a few more moments for Henry to stand up, gather his senses and feel the blood rush through his legs.

Eventually, Henry stood up and walked steadily towards the stairs. He stepped onto the first step softly, praying it would not creak. He sighed and then walked up very slowly. At the top of the stairs, he turned and walked steadily down the corridor, careful not to let the floorboards creak. Henry undid the catch on the door and pushed it steadily.

He was welcomed by a moonlit night. Ahead of him sat the shadow of a dark forest. Henry did not have a plan and had no idea where he was or where he was going, all he knew was that he had to get as far away from the rickety old house as possible. He jogged determinedly for a good half hour before slowing down to a trot and then a walk.

Some time passed. The forest was lighting up and Henry could see around him more clearly. He was far enough now, he thought, to rest awhile. Henry sat in quiet contemplation against a tree. An owl hooted around him and flew from branch to branch, it disappeared now and again only to return moments later. The forest was probably infested with owls thought Henry. The owl perched itself on a branch ahead of him. It hooted shyly and turned its head from one side to another before running its curved beak through its feathers.

"Good morning little fellow," whispered Henry cheekily as the owl continued grooming itself.

~ 21 ~

Bowman Glover Monson

Saul jolted awake from a deep sleep.

"Saul!" cried Ruby, "we're late!"

"What? No!" groaned Saul. He shot up, trotted around the dark room looking for his clothes and fell over a couple of times.

"For crying out loud, just get ready will you?"

"Where did I put my trousers?"

"How many times have I told you to fold them up and put them in a cupboard Saul," replied Ruby angrily. "Here," she added picking up the trousers from the corner in the room where Saul had thrown them the night before.

"What's the time?" he asked as he ran around looking for his shoes.

"Around half-past five," Ruby replied running to her bag. "We were supposed to leave half an hour ago!"

Despite all the elaborate planning, they were already behind schedule. They crept out of the room and walked quietly down the long corridor which, until now, had never seemed so long.

Around thirty krays were lying in slumber. Suddenly one of them lifted its head to within a foot of Ruby and looked straight at her. Its warm breath stroked her face. There was a stunned silence that seemed to last an eternity with neither the kray nor Ruby moving. Saul had vivid recollections of his near-death experience with the walvark and watched on helplessly, wanting to shout to Ruby to run back quickly but not daring to utter a sound.

"There there," whispered Ruby calmly. "Sleepy time." Remarkably, the kray put its head back down.

"I don't know how you do that," Saul muttered, shaking his head incredulously. "Now let's get a move on."

"Where's my kray?" asked Ruby.

"Your kray?"

"The kray I travelled on to Kirk Heidengaard," she said as she walked around frantically. *"Here!"*

"The saddle only carries one or two people," Saul said looking up at the line of saddles on the walls of the stables. "We have to take two krays."

They kicked themselves for not having thought of this earlier.

"Where's your kray?" queried Ruby.

"Err... I don't know, does it really matter, let's just get another one and go, we're losing time!" Saul replied impatiently.

"We shouldn't Saul. The kray will feel more comfortable with you if you've already travelled together."

"*It* will feel more comfortable with *me*?" Saul gesticulated. "That's taking it too far Ruby. Let's just get onto a kray and leave and—"

"Ah, here we are," Ruby said pointing at a kray and walking up to it. "The saddles quick!"

Moments later, with a collective sigh of relief, they were floating high above the fort towards the Forest of Maydor. Saul took a cursory glance down to see if anybody had noticed, but the fort quickly became a distant spot in the landscape as the kray tore through the sky with its customary vigour.

*

As the day progressed, Henry felt tired and hungry. But with every rustle of the trees behind him and every chirrup or tweet of a bird, he became more determined to keep going until he reached a town or village.

Henry stopped suddenly. He had been so engrossed in his thoughts he had not noticed a lonely cottage announcing itself in an open space.

He surveyed the cottage and space around it carefully. It seemed empty. He walked to the door and knocked gently. There was no answer. He turned the handle, it was locked. Next Henry walked around to the back. The back door opened with a soft creak. Henry waited a moment before walking in cautiously.

It was a busy kitchen. Pots, pans, and utensils lay untidily around the sink. Henry's attention was drawn to bread and fruit which lay invitingly on the kitchen table. Without thinking, he pushed some fruit into his bag and began gnawing on the bread hungrily. Next, he wandered around the kitchen, looking through the shelves and inside the cupboards for more food.

Content that he had enough food to last a couple of days, Henry prepared to set off. He stepped out of the door, looked at the forest for a few moments, and then sat down at the door.

The trees, the greenery, and the foliage that he had just spent more than a day wandering through made his stomach churn. He could not face going back into the forest. Henry weighed this up momentarily before deciding to rest a while. He would resume his journey later in the day.

He walked back in and decided to explore the cottage. He walked through the kitchen into a small corridor, in turn leading to a small room at the front of the cottage. An armchair sat opposite a fireplace, and for a moment, Henry thought about resting here before deciding to check upstairs.

The bedsheets in the first bedroom were strewn across the bed. Whoever lived here must have left in a rush. The second room was just big enough to have a small bed and a desk. It was a child's room. The bed was covered by a beautiful blanket woven with pretty pictures of ducks, cats, and dogs.

Henry walked downstairs into the living room and sunk into an armchair. A strange eerie but peaceful silence filled the air, disturbed now and again by the tweeting of a bird in the forest, the chirruping of a grasshopper, or the hooting of an owl. *There's that owl again,* he thought. Henry passed the time lazily looking through the window eyeing the trees and leaves rustling gently in the wind.

Soon, darkness set in, and Henry considered his next move. The right thing to do was to leave right now. Although the cottage looked abandoned, he could not risk the owner returning. But again, the thought of crossing through the forest and bumping into the searchers made him shudder with anxiety. These thoughts churned away before Henry finally decided to stay and leave early in the morning.

Later that evening, Henry walked upstairs and dropped his bag on the table in the child's room. He settled himself on the bed and soon fell into a deep sleep.

*

Henry was awoken by a frightful banging sound. He sat up frightened out of his wits.

"It's abandoned I reckon!" shouted a voice under the window. "Let's move on!"

"Can't take a chance Aramond!" called a second voice. "Let's have a look inside!"

What now? thought Henry.

The kitchen door opened and banged shut sending a tremor through the cottage. Two pairs of shoes walked around the kitchen, through the corridor and into the front room. Then the footsteps climbed up the staircase.

Henry looked frantically out of the window. It was a steep drop, he would hurt himself if he jumped out. He looked around the dark room and without another thought slid quietly under the bed, pushing himself firmly against the wall.

Suddenly a horrible thought struck Henry. His bag was sitting on the table! He crawled across the dark floor quietly, pulled the bag down gently, and slid back underneath as the door opened. A sturdy light spread across the floor, and a pair of shoes walked into the room. Henry's heart was pounding in his throat, loud enough, thought Henry, for the intruder to hear it.

"Let's rest here tonight Aramond," suggested the voice in the room.

No! thought Henry.

"Rayman, it's not often that a good idea crosses that demented mind of yours," returned Aramond from the second bedroom.

"It'll be nice to have a proper bed for the night," murmured Rayman lifting his feet onto the bed. The bed sunk to within an inch of Henry's nose. Rayman shifted around the bed before settling down.

"I wonder where that cretin got to," said Aramond.

"I want to know why the children are so important," returned the second voice. "Shooting around the countryside to search for three miscreants isn't how I'd planned to spend the week."

Aramond and Rayman continued talking for what seemed an eternity before Rayman fell sound asleep. He snored like a rattle and constantly tossed and turned, causing the mattress to sink and rise beneath him.

Finally, Henry gathered his thoughts. The thought of lying under the bed all night was disconcerting. What now? Should he sneak out? Rayman was asleep, but what if Aramond was awake, perhaps even sitting downstairs?

In the end, Henry decided to stay put. He lay under the bed, trembling at every loud snore and movement.

*

"Rayman!" screamed Aramond's voice.

Henry awoke to a frightening shuffling banging sound next door. The bed moved violently as Rayman jumped up and tore out of the room.

Banging, shouting, and a tirade of cursing and swearing filled the room next door. Now and again, Aramond or Rayman cried in pain. There was a deafening scream, something hit the wall. There was more scuffling and shouting, and then a second loud thud. Someone or something had landed heavily on the floor.

Now there was silence. Henry listened carefully. Nothing stirred.

A pair of boots, stiffer and heavier than those of Rayman and Aramond, walked around the room next door, dragged something across the floor into the corridor, down the stairs and out of the house. A while later, the boots climbed up the stairs, into the room next door and then back down and out again.

Henry lay under the bed listening intently.

A while later, the boots walked up the stairs and stopped outside the small bedroom. The door crept open. A pair of brown boots walked up to the bed and stopped still. Henry held his breath.

"Come out from under there," murmured a deep vibrating voice.

Henry shuddered.

"I said come out. I know you're there. We can do this the easy way, or the messy way," asserted the voice. Henry gasped as the vague outline of an axe landed with a thud on the floor!

Henry felt paralysed with fear.

"Your two friends are dead," announced the voice chillingly. "You'll be joining them if you don't come out."

Henry pulled himself out slowly and stood up. A huge bald bearded man looked down at him. A pair of small cynical black eyes sat beneath his bushy eyebrows. A heavy beard and moustache covered his face. He held a huge threatening axe.

The man seemed as surprised to see Henry as Henry was shocked to see him.

"Please sir," Henry gulped, his mind racing wildly. "They're not my friends. I can explain, I'm not with those men and—"

"What were searchers doing in my house?" interrupted the bearded man.

"They were… they were looking for me," returned Henry. "I… I was hiding from them. I had to hide here. I didn't mean to but…" Henry's voice trailed away.

The bearded man thought for a few moments. The angry look on his face changed subtly and became less tempestuous.

"Follow me."

He led Henry down the stairs into the kitchen. Next, he lit a lamp and placed it on the windowsill. The kitchen brightened up, and for the first time, Henry saw him properly.

"Why were they after you?" he asked calmly.

"It's not really me they're after," said Henry. "They're after a friend called Rufus."

"Rufus?"

"Yes."

"And why do they want this *Rufus?*"

"I'm not sure. They've been after him since we arrived at Kirk Heidengaard."

"That's miles away."

"Yes."

"Is he a fugitive?"

"Fugitive?"

"An escaped prisoner."

"No. Definitely not."

"Then why do they want him?"

"I… I don't know. He's a good man honestly."

The bearded man thought about this for a little while. The candlelight cast eerie shadows over his face.

"You've picked your enemies badly," he boomed. "The searchers are… very bad."

"I know. They kidnapped me and kept me in a cellar, but I escaped. I didn't mean to stay here long, just one night and…" The bearded man walked to the sink. He filled a kettle and placed it on the stove. He walked back a few moments later with two mugs of tea and nodded towards the table.

"The searchers will be out prowling for you and their missing friends." He looked firmly at Henry with his beady eyes, making Henry feel very uncomfortable. There was something very raw about this man. His recluse-like manner, the menacing look in his tiny eyes.

"Did you…?" Henry wanted to ask if the man had killed the two searchers. A stiff silence answered the question.

"I'm Henry."

"Bowman Glover Monson."

"I need to get to Port Newton," Henry ventured.

"That's three days away," Bowman muttered after an unsteady pause. "It's too far to reach on your own. You'll be lucky to get within a day of the Port without being chased and caught by the searchers. They're trained hunters, it's a wonder you've got this far in one piece to be honest."

"But I *have* to go there," asserted Henry timidly. "My friends'll be waiting. They'll leave without me if I don't get there in time."

Bowman thought about this for a while.

"Stay here for a day or two," he began. "That'll get the searchers off the trail. I have a good friend at Timpson Halls, he'll take you to Port Newton safely."

Henry was desperate to reach Port Newton. However, the prospect of the searchers being on his back the whole distance was frightening.

"That would be wonderful," said Henry smiling.

"Time to rest Henry."

*

Henry awoke to the sound of clanking cooking utensils downstairs. He looked around the room lazily, eyeing the chair, the curtains, and the box of toys before sinking back into his pillow.

Bowman had prepared toast, beans, and ham. It was the most welcoming sight Henry had seen in days. There was a sprinkling of polite conversation as they ate, *had Henry rested well? The breakfast was wonderful, it was a nice cottage*. Henry began to feel at ease with Bowman.

It was a restful day. Henry whiled away part of the morning on a bench outside the cottage watching the trees in the forest sway softly from side to side.

Later, Henry returned to the bedroom. He ran his eyes across a stack of books sitting on the dressing table and pulled out a book called *Sorcerers and Warlocks: Dispute, Turmoil, and Anarchy*. He put it back and pulled out *The Last of the Druid Kings*. Henry flicked through the pages inquisitively before settling on *A Short History of the Petonian Council: of Druids, Sorcerers, and Alchemists.*

*

"Lunch will be ready soon," said Bowman.

The commotion from the previous night had taken its toll, and Henry had fallen asleep. The book lay on the bed and sunshine was beaming through the window.

"I need to pop out after lunch," said Bowman. "I'll be gone a while. Don't wait up for me. There's some bread, and salad in the kitchen, make yourself a sandwich."

Later, Bowman slung his axe over a shoulder and a bag over the other and disappeared into the forest, leaving Henry to wonder why Bowman had to have his axe with him.

The evening crept in, and the sounds of the forest changed to announce the nightlife. As Henry sat down to eat in the lamp-lit kitchen, he began to feel anxious. What if the searchers returned in Bowman's absence?

*

Henry awoke deep into the night, a restless bundle of nerves. He could not stop thinking about Bowman's strange departure into the forest and the axe. But what Henry found most unnerving was the room he was staying in. Whose room was it? Did Bowman have a child, if so where was he? Maybe he kidnapped children and sold them to slave traders. *Maybe he's an axe murderer,* thought Henry.

Suddenly, the kitchen door closed shut. Bowman walked up the stairs into his room. He shuffled around for a while. Everything went quiet.

Sometime later, there was a quiet movement next door. Bowman was shuffling around again. What was he doing?

Henry listened intently. The door to Bowman's bedroom opened, Henry glued his eyes to the bedroom door. Nothing happened. Now, Henry heard Bowman treading softly down the stairs and out of the cottage.

Henry jumped to the window to see Bowman's shadow walking into the forest, a lantern over one shoulder, his axe over the other.

If Bowman had wanted to harm me, thought Henry, *he would've done it by now.* He could have done it at any point in the evening. Henry was helpless and would not stand a chance against an axe-wielding madman. If the plan was to sell him to slave traders, Bowman would have tied Henry up to prevent his escape until the traders arrived. The axeman had not harmed Henry. Instead, Henry had been fed and given a comfortable room to stay in. *That's not what axe murderers do* thought Henry. With these thoughts, he lay down and against all his intentions fell into a deep sleep.

*

"Did you have a child living here?" asked Henry at the breakfast table.

"Yes," Bowman replied after an unsteady silence. "My son. He's been gone quite a while."

"The war, right?"

Bowman nodded and carried on eating. Another silence surrounded the table.

"My son and wife disappeared thirteen years ago. He must be fourteen now, a big lad I'll wonder."

There was a soft twinkle in his eye. This was the kink in Bowman's armour. Henry felt a sudden surge of confidence. Strangely, he could feel the presence of a boy in the house, the bedroom, the kitchen, the living room, everything made him feel that Bowman's son was still here.

"Do you think he's still alive?"

"I'm sure of it. I err… I hear his voice now and again," Bowman replied quietly.

"That's why you went into the forest last night, right?"

Bowman raised an eyebrow and looked at Henry inquisitively. He nodded and carried on eating his toast. Henry wanted to say that the voice was either Bowman's imagination or the wind in the forest, whichever it was, he had so wanted to hear his son's voice that he was now imagining it. But this was not what Bowman wanted to hear.

"We'll leave later in the afternoon," said Bowman.

"I'm sorry to have imposed like this," replied Henry with a smile."It's the least I can do." Bowman took a sip of his tea. "It's strange, but you… you remind me of my son." his voice broke off and he coughed to try and hide his sadness.

"I'm sure he's out there somewhere," said Henry, almost believing it himself. "You'll find him and—"

"The pantry quick!" said Bowman getting up quickly.

There was a movement outside the kitchen window. Bowman collected his axe from behind the kitchen door and walked to the cottage door. There was a relentless beating on the door.

Henry walked into a dark pantry and pulled the door shut. Three of the walls were lined with shelves, stacked with utensils and small containers. A small window sat at the top of one of the walls. Henry pasted himself behind the door listening intently for any sound.

"You're welcome to search the cottage," said Bowman calmly.

"Do you think we'll fall for that?" said the voice of Edgerton.

Henry's heart pounded in his throat. He calculated his options quickly. He could dart through the kitchen and out into the forest, but he risked getting caught in the kitchen or outside near the kitchen door, someone was bound to be waiting there for him.

"Edgerton! Upstairs!" ordered Rankin from the kitchen.

Henry looked up at the tiny window and put his foot tentatively on one of the shelves. It was sturdy.

"The consequences of hiding a wanted man are pretty severe!" Rankin was outside the pantry door!

Henry climbed steadily up towards the window, careful not to exert too much pressure on the shelves lest they came crashing down. He removed the latch from the window and pushed softly at the window, it opened just as the shelf beneath him gave way with a crashing clatter! Henry pulled himself out of the window.

The pantry door opened. *"Outside Edgerton, he's escaping!"* Rankin reached for Henry's ankles.

Henry desperately tried to pull himself up. Somebody grabbed his arms. He was caught!

~ 23 ~

Amaruk

The early morning rays of Solarius rose over the horizon, filled from one end to the other by the Forest of Maydor.

As Saul and Ruby got closer, a thick blanket of trees stretched below them with barely an opening in sight. They did not know where to begin looking. They searched for everything and anything, an opening, a roof peering above the trees, the smoke of a chimney, anything. Occasionally, one or the other of them swooped down to the roof of the forest. They were now within touching distance of the tips of the trees, still, they could not find an opening.

Half an hour passed. All the while, Saul and Ruby looked around aimlessly for a sign or clue. Each powerful flap of the kray's wings further disheartened them.

"It's useless!" shouted Saul. "Where do we start?"

Ruby pursed her lips in agreement and tried to keep her eyes fixed beneath her. *"How long has it been?"*

"Around an hour I reckon."

Suddenly a gentle swishing sound pressed past Saul's ear, he looked up and saw a golden eagle! He was convinced it was the same golden eagle that had delivered the note! It swooped up above them, turned around and flew back in the opposite direction.

"Ruby! The eagle. Look!"

Saul and Ruby turned the krays and tore behind the eagle. It swooped swiftly through the air. Now it slowed down, drifted downwards before perching itself on a tree. Saul and Ruby looked at each other enthusiastically.

"Saul," said Ruby looking down at the forest. *"What the devil is that?"*

The trees below them were moving wildly as if a gale-force wind was tearing through the forest. Saul and Ruby gasped as a clump of trees fell downwards. Henry was in deep trouble, they dared not imagine what was going on. Instinctively they guided the kray down closer to the forest.

"Over there, look!" shouted Ruby pointing forward.

Two tiny figures were scampering wildly away from the forest.

"Henry!" cried Saul.

He tugged the reins of the kray and shot downwards. They got closer and saw the small frame of a girl wearing a tatty torn dress at the front. Saul tilted his head softly and squinted his eyes, noticing disappointedly, that the boy behind her was not Henry. Both children were bald. The boy was small and skinny. He ran aimlessly with a limp, and at any moment now, thought Saul, he would fall flat on his face.

"What are they running from?" quizzed Ruby as they crossed over the edge of the forest down to within a hundred yards of the children.

A terrifying roar tore shot out behind them. Saul and Ruby turned and gasped as two huge ferocious beasts emerged from the forest.

"Amaruk!" they both screamed, remembering the vivid description that Jarrett had given.

Nothing that Jarrett had told them could have prepared them for what they saw. Although the amaruk shared some of the features of the sowren, it was brown, had a larger jaw and much larger paws. A ferocious look was sprawled across its face as it tore across the ground towards the two children.

The two children were fifty yards ahead of Saul and Ruby, but the amaruk was only fifty yards behind the kray and catching up very quickly. If Saul stopped to collect the children, the amaruk would be onto them.

Saul pushed down closer to the ground. *"I'm here to help!"*

The boy turned around. His face contorted horribly as he saw the fearsome sight of the kray.

"Over us!" yelled the girl gesturing wildly with her arms. *"Over us, quick!"*

Saul threw an incredulous glance at Ruby. *"I'm here to help!"* he cried again, now within ten yards. *"Keep running until we get to a safe place and then—"*

"Bring... the krays... over us!" panted the girl. "They'll know what to do!"

Saul did not see how this would help, but steadily he guided the kray directly over the boy and girl.

The amaruk was forty yards away now.

"Down!" she cried.

"What?" screamed Saul.

"Bring the kray... down... near us!"

"But that's crazy you'll be—"

"Shut up and do it!" the girl screamed, nearly falling over.

Saul looked around momentarily. The amaruk was thirty yards away now, Saul or Ruby had to do something.

Then, without Saul's intervention, the kray glided downwards, its' front two legs stretched down as if about to land. Now, the kray slowed down and hovered gently above the children. The amaruk was twenty yards away now, Saul had to pull the kray up!

"We can't... land! That thing will be onto us!" Saul screamed pulling the reins up hopelessly.

"Vince! Reach up and let the kray take you!" the girl cried frantically.

"No!" cried the boy in return.

"No!" screamed Saul "Take you? You silly girl you're—"

"Vince, you have to trust me, raise your arms, the kray won't hurt you!"

What happened next left Saul feeling shocked, helpless, and exasperated. With a mind of its own, the kray came further to the ground, closer and closer to the two children, its legs now completely outstretched. In an instant, the kray took hold of both the children, one in each of its huge claws!

"No!" screamed Saul pulling the reins as hard as he could. "What are you doing? Stupid animal, you'll kill them!"

The kray shot up into the air as the huge fanged mouth of the amaruk closed tightly behind them, missing the kray by a whisker. Saul and Ruby were lost for words. Then, suddenly, another horrifying thought struck Saul. If the kray let go now, the two children would be finished. He had to get the kray down to ground level so they could somehow, wriggle free. He loosened the reins and hit his foot against the side of the kray. It did not respond. He did it again. The kray did not respond.

"Stupid, stupid animal!"

"Saul!" came the voice of Ruby.

"Ruby we have to get the kray to—"

"It won't harm them!"

"But if it let's go—"

"Listen to me!" yelled Ruby wildly. "Look at the kray."

Saul peered around the neck of the kray and saw the girl cocooned comfortably in the claws of the kray. The boy was held just as comfortably in the other claw. The sight of the fearsome terrifying kray holding the two children like a pair of small chicks was beyond belief. Somehow, deep down, Saul knew that the two children were perfectly safe.

The kray flew on for a while longer, each flap of its powerful wings putting a few more yards between it and the amaruk. The forest fell away in the distance behind them, the amaruk was nowhere to be seen. The kray began to descend slowly.

"Vince!" the girl screamed. "When I say, you have to jump, do you understand?"

"Yes," he replied feebly.

"Hold on!"

The kray slowed down, now it was hovering.

"Jump!"

The two children jumped and landed with a tumble. The kray flew forward a few yards and landed comfortably. Saul and Ruby jumped off and ran to the two children.

"Thank you," cried the girl throwing her arms around Ruby. She clung tightly to her, sobbing, and crying quietly.

Meanwhile, the boy stood in a confused dazed state, and, like Saul and Ruby, struggled to comprehend everything that had just happened.

Saul walked to him and put an arm around him. The two children were so thin and bony that Saul and Ruby wondered how they had mustered the energy to run from the amaruk.

"You're safe now my friend," Saul said quietly. The boy rested his head on Saul's shoulder. "Why were those… things, chasing you?"

"We escaped," Vince replied.

"Escaped?"

"From the mines."

Saul and Ruby looked at each other excitedly.

"Which mines?" Ruby asked.

"The Catellan Mines."

Saul raised his eyebrows. "Were there more children there?"

Vince nodded. "Was... was there another boy with you, wearing glasses, about my age and height?"

Vince thought about this for a moment. "No."

"His name's Henry," said Saul as if that might help. "He's a bit shorter than me, wears round glasses."

Vince shook his head. "There were only five others. But not your age or height. They're all older than us. Maybe sixteen or seventeen years old."

"You're absolutely sure?" queried Ruby.

Vince nodded. A wave of frustration filled Saul and Ruby's faces.

"Did anybody else escape with you or in the last few days?" Ruby asked.

"No just Jessy and me. But the ice mines are full of children," said Vince.

Ruby raised her eyebrows. "Ice mines?"

"Yes."

"How far are the ice mines?"

"Probably two weeks on a kray."

"Hmm. Henry couldn't be there," Ruby said quietly to Saul.

"Maybe we were sent here to rescue these two children and not Henry," began Saul. "They would have had no chance against that amaruk and…"

Ruby had turned sharply towards the girl. While Saul and Ruby had been talking to Vince, the girl had moved up to the krays and was stroking their terrifying jaws and rubbing her face on them. Saul gasped, and for the first time, Ruby saw why everyone felt nervous about her and the kray.

"You said your name's Jessy right?"

The girl nodded. Saul looked at Jessy and the kray for a while.

"Is your father Caleb?"

"How do you know?" she asked anxiously.

"Well, how can I put this? We're with your father and—"

"—he's back at Fort Delmar. You're brother too—"

"—we've been with him for the last few weeks." Saul and Ruby could not control their excitement, and as they spoke, Jessy's face lit up in excitement.

"They're at Fort Delmar. They've been searching for a long time," continued Saul.

"We're going to take you to them," Ruby announced.

"But where's your mother?" asked Saul.

"I think she's still in the mines," replied Jessy tentatively. "She managed to get us out, but she couldn't escape. She's probably still there."

As they flew back over the immense forest, Saul and Ruby cast warm glances at Jessy and Vince. Saul and Ruby could not imagine the suffering they had endured in the mines, and it seemed to make their own predicament seem meagre in comparison. They carried mixed feelings about the strange adventure. Whilst glad to have saved Vince and Jessy from certain doom, they were desperately worried about Henry.

During the journey back, Ruby and Jessy did not stop speaking. Ruby told her everything she could about Caleb and Jordan, particularly about their determined search. With each word and anecdote, Jessy felt ever more desperate to get to the Fort and see for herself that this was not a dream.

As they approached the fort, a group gathered to watch the landing. Somewhere in the crowd, Saul and Ruby saw Jordan running angrily towards the stables.

"Do you know how much trouble I'll be in when father gets back?" he screamed as Saul climbed off.

"Clear the way, clear the way," called a monotonous voice revealing itself to be the small figure of Mistie Herma. "Now that was stupid, there'll be trouble for you… who are these children?"

"Just can't stay out of mischief can you?" came the unhelpful voice of Junus Palfrey. This was getting worse. "You can't just take a kray because you think you can ride one, do you know how dangerous…" Junus Palfrey stopped midstream as he watched the thin figure of Jessy sitting on the saddle behind Ruby looking confused. "My. Is this—?"

"Jessy and Vince," Ruby announced proudly.

A shocked silence filled the air as Jessy stepped unsteadily off the kray.

"It can't be," Jordan muttered quietly. "How did you…" Jordan stopped to think for a moment.

"It doesn't matter how it happened, what matters is that Jessy is safe," Saul said loftily. "And if it wasn't for us, well…" Saul left the rest of the sentence unfinished.

For a moment Jessy stood looking at Jordan from a distance. A tear trickled down her cheek and she nearly fell over as she ran towards Jordan and gave him a warm tearful hug.

Ruby gestured softly to Saul. "Let's get Vince to Rufus," she said quietly.

*

"Grandon Smith at your service," came a booming voice. "We're here to rescue you," he announced as he pulled Henry out of the window.

Henry landed on the grass and leapt to his feet.

"You have to do what we say." Grandon pointed towards the forest "See that thicket of trees?"

Henry nodded.

"We have to get there. There are only two of us and this," he lifted his quadbow. "And one bag of arrows I'm afraid, hadn't guessed the place would be crawling with so many searchers."

"They're around the back!" screamed a voice.

"There are nine, maybe ten of them," continued Grandon calmly. "Go through that thicket. Caleb is waiting a hundred or so yards in. Don't wait for me just keep running until you get there. On my mark try to run as fast as you can, I'll try to cover you."

"Try?"

"Run!"

Henry tore ahead of Grandon, his heart pounding with every step. The muscles in his legs were aching as he tried to push himself further and further as fast as possible across the open ground into the safety of the forest.

"Don't stop keep going," said Grandon calmly as he followed on Henry's heels.

"Over there look!" boomed a voice at the front of the cottage.

An arrow tore past Grandon's shoulder sending him off balance. He steadied himself and continued running.

"I've got you covered. Don't stop!" boomed Grandon.

He turned around suddenly, aimed his quadbow and fired it at three searchers who were in hot pursuit. One of them screamed and fell holding his thigh, the other two fired back, both arrows missing Grandon by an inch.

Henry looked back frantically and recognised Edgerton and Rankin. Four more searchers were behind them. An arrow whizzed past Henry's head, he ran faster, completely oblivious of the branches around him.

Finally, he saw the opening ahead of him.

"Caleb!" shouted Grandon.

Two krays were lying in wait behind Caleb. Henry heard a scuffling sound behind him. He turned to see Grandon punch Edgerton in the jaw. Edgerton went crashing down. Three searchers lined up their quadbows. Henry jumped onto the kray, Caleb followed behind him. Moments later, the kray shot upwards and then hovered over the opening for a while.

"Let's be sure he's got on," suggested Caleb.

Two searchers had caught up with Grandon. His fist shot up and struck one squarely under the chin. The searcher was lifted off his feet and crashed into a tree. Then Grandon's foot landed in the chest of the second searcher sending him sprawling to the ground. Grandon reached the kray and climbed on. Rankin grabbed his ankle and pulled him down.

Suddenly the kray screeched, reached around with its huge jaws, took hold of Rankin by his arm, and flung him upwards through the trees. Henry was horrified to see that Rankin's arm had been ripped off from the elbow!

Rankin lay on the floor in anguish as Edgerton retreated to help him. Three more searchers had caught up with Grandon, and together they fired a stream of arrows through the forest, every one of them, somehow, miraculously, missing Grandon. Yet another moment later, Grandon's kray shot upwards, and within seconds, they were high in the sky clasping the saddle of the kray, moved, and shaken by the adventure, but unharmed and safe.

"We have to save Bowman," murmured Henry. *"They'll kill him!"*

Caleb's gaze was transfixed on the journey ahead of him.

"Listen!" cried Henry deliriously. "We have to help him! We have to help Bowman!"

"It's too risky. Let's get you to the fort. Maybe Grandon and I can come back and help him."

"Maybe?" muttered Henry. He pursed his lips together and took deep breaths as he thought about Bowman's predicament. Sure, they could not go back to save him without endangering themselves, but Henry hoped that somehow, Bowman had escaped while the searchers had been chasing them.

~ 24 ~

War Plans

Saul, Ruby, Henry, and Jordan had spent the afternoon wandering the fort and reminiscing on their remarkable adventures. A pleasant warm glow emanated gently from the courtyard lamps as dusk fell across Fort Delmar.

They headed to the square and were met by a wonderful musical carnival. Groups of sorcerers, giants, and vampires were engaged in jovial conversation, small groups played music and sang heartily.

"You've *got* to hear this," insisted Jordan leading Saul, Ruby, and Henry to a small crowd gathered at one side. "The mesmeric fiddlers," he announced.

Five violinists played in the middle of the crowd creating a musical melody that charmed and enthralled the senses of the captivated audience.

"Is that Mistie?" queried Ruby. Four of the violinists were beautiful slender long-haired ladies, the fifth was indeed the short stumpy figure of Mistie Herma, playing a violin with an elegance contrasting sharply against the grumpiness of her natural demeanour. The fiddlers cast knowing glances at each other and the audience as their fiddles flew over the strings with precise musical harmony, all five fiddles playing as one creating an enlightening musical resonance.

It was a while before the children moved on, and when they did, they walked towards another, very macabre group.

"The Vampiric Quintet," announced Jordan excitedly. "These guys are so good."

Five vampires, including Siraf stood plucking the sonorous strings of a double bass to create an eerie spectacular rhythm. Their tall gaunt figures, coupled with the spooky smiles spread across their thin white faces, presented one of the eeriest sights the children had ever seen.

The music was extraordinary. The children were completely dazed and gripped by the sound. Something inside them was stirring, and every string plucked by the ghoulish group seemed to warm their blood and send them further and further into a hypnotic trance.

"Ahh, Ruby, thank you for your very kind offer of help," said Ryder as he and Rufus approached the children. "I wonder if you and Henry could help set up and clear the dining hall."

"Clear the—?"

"Err... it's no problem, we'll be happy to help out," promised Ruby interrupting Henry.

"Saul can help in the war room," proposed Rufus.

"The war room, are you sure?" queried Ryder cynically.

"Yes, we could do with a hand moving all those maps around, don't you think?"

Saul raised his eyebrows and shrugged his shoulders at Henry and Ruby apologetically. During the day, they had become aware of a secretive gathering in the meeting room on the ground floor of their living quarters. The entrance was now guarded by a giant who only allowed the children and a select group of sorcerers in and out.

"You volunteered us for work?" began Henry sternly as they headed back to their rooms.

"Well, I thought we could make ourselves useful, given we're going to be here for a few days and—"

"Don't you think it would have been courteous to at least ask us, before *volunteering* us?"

"So, what do you propose we do all day Henry? Do you think we—"

"Calm down both of you," interrupted Saul as they turned into the corridor leading to their room.

"It's alright for you to say, *calm down*. You're not the one who's going to be stuck in the dining room every evening—"

"And morning," murmured Ruby.

"Morning as well?" retorted Henry.

Saul left Ruby and Henry to continue arguing for a little longer, secretly feeling quite excited about the work in the War Room.

*

The following morning, Saul entered the war room shyly and began his work with subdued caution.

Throughout the day, he moved maps from table to table at the behest of the small groups presiding over them. He brought in boxes of miniature lead soldiers. The groups spread these around the maps to organise the movement of sorcerers around the state. All the while, Saul was a curiously excited observer, feeling uneasy but privileged to be hearing intimate plans.

"The biggest challenge," began Rothner, he ran his hand over a collection of lead soldiers sitting on a map, instantly, the lead figures slid across the map to another point on the map, "is that we don't have enough soldiers. Our army is too small compared to what the Gorans will throw at us. If we're serious about putting up a fight, then we should be thinking about extending our reach."

Rothner ran his hand over another section of the map and the figures slid across to the spot marked with the words *Garson's Well.* Saul watched all this, his eyes wide open in disbelief.

"Extending our reach?" queried Theran.

"Yes. Look I know it sounds wild, but we should be speaking to the centaurs, minotaurs, satyrs, hawkmen, and fauns and bringing them to our side," an uncomfortable murmur spread around the room. "After all, the Gorans are probably already speaking to the trolls and goblins."

"Good point," replied Theran. "But the centaurs won't get involved in the wars of men and—"

"I know I know," said Rothner. "But that was fifty years ago. Things have changed since then, haven't they? Once they know what's coming, I'm sure they'll be just as anxious as we are."

"And," Theran continued firmly, "we didn't exactly finish on the best of terms with the minotaurs did we?"

Another murmur filled the room. *Terrible situation* said someone, *very undignified if you ask me* added another.

"Look the bottom line is that we have to build our own army of sorcerers," continued Theran. "We haven't got time to be gallivanting around Petonia recruiting beings that have all kinds of grievances and problems with us. Besides, we're armed with krays. Nobody else has krays." there was a sporadic murmuring of quiet agreement.

"Did anybody ever hear anything about the hermit in Gaspar Harland?" Doe Festers asked.

"The dragon tamer?" Theran asked.

"Yes. Don't get me wrong, krays are wonderful creatures, but imagine an army of trained dragons," Doe Festers said excitedly. An eager murmur filled the air.

"A rumour, nothing more. Nobody's ever tamed a dragon," replied Junus Palfrey dismissively. "It's futile, they're too wild, completely untameable."

For the rest of the day, plans were made, maps were moved around, ideas were aired, and thoughts and opinions were shared. By the end of it, Saul felt quite exhausted from moving so many boxes around and setting up so many maps.

*

After dinner, Saul, Ruby, Henry, and Jordan retired to a hill at the edge of the fort and sat looking lazily over the distant black sea.

"The council's preparing for war."

Henry raised his eyebrows. "War?"

"But first they plan to raid the Mines of Catellan. Apparently, most of the important sorcerers are being held there."

"Hey that's where your mother's being held," remarked Ruby excitedly.

"If she's still there," Jordan replied guardedly.

"Don't be so glum Jordan. Where else could she be?" queried Ruby. "She was there just a few days ago before Jessy and Vince escaped, she hasn't gone anywhere."

"I suppose this explains all the arms training that's been going on," said Henry. "And anyway, how do we fit into all this? I mean shouldn't we be getting home soon? Hasn't Ambrose Dunster appeared yet?"

"Well, this is it. Ambrose Dunster was supposed to meet here, but now he's not meeting the council until the raid," Saul said resignedly.

Henry and Ruby sighed.

"This is getting worse and worse. I presume that once we get there, no doubt having risked life and limb again, they'll say *oh sorry, he hasn't arrived, but he'll definitely be at such-and-such place,"* said Henry in a sarcastic tone.

"Where are Jessy and Vince?" asked Ruby trying to change the subject.

"They're still in the hospital ward," replied Jordan.

"Are they alright?"

"They're fine. Just suffering from exhaustion and need some rest," Jordan said. "They'll be there for a few days. Dad's with them pretty much all the time."

It was getting dark by the time they headed for the bedroom. They walked through the busy square and were met by Rufus.

"Ahh, there you are," he began. "I've been looking for you. Rabin would like you three to begin some arms training tomorrow," he announced.

"Arms training?" queried Henry.

Rufus nodded.

"You may as well get busy, we're here for five more days. Your training begins early in the morning, be at the ground no later than eight. Ask for Grandon Smith when you get there," Rufus added before walking away.

"Err... does that mean we don't have to work in the great hall?" asked Henry hopefully.

"No such luck I'm afraid. Arms training in the day and then be in the hall an hour before dinner," Rufus replied. "But if it helps you can skip the morning chores."

"And the war room—?" queried Saul.

"I'm sure we can get Junus to move the maps around for a few days."

Saul sighed in quiet disappointment.

"Henry," said Rufus in an urgent tone. "Caleb went back last night."

"Back where?"

"To find Bowman." Henry raised his eyebrows expectantly. "It's not great news I'm afraid."

"Why?"

"The cottage was… it was burned down."

Henry gasped. "Was Bowman—"

"I'm sure he got away and—"

"You're sure? Did you find him?"

"I didn't go, Caleb went and—"

"Did Caleb find him?"

"Not really, he—"

"Did he bother even looking?"

"If you'll let me finish what I'm saying," said Rufus calmly. "He *did* look. Caleb went into the burnt ruins of the cottage. Bowman wasn't there."

"You're… I mean is Caleb sure of it?"

"Yes. Absolutely sure," said Rufus assertively. "Bowman must have escaped before the searchers got back to burn it down."

Henry thought long and hard about this.

"I'm sorry Henry," said Rufus assuringly. "But I'm sure Bowman is fine," he added unconvincingly before turning away.

For the rest of the evening, Henry was gloomy and anxious. He could not help feeling guilty that he had put Bowman into a dangerous position.

Henry did not stop thinking about it all evening. Later Saul, Ruby, and Henry sat in the bedroom. Henry sat alone looking out of the window.

"I wouldn't worry," said Ruby across the room. "Bowman's very strong and courageous by the sounds of it, and I'm sure he would've been able to take them on."

"I know but… I'm the reason the searchers went after him. He was just helping me and…" Henry went quiet. "I hope he's safe," he murmured.

For the rest of the day, it was impossible to get Henry out of his misery. Time and time again he regretted walking into the cottage and putting Bowman in such danger, and no amount of reasoning from Saul, Ruby, or Jordan could get him out of his regret.

*

The training grounds sat in a huge field against an array of stone buildings. The area was brimming with activity. On one side, a group of tall strong men launched spears towards targets sitting hundreds of yards away. The spears tore into their targets with superb accuracy.

"Fire!" shouted the voice of a tall lady. The children turned suddenly to see ten heavy rocks hurled into the air by a set of huge catapults.

Another group, who stood facing away while this happened, turned around suddenly, raised their hands, and hurled a white bolt of lightning which sent the rocks exploding into tiny pieces.

"Wow!" muttered Henry.

Ahead of them, a group of archers were firing a torrent of arrows at targets a hundred yards away, invariably hitting their mark every time. Grandon Smith, the tall blond-haired wide-mouthed thick moustached man that had rescued Henry a few days earlier, stood in a militaristic manner overseeing the training.

"Ready… fire!"

Ten sorcerers sent a shower of arrows swishing through the air. The arrows landed with a burst of thuds that sounded like heavy rain falling on a tin roof.

"Fire two on your ready!" he boomed as the children approached him.

The targets were moved five yards away and now looked like a large dot in the distance. The sorcerers fine-tuned what seemed like a bolt on the side of the bow. They raised the quadbow, closed one eye and looked fixedly down the line of the bow at the distant target.

"Ready… fire!" boomed Grandon.

The arrows shot out with a loud whizzing sound and landed at their targets with a tremendous rattle.

"Number seven out by one!" shouted a voice in the distance.

"Giles, that's one out again. Sharpen up!" boomed Grandon.

"Sir?" began Saul, anxious he was disturbing the training.

"Grandon Smith at your service," replied the man bowing with a flamboyant courtesy.

"Grandon Smith sir?"

"Just Grandon will do," he replied. *"Ready… fire!"* he boomed, causing the children to jump. A torrent of arrows whizzed through the air again and hit their targets with a methodical thud.

"Full house!" came a cry from the distance.

"Well done, take a break!" boomed Grandon. "Good one Giles," he said quietly to one of the archers.

A chorus of murmuring filled the air as the sorcerers laid down their quadbows and sat on the grass talking busily and drinking water.

"We've been sent by Rufus for arms training," announced Saul anxiously.

Grandon eyed them from head to foot giving the impression that they were probably not even capable of holding up a bow, let alone firing one.

"Yes, I was told about the err… training," he said hesitantly. "I think you," he pointed at Ruby, "should learn to handle a sword for a day or so before taking quadbow training. You may have problems handling this," he added throwing a quadbow each to Saul and Henry.

It was much heavier than it looked, and they nearly fell over backwards as the bow landed awkwardly in their arms.

"Ah, here she is," said Grandon. A tall slender lady approached them.

"Ruby?" she asked holding out her hand. Ruby nodded and shook the hand. "I'm Celia Abbey. And you must be Henry and Saul."

Celia looked searchingly at the children. Celia had light brown skin. Her black hair flowed softly down just below her shoulders and her soft kind voice gave her a personable personality.

"Have you used a sword before?" she asked turning to Ruby.

"Err no," Ruby replied, taken aback by the question.

"Not to worry. Let's head off to the west side of the fort. It's quieter there."

The first hour of quadbow training was tough. Whenever Saul and Henry fired the bow, the force of the arrows pushed them back in the opposite direction, and once or twice, one or the other landed embarrassingly on their backsides. If that was not bad enough, arrows flew in almost every direction but the target.

"Err... bring the targets back a bit will you Frederick?" ordered Grandon hesitantly. "A err... bit closer please."

The target was only yards away by the time Saul and Henry finally managed to get an arrow onto it.

"We're hopeless," sighed Henry loudly when Grandon allowed them to take a break.

"Not to worry," said Grandon handing Saul a pitcher of water. "We'll make archers out of you yet. The trick is to be pushing forward when you fire the arrows, that will compensate the force of the arrows."

Saul and Henry nodded.

"Sir... I mean Grandon," began Henry after a moment.

Grandon turned around and looked at Henry. "I never really thanked you for helping me. I don't think I'd ever be able to repay you but—"

"Nonsense, you don't have to thank me for that," Grandon said with a surprised look on his face. "It's what I do. I rescue people, I seek them, I find them," he said proudly. "I'm a scentia you know," he added quietly.

"Yes," said Saul and Henry together.

Grandon was inspecting a bag of arrows. He pulled each one out, lined it up with his eye, looked down it, and then placed it in one of two boxes.

"We had a pretty good idea of the direction the searchers took when they left Kirk Heidengaard. I had a lot of information coming back to me and was positive you were in the forest somewhere. The only question was where? It's a *biggy* that one.

"Once we realised where you were and that a gang of searchers was trawling through the forest, we knew it was a battle against time."

A sharp glint in his eye indicated he was in his element. Grandon liked nothing better to talk about than a good old mission.

"Now," he said in a militaristic tone. "How to get through that forest to the cottage. That needed a lot of thought. Now I think about it, it reminds me of the time I rescued Doctor Hindengeld from the Notheric Volcanic Range. Have I told you about that? No? Well, that was a tough one that, took two days and—"

Grandon went on for a while, with Saul and Henry looking artificially awe-struck by the ingenuity that Grandon had applied in numerous rescue missions. He needed an excuse to talk about his intrinsically delivered rescue mission and they had delivered it.

By the afternoon, Henry's target had moved back a few yards and he was hitting a lot more of it. However, Saul was still having a terrible time. His arm twitched nervously whenever he pulled the trigger, sending the arrows everywhere but within a yard of the target. Saul became anxious and annoyed at the distinct lack of progress.

Focus, he thought angrily each time, he lined up the bow. But despite his increasing determination, he continued missing the target.

"Don't worry Saul," boomed Grandon in a patronising tone as they approached the central square late that afternoon. "Practice makes perfect, that's what I always say. Keep it going for the next few days, I'm sure you'll get better. Your arms'll be sore tomorrow morning, but be sure to turn up on time."

Meanwhile, Ruby was having a wonderful day. She was awe-stricken by Celia, the expert swordswoman. The first hour of Ruby's lesson was spent holding the sword up and moving it accurately but quickly between two posts.

"That's… wonderful," smiled Celia clearly impressed with Ruby's progress. "Quite remarkable for someone who's never used a sword before."

This inspired Ruby further, and later, by which time Ruby was striking two posts while swapping the sword from one hand to the other each time, Celia stood back and admired Ruby's progress.

Celia was intrigued by Saul, Ruby, and Henry's accidental arrival in the Netherworld. She was keen to know about the journey into the Netherworld and was horrified by their experiences of the last few weeks.

That evening, Ruby's enthusiasm spilt over the dining table and she could not help leading every other conversation into another praising melody about Celia.

"And you know what?" she said excitedly as they carried a pile of plates into the kitchen. "She's so fast, the sword looks like a gust of wind in her hands."

"I'm sure it does," murmured Henry quietly.

"She's an expert in archery you know, that's just a hobby, she learned how to fire quadbows when she was really young," Saul and Henry reared their heads back at Ruby's dismissiveness. To suggest that archery was *just a hobby,* to them, having spent the best part of the day trying to get an arrow onto a target was bordering on impertinence.

"She spent ten years learning the art of combat at the University of Warford. And you know what, she came top of the class! Have you heard about the University of Warford? It's the best University in Petonia, you have to pass lots of exams and stuff to get in and—"

Saul and Henry were quietly wishing Ruby would stop. Celia seemed like a wonderful person, and learning sword fighting seemed exciting, but this had gone on too long.

"This is quite heavy Saul," said Ruby lifting Saul's sword as soon as they walked back into the room. She waved it methodically in the air. "I don't know how you carried it from Kirk Heidengaard."

The following morning, despite their aching arms, Saul and Henry could not get to the training ground fast enough. They ran the whole distance and perched themselves near the archers with active enthusiasm.

It was another tough day, and Saul was determined to focus on hitting the target. But as the day drew on, Saul's target remained rooted to the same spot, while Henry's inched further away. By the afternoon, it was lined up next to the targets of the sorcerers.

"That's... a remarkable improvement Henry," commented Grandon at the end of the day. "Seem to have a natural skill," he added with a wink. "And err… don't worry too much Saul. Keep it together and all that. Practice makes perfect, it's probably a confidence thing."

"I don't know what it is, now and again I just twitch and… well..."

"Two more days Saul and we'll get the twitch out of you."

"Grandon?" began Saul as they walked back to the central square at the end of the day. A group of sorcerers were shooting bolts of light with awe-inspiring precision at rocks in the air. "Why do the sorcerers bother learning to fight when you could quite easily destroy your enemy, just by using your powers?"

"These powers demand huge responsibility Saul," replied Grandon.

"Not even when our lives are at threat?" asked Henry.

"Err… lives at threat? What do you mean?"

"I would've thought the chase through Kirk Heidengaard to be quite *life-threatening*. I don't see why Rufus, Althea, and Jarrett didn't—"

"Yes, I, err... heard about that," said Grandon with a knotted brow. "It's not as easy as that. You see, the Arkan Decree creates many difficulties. If witnesses had reported that the council had brandished their powers in the alleyways of Kirk Heidengaard, there would've been a major operation to capture the sorcerers responsible. That does us no good, especially when we're trying to build an army, not decapitate one."

"The sooner we repeal the Arkan Decree the better," he muttered frustratedly under his breath, seeing that Saul and Henry were not convinced. "In any case, you're safe, that's what matters and we're not letting you out of our sight again."

*

After dinner, Grandon Smith stepped onto the stage, rattled a spoon against a glass and then proceeded to provide an update on the training.

"We're doing well," he smiled. "Thirteen years in the wilderness have made us a bit rusty, but ninety fighters have been training day and night, and we can probably increase the training to accommodate another twenty. However, weapons and armoury are a big problem."

He droned on for quite a while, sharing numbers and details on how many arrows and quadbows they had and the problems of delayed arms shipments.

"The Makelonian forges have been very helpful," he continued. "We've fooled them into thinking that we're a Petonian regiment and they've been sending us supplies quite promptly," there was a murmur of laughter. "However—"

The big wooden door to the hall creaked open loudly and a brown cloaked figure walked through. His hood hid his face and his long black boots echoed through the dining hall. He carried a bag over one shoulder and a staff in his right hand, resembling the lonely figure of Rufus when he had first appeared in Edgings Burrows.

"I think that's Rufus' brother Luru," whispered Jordan.

By the time he reached the front of the hall, every head in the great hall was affixed on the strange figure.

The cloaked man walked up to the stage, climbed up and bowed courteously to Rabin before entering into a quiet conversation with him, Rufus, Jarrett, and Grandon. Everyone in the hall sat in pin-drop silence at the edge of their seats.

Eventually, Rabin stood up. The hooded man shuffled next to him. His fingers were wrapped around the staff, three fingers on each hand wore a ring capped with a coloured stone. Still, he did not remove his hood.

"Critical discussions began at the parliament two weeks ago," began Rabin. "We've been hopeful of a successful renegotiation of the Arkan decree. If the negotiations go our way, Petonia will have greater rights, we'll be able to build an army. If they fail, we'll probably enter another long war."

"The negotiations began with excitement and determination, and for two days, it seemed that the Gorans were giving way." Rabin stopped, and the hooded man whispered something to him.

"Goran agreed to withdraw troops from Petonia. There was even a positive discussion about the ownership and control of mines and the restrictions on troops. An exciting optimistic mood filled the parliament. But on the third day, there was a disturbing development." Rabin listened to the hooded man.

"That day, a Petonian attendant charged into the parliament to announce that the treasure vaults lying beneath the parliament had been raided. Important treasures, dating back centuries, were stolen," a collective gasp of astonishment filled the room.

"There was chaos. A fierce exchange of blame, claim and counter-claim was followed by scuffles and brawls. Petonian soldiers stormed the palace to restore calm and eventually, the Gorans left in a fit of rage, promising dire consequences, for being accused of the theft.

"I'm afraid that the outcome of the negotiations was nothing more than an entrenched determination to settle things on a battlefield. Late that night, King Isal and the Petonian Parliament declared war."

Murmurs of shocked discussion permeated through the hall. Grandon rattled his spoon on a glass and steadily the hall became quiet again.

"Do we know who did it?" asked someone from the floor.

The hooded man whispered into Rabin's ear.

"No," replied Rabin. "On the one hand, we don't believe Petonia would sabotage the negotiations in this way. But then why would the Gorans travel all that way just to sabotage the negotiations?

"How does this affect our plans?" asked someone at the front.

"We must continue with our plans," announced Rabin. "We were optimistic about the negotiations but weren't waiting for the outcome. We set off in two days for the final stage of this mission."

The hooded man bowed courteously to Rabin and walked out as mysteriously as he had arrived.

*

The following morning, Henry resumed his crossbow training, however, Saul was summoned to the war room after breakfast. If anything, thought Saul frustratedly, he was the one that needed the training, not Henry.

More chairs were brought in for Siraf, two more vampires and two giants whose heads floated a foot below the ceiling. More maps covered each of the four walls and, as if there were not enough maps in the room already, Saul helped Junus Palfrey carry two more chests in.

The discussion now focussed on the Mines of Catellan which sat a day away from Port Newton. Hundreds of slaves worked in the mine. They lived in decrepit conditions. Amongst them were many important sorcerers. This was the mine that Jessy and Vince had escaped from. Jordan's mother was somewhere in this mine and this kept Saul intrigued. He kept his ears close to the table and curbed his excitement throughout the day, promising to update Jordan at the dinner table.

The mines were strongly protected, and the sorcerers would have to infiltrate a deep maze of tunnels. Grandon and Theran spent much of the morning around complex maps and drawings and meticulously calculated the time it would take to get into the mines, the time it might take for reinforcements to arrive from Galetonia, a nearby Goran army encampment, and the time it would take to get to a nearby shipping port in case the sorcerers had to escape in that direction.

"The regiment in Galetonia is two hours from the mine," announced Grandon later that afternoon. "The road into the mine is very good. The regiment is only a hundred strong, so even if they arrive before we've finished, we'll be able to deal with them quite easily.

"There are seventy-one of us, and four children."

"We're taking the children with us?" asked Junus.

"Yes."

"Into the heart of a battle?"

"Yes. After the Kirk Heidengaard debacle, Rabin wants them to stay with us at all times."

"There's a lot of uncertainty about the layout of the mines," Grandon continued. "The only map we have is a year old, and a mine can change quite remarkably in a year," he added gesturing to Theran.

"Yes," interjected Theran. "Over the year, the mine shafts will have gone much further and deeper, there might be new mine shafts, others might now be blocked off. Our calculations could easily be out by two or three hundred yards."

"There are three entrances to the mine," continued Theran. "North, South and West. The North and West entrances are very busy. The South entrance is used for administration, deliveries, and dignitaries.

"This is probably one of the largest mines in Petonia, we've never seen anything like it. The walking distance between each entrance is half an hour which works in our favour," Theran tapped a map on the wall.

"We've organised three parties, one for each entrance. Each party will position itself at a vantage point two hundred yards from the entrance and wait for a single green flare. That's your cue to action.

"The North group led by Rothner sets up our decoy. You'll launch a decoy attack at the entrance to attract soldiers from the other two entrances. When that happens, the South and West groups will enter the mine. You'll have an hour to enter and follow the routes we're providing you. Memorise them carefully, one wrong turn could jeopardise everything."

Theran looked at Saul who jumped up absent-mindedly and brought two rolled-up maps to the wall.

"Do we know how many prisoners are in the mine?" asked Junus.

"No."

"How will we protect them once they're out? There could be hundreds perhaps thousands of people, maybe even an army on our back," asked Junus sceptically.

"We have a plan." Mistie stood up and walked to the front of the room. "Not that one. Pay attention," she muttered disapprovingly as Saul pulled out a map.

"We're moving the prisoners to these five locations," she pointed to five places on the map. "Around a hundred nark carts will arrive with medical supplies. We'll tend to the immediate medical needs of the prisoners and then Berto, Rothner, Arak, Ambrose Dunster, and I will lead them to safety."

Saul's ears pricked up at the mention of Ambrose Dunster.

"As I've outlined," Theran announced. "Rothner will approach the North entrance and hold the soldiers for an hour before retreating." Rothner nodded.

"Once we're in, we rescue everyone," said Theran. "We don't differentiate between our friends and other prisoners. We rescue everybody is that understood?"

A begrudging murmur of agreement trickled through the room.

"Some of the mine shafts are around two miles deep. Make sure you look out for these rest areas," Theran pointed at a complex array of lines running through one of the maps and then at areas on the maps which were outlined in a black box. "The prisoners work very long hours in rotation, so they may be resting here. Everyone exits out of the Southern entrance," Theran circled an area representing the Southern entrance. "If you follow these routes," he swiped his stick at several mine shafts, "you'll all end up near the Southern entrance."

"And another thing," he continued. "Nobody other than Rabin, Rufus, and those in this room know about these plans. Make sure it stays that way."

*

Saul, Ruby, Henry, and Jordan stayed up late into the night wandering the grounds aimlessly and soaking up the carnival-like atmosphere. They jostled their way through busy groups and crowds, in the end deciding to sit on a bench near the entrance to the fort.

The mood here was remarkably different. Heavy anxiety hung in the air as groups of sorcerers gathered in preparation to leave for the mines. Saul and Henry recognised a few of them from their quadbow training. They were prepared for battle. Each one carried a quadbow, a small bag full of arrows on their back and a sword at their side.

Soon, just as many narks clambered steadily through the gates. There was a hive of activity as sorcerers climbed on and then disappeared into the night leaving an eerie silence behind them.

~ 25 ~

The Mines of Catellan

The following morning, Saul, Ruby, and Henry walked tiredly down the stairs and had a quick breakfast with Jordan before gathering in the square with the rest of the group for the impending departures.

The party-like mood of the last few days was replaced by a tangle of anxious nerves which hung in the air throughout the fort.

The anxiety was plain to see on Jordan and Caleb's faces. Jordan's mother was in the Catellan mine, and after years of searching, they were hours away from being reunited. The wiser side of Saul, Ruby, and Henry wanted to encourage Jordan to dampen his excitement, but that was much easier said than done.

Not long after, the children found themselves flying away into the morning sky. As the first rays of solarius peered up over the distant horizon, the travellers were greeted in the distance by a clump of hills and valleys. Dozens of well-worn paths led downwards deep into the Valley of Catellan. A complex crop of wooden buildings stood against one of the many hills.

The krays swooped down and landed behind a hill overlooking the valley. The group disembarked and waited patiently. Before long, a gaggle of narks appeared in the distance. The green flare shot up.

"Berto and Junus are staying behind to watch over you," announced Theran. He turned to Berto and Junus. "I'm leaving these," he pointed to four quadbows and a chest of arrows. "You won't need them, but…" Theran did not finish the sentence.

A moment later, Berto, Junus, and the children watched the group disappear into the entrance to the mines. Dawn was breaking over the hills by the time the lonely figures entered the mesh of buildings.

The morning grew brighter, and the children watched the mine entrance with agonising impatience for signs of movement. Meanwhile, Berto and Junus busied themselves in hushed speculation about the events in the parliament, the likelihood of a traitor in their midst, and the identity of the strange cloaked man.

"Do you remember Luru?" queried Junus.

"The sorcerer of Engor?"

"Yes, Rufus' brother. He was sent to the Petonian parliament fourteen years ago."

"Yes, but it can't be him because I think he moved to Englesburg. And anyway—"

"Look!" exclaimed Ruby, pointing to the distant horizon far to their right.

An anxious look spread over Berto and Junus' faces as they saw a vague line of what looked like ants was creeping towards the mines. A garrison of soldiers was marching in steady formation.

"Now listen," urged Junus. "We've been betrayed. That regiment should be miles away. Berto and I are entering the mines to warn everyone. By the time we return, the regiment will still be some distance away and—"

"Stay here and don't move," interrupted Berto. "Don't leave the kray, don't go for a walk and whatever happens, stay away from the mines. Is that clear?"

"You can't leave us here alone," said Ruby. "You heard what Rufus said, you have to—"

"We have to warn them."

"But what about us, what if—"

"There's no time, many lives depend on it."

"You'll be safe here," interjected Berto more calmly. "You're out of sight and out of reach."

Collectively, they watched the thin line move steadily towards the mines. The children knew Junus and Berto had to go down and warn the others, however, the horrible experience of Kirk Heidengaard still made their nerves tingle.

"If anything happens, get onto the kray and fly away," said Junus.

"You have some quadbows and arrows," said Berto comfortingly. "I'm sure you won't need to use them though," he added unconvincingly.

A moment later, Berto and Junus Palfrey rushed off down the hill and eventually disappeared into the mines.

"There must be hundreds," gasped Jordan quietly. The line of soldiers grew longer and stretched steadily closer to the mines.

"Jarrett and Rothner checked the garrison a few times," said Saul quietly. "They received a daily account of it, I heard them in the war room, they said there were only a hundred soldiers and—"

"There's more than a hundred Saul," said Ruby.

"We have to do something. Everyone'll be trapped inside the mines," murmured Jordan.

"We *don't* have to do anything," replied Ruby curtly. "They'll be back soon. We're hours away from getting home, let's not do anything silly."

"And how do we get home if all the sorcerers are killed?" asked Saul.

"Well—"

"Junus shouldn't have gone," complained Henry. "He's supposed to be looking after us!"

They sat in frozen silence for a few moments, peering anxiously over the hill and watching the line grow longer and longer.

"We have to do *something*," stressed Saul. He walked to the quadbows, opened the chest of arrows, and placed a handful in a bag on the side of the kray. "We can fly one of the most feared beasts in the Netherworld. I mean just the sight of a kray tearing down towards you will frighten the daylights out of anybody right?"

"And we can fire a quadbow," said Henry getting up. "Well, Saul and I can." How glad Saul and Henry now were of spending those hours learning how to fire a quadbow.

"Me too," chipped in Jordan.

"You can fire a quadbow?" queried Saul.

"Yes, it's easy I learned when I was a child," replied Jordan dismissively. Saul's jaw dropped.

Ruby jumped up and led four krays towards them stroking the face of one of them gently and seemingly whispering to it.

Meanwhile, Saul opened the box of arrows and passed a bunch of arrows and a quad bow each to Ruby, Henry, and Jordan.

"Saul I've never fired one of these before," said Ruby.

Saul thought about this for a moment "You'll just have to work it out," he replied as he tied a quadbow to each saddle. "Be careful when you load—"

"Look," began Henry noticing Ruby's worried look. Henry proceeded to demonstrate how to hold the bow, reload it and then fire it. Ruby took the quadbow, lined it up and pointed it at a tree a hundred yards away.

"Err, that's quite far," said Henry. "Try this tree," he pointed to a tree a few yards away.

"It's not easy," began Saul "I—"

TWANG! Four arrows sunk into a tree, much further away from the first tree and vibrated wildly for a few moments.

Saul's heart sank. How was it possible, he wondered, for Ruby to pick up a quadbow and fire it so accurately when his hours of training resulted in most arrows avoiding the target like the plague?

Henry raised an eyebrow. "Beginners luck?" he proposed with a cheeky smile before noticing the stern look on Ruby's face.

"Good luck," said Saul grudgingly before climbing onto the kray. Moments later four krays were circling the sky high above the approaching army.

The children turned their attention between the mine entrance and the line of soldiers. It had seemed a good idea at the time, but now they were in the air, nobody seemed to know what to do. They had clumsily loaded their quadbow and seemed to be waiting for someone else to make the first move.

Suddenly, Saul's kray let out a deafening roar which frightened the children. Although Ruby had heard the roar of a kray in Balson Mees, neither Saul nor Henry had heard any of their krays utter anything more than a steady purr. Even Jordan, fully accustomed to the kray's habits, raised a curious eyebrow.

An instant later, Henry's kray responded with a thunderous roar, and then all four krays were roaring sporadically. With each loud roar, the children felt a surge of bravery flow through their veins.

The commotion in the air had not gone unnoticed. Far below them, the line of soldiers had stopped moving, and was in busy conversation, pointing up to the sky now and again.

With the reins in one hand and the quadbow in the other, Henry sent the beast hurtling downwards. He got closer and aimed the quadbow at the middle of the army. Now, he was within shooting range and could see the frightened faces below him. Suddenly, the kray let out another terrifying roar. Henry felt the sound travel through the lungs beneath him and out through the long neck. At that moment, he remembered the ordeal he had suffered at the hands of Edgerton and Rankin. A scowl of determination filled his face, and a surge of anger tore through his body.

As the fearsome beast came closer, the soldiers began to disperse in a frightened panic. It was too late. Henry fired the quadbow, sending four arrows tearing into a group of soldiers. Henry pulled the reigns sharply, the kray shot upwards leaving shouts and screams behind him. Dozens of arrows struck the kray as it ascended upwards, bouncing harmlessly off its hard leathery skin.

"Yes! Yes!" screamed Henry as the kray stopped to a hovering standstill in mid-air. Blood pumped through his veins, his heart was beating wildly.

In that streaky moment, if they ever needed reminding, the children realised why the kray was such a fearsome creature in battle. The sight of a kray descending at lightning speed was enough to frighten and demoralise the toughest of opponents and, importantly, mere arrows and spears could not pierce its tough leathery skin.

Saul, Ruby, and Jordan watched Henry's assault in admiration. Then, Saul shot downwards, quadbow lined up carefully. *Now's not the time to misfire,* he told himself anxiously. He got closer and became more nervous. *Focus!* he kept saying. Saul was within shooting range. He pulled the trigger. One arrow tore into a soldier, but the other three landed harmlessly into the ground. Saul grimaced as the kray shot upwards. He would be out of arrows soon at this rate!

Saul approached a second time, his face bearing a frozen determined look. He pointed the quadbow to the centre of a group of soldiers. *Focus!* He fired the quadbow, this time two arrows hit the soldiers. He was out by two, but two had hit! Now each time he flew down, he landed two, sometimes three arrows into the group. He was not completely pleased with the result, but at least his confidence had not capitulated.

Kray after kray tore downwards in quick formation, leaving mayhem behind. With each descent, the army was turning into a disorganised wreck. Added to that, Saul, Ruby, Henry, and Jordan were lifted with the knowledge that the Galetonian regiment had become so preoccupied with the attack of the krays that they had stopped moving towards the mines.

But now, with each advance, the regiment was becoming more organised, and the descent of the kray was being met with a more coordinated response. As the kray swooped down towards the regiment, the soldiers lined themselves up, bows and spears at the ready, and as the kray came within striking distance, it was met with a shower of arrows.

Saul hugged the kray tightly each time he shot upwards. A whizzing sound flew past his ears as arrows flew within inches of his head. *This is getting too risky,* thought Saul as a spear whooshed past his head.

As Saul approached for the eighth or ninth time, he noticed alarmingly that he only had a handful of arrows left. This had to be the last excursion. The kray tore downward, and as he got closer, Saul heard the familiar whizzing sound of arrows flying past.

"Ouch!" screamed Saul.

Saul grasped his shoulder in pain. An arrow had hit his injured shoulder! The quadbow slipped out of his hand. Saul lost his balance. He tipped to one side and fell off the kray landing painfully on his foot into a thorny bush.

Saul gasped in agony. He lay in the bush holding his ankle, grimacing in pain. Through the corner of his eye, Saul saw dozens of Galetonian soldiers charging towards him. But behind them some distance away, Saul saw the brown cloaks of sorcerers running in. Reinforcements had arrived!

Five Galetonian soldiers were loading up their quadbows. They were ten yards away, at any moment, they would fire, but why didn't the sorcerers strike? One of the soldiers raised his bow and aimed it at Saul. In a moment, Saul thought, he would be finished. He limped up in a panic and raised his hands in front of him.

"No!" He screamed.

Instantaneously, in a strange wondrous blur, somehow, weirdly, the five soldiers were lifted off their feet and landed twenty or so yards away as if dragged by a powerful tornado.

Saul stood with his eyes wide open, his mouth gaping in astonishment. Three sorcerers were fighting the Galetonian soldiers. Did the sorcerers do that?

"What are you waiting for?" screamed Henry. He was standing a few yards away gesturing frantically for Saul to climb onto his kray. Saul limped unsteadily towards him but fell in a heap.

"My ankle!"

Henry ran to Saul. He lifted Saul's arm over his shoulder and half-dragged him up to the kray.

"Did you see what the sorcerers did?" asked Saul painfully as the kray hovered in the safety of the air.

Saul and Henry looked down at the incredible battle taking place far below them. Each sorcerer was surrounded by four or five soldiers. Their staffs flew around their body in a blur and soldiers fell in a heap around them.

Ruby flew over next to Jordan. "There's only twenty-three of them!" she screamed "They can't hold the Galetonians much longer!"

"We haven't got any arrows left Ruby," began Jordan. "Let's hold tight and hope the sorcerers return." They retreated downwards and joined Saul and Henry at the top of the hill.

Soon the reinforcements began retreating backwards, the Galetonian soldiers were on a charge. One of the sorcerers fell to the floor holding an arrow lodged painfully in his shoulder.

"Why won't they come out of the mines!" exclaimed Henry with gritted teeth. "What's holding them?"

The children looked from the mines to the reinforcements. There was no sign of anybody emerging. Meanwhile, the reinforcements were being pushed back towards the entrance to the mines.

"We have to help them. We have to do something," said Saul quietly.

"Saul we're out of arrows and—"

Saul limped over to the kray and pulled himself up.

"What are you doing?" questioned Henry incredulously. "You need to rest, you can't—"

The kray shot upwards leaving a gust of wind behind.

The soldiers were now five hundred yards from the mine entrance and getting closer as each moment passed by. Two more of the reinforcements were down. They were losing the battle.

Instinctively, Saul flew down towards the Galetonians. The kray got lower and lower before straightening up so that it was almost gliding across the ground. Then, in a moment of ingenious madness, Saul guided the kray towards a group of Galetonian soldiers. The kray let out a thunderous roar as it approached the soldiers and then lashed wildly with its mouth, tearing through the soldiers. Saul was surrounded by the screams of soldiers, sent flying in all directions. The kray grabbed two or three soldiers with each of its huge claws, flew upwards and then let go of the soldiers sending them hurtling downwards into the ground.

When Saul turned around to look down behind him, he was met with a trail of destruction. An untidy bruised line of Galetonian soldiers lay on the flooor, many of them crying in agony.

Ruby, Henry, and Jordan watched with their mouths wide open in shock.

"Bloody genius!" cried Henry in disbelief.

Without another word, Ruby, Henry, and Jordan ran to their krays, shot into the air, and followed Saul's lead. As they tore through the Galetonian regiment, soldiers were sent flying and yelling in pain. Steadily, the Galetonians retreated away from the mines. Soon, there were no Galetonian soldiers in sight.

"We've done it!" screamed Ruby.

The children gathered tiredly at the top of the hill and looked down towards a barren valley. Dozens of soldiers lay on the ground crying in agony.

*

The sky turned gloomy. A soft wind swept the valley and the atmosphere felt as if a storm was brewing.

"Look!" cried Jordan suddenly. Three people were emerging from the entrance. They were followed by many more, and soon, a long line of people stretched up the hill. Berto Manser and Mistie Herma were leading the group. They were followed by Jarrett, his gaze affixed confusedly at the dead and injured soldiers a few hundred yards from the mines. Scattered throughout the line, the children recognised some of the reinforcements.

All the while, the four children were desperately keen to see Caleb walking out, and to catch a sight of Jordan's mother. Suddenly, Jordan tore off down the hill and deep into the thicket of prisoners emerging from the mines. He looked one way, then another, and then another, desperate to find his father.

The group got closer to the top of the hill, Saul, Ruby, and Henry were shocked by the sight of hundreds of thin, starved prisoners, walking up slowly, many holding onto each other. Their clothes were tattered, ripped and dirty, and their dust-covered faces were sunken to the bone. For a while, the children stood in shock, unable to comprehend the sight.

Instinctively, Ruby clambered down the hill and offered her shoulder to a thin woman. The lady smiled wearily and limped alongside unsteadily. Her shrivelled face was covered in dirt, she was very light, her arms were as thin as a stick, and her eyes were sunken in, giving the impression of a walking skeleton. Henry and Jordan followed Ruby and soon all three were helping the prisoners climb up to the top of the hill.

Soon, hundreds of prisoners sat or lay exhausted on the grass. The sorcerers and the children walked amongst them offering bread, food, and water.

The children had never imagined such decrepit conditions and were overwhelmed by the sight. The battle coupled with the gruelling sight of the prisoners had become too much to bear.

Ruby closed her eyes for a moment, overcome with emotion and finding it difficult to absorb everything around her. Now and again, as she helped another prisoner climb up the hill, she pursed her lips tightly and wiped a tear as it trickled down her cheek.

"How do we get the prisoners back to Port Newton?" asked Henry. "They won't last an hour on the road."

"There should be around a hundred narks—"

A low drummy rattling noise filled the air. A trail of dust rose upwards in the distance. At the head of this commotion, dozens of narks charged forward pulling long carts behind them. The narks gathered at the top of the hill. Berto Manser moved ahead and lined up the carts.

"Give us a hand," muttered Althea. "We need to get them away quickly." Ruby and Henry jumped up instinctively and joined the sorcerers in helping the prisoners onto the carts.

As each cart was filled with tired, exhausted, and hungry prisoners, the carts set off in different directions led by two, sometimes three sorcerers. Celia, Caleb, Rothner, Saul, Henry, Ruby, and Jordan watched the trail of dust settle in the distance. A while later, Saul, Ruby, and Henry sat together in quiet contemplation looking out across the hill towards the empty mine.

Saul looked over to see Caleb, Rothner, and Jordan engaged in a busy conversation. Caleb looked agitated and Jordan carried an anxious disappointed look. It was clear that Jordan had not found his mother, this thought gave Saul a heavy heart.

An uncomfortable silence filled the air when Jordan joined them a few moments later. Nobody seemed to know what to ask or say. Nobody wanted to ask the question they all knew the answer to.

"They..." began Jordan with a quivery voice. "My mother wasn't... she wasn't in the mine," he stammered. Jordan's lips were pursed tightly together. A tear trickled down his cheek and he let out a slow frustrated sigh.

"I'm really sorry," said Henry. He stepped closer to Jordan and put his hand on Jordan's shoulder.

Nobody spoke for a few moments.

"Is it possible," began Saul, keen to break the uncomfortable silence. "That there's anyone still left in the mines? I mean the mines went pretty deep and how do we know they covered all the shafts?"

"No," said Jordan abruptly. "They swept the mines very carefully. Jarrett even led them through some unused mines to be on the safe side. That's why it took so long to get out. She wasn't there," he added quietly. A gust of wind ruffled their hair as they stood looking over the hill towards the mine, somehow hoping that Jordan's mother would suddenly materialise out of the mines. "But we do have some important information. My mother was transported to this mine with five other prisoners," he continued. "It's the most positive news to date. She's alive, and she was here just two weeks ago."

"Well," began Ruby not sure about whether to feel happy or sad, "you're getting closer and closer to finding her," she said with the only comforting words she could find.

"Yes. Father's trying to raise my spirits. Besides, we've found Jessy thanks to you. And that's a lot closer than where we were a month ago. Look, I really appreciate what you've done for us. You've been like a family to me," said Jordan after a while.

Saul, Ruby, and Henry smiled.

"Was your mum kept here for a while?" asked Ruby.

"For a little while, but then she was taken away, a little while after Jessy escaped."

"Which means she may not be far from here," suggested Ruby excitedly.

"Yes. Once we've got you back to Kirby Hall, father wants to return and search the area."

~ 26 ~

Homeward Bound

They travelled back to Kirby Hall through three magical sunsets into a quiet dreamy night. The kray floated gently over the dark countryside, lit up beautifully by the steady glow of villages and towns far below them. The steady *woosh* of the kray's wings was strangely therapeutic and made the children feel dreary and sleepy.

Caleb was visibly agitated throughout the whole journey. He was desperate to get back to Jessy and was continually thinking about the daughter he had only just become reunited with. But added to that, he harboured a desperate anxiety to come back to the valley and the surrounding area to resume his search. He and Jordan would be back within a day, and although it was unlikely his wife would have got far, every moment he lost, now felt like an agonising annoyance.

*

"Open the door Saul," murmured Ruby dreamily.

"What?"

"The door. Someone's knocking on it."

"Door?"

There was a loud knock on the door to the living room.

"Oh, the door, why can't you—?"

"Shut up and open it Saul," returned Ruby turning over and sinking into the pillow.

It took Saul a few moments to realise they were back at Kirby Hall. He dragged himself out of bed and squinted his eyes as he walked into the bright lounge.

"How many times do I have to knock? Do you think I have nothing better to do all day boy?"

"Good morning Mistie, sorry about—"

"Morning? It's well past midday," she barked. "Ambrose is meeting you at sunset."

"He's here?"

"Yes of course," replied Mistie. "Your school clothes are in the wardrobe, you might want to get back into them. Don't be too late he won't have much time to get you home. There's still food in the dining hall, you'd better be quick," Mistie said before walking out.

"She was nicer than normal. Do you think she'll miss us?" asked Saul sarcastically.

In all the commotion of the previous day, they had completely forgotten about Ambrose. Now that it dawned on them, Saul, Ruby, and Henry did not know how to react to the news.

"Doesn't it feel strange to be getting back into these?" asked Henry pulling on his school shirt. "I'm sure I've lost some weight," he added pulling the shirt from around the stomach.

There was another knock on the door. Ruby opened it to let in Jordan, Jessy, and Vince. Saul, Ruby, and Henry hugged them wildly and felt a surge of joy and relief to see Jessy and Vince.

They were looking remarkably better. The colour had returned to their cheeks, their hair was growing, and they looked much more assured and confident.

"We heard that you'll be going soon," said Jordan with a quivery voice.

"Yes," said Ruby. "We'll probably be gone by the evening."

An uncomfortable silence filled the room.

"Let's go for a walk after lunch," suggested Henry excitedly, changing the subject.

Later, they charged through the wonderful gardens, down the hill towards the beautiful landscape that surrounded Kirby Hall. Soon they were in the orange forest and a little while later, at the shores of Kirby Lake. It did not take long for the kherk to swim past, and within an instant, Jordan had jumped into the lake.

"Come on what are you waiting for?" he cried as the kherk raised its head out of the water for the third or fourth time.

"You even think about it Saul and—"

"I'd errr... better not!" Saul shouted, mindful of Ruby's stern expression.

The children sat on the shore of the lake looking out at the orange forest and the wonderful landscape. Now and again, the kherk shot out of the lake accompanied by a loud excited scream from Jordan.

Saul, Ruby, and Henry whiled the time away getting to know Jessy and Vince. Jessy was a tender soul, she spoke with a soft voice and rarely stopped smiling.

Notwithstanding the terrible experiences he had endured in the mines, Vince was surprisingly boisterous and confident. He had been separated from his father a year ago and had endured horrible traumas in the time since.

Saul, Ruby, and Henry wondered quietly what Jessy and Vince had been through. What were the conditions like in the mine? How did they escape? How had they ended up in the Forest of Maydor? But the trauma they had already endured made this a very difficult question to raise.

*

Later that afternoon, now feeling tired and hungry, the children walked back up the hill and into the gardens.

"Ruby, Saul, and Henry if I'm not mistaken?" asked a soft voice behind them as they stepped into the garden.

They turned around and were met by a tall thin serious-looking man who looked out of place in the Netherworld. He wore round spectacles, a smart tan suit and a blue shirt. His left eye twitched distractingly now and again.

"Ambrose Dunster at your service," he said extending his hand.

The children shook his hand gladly in turn. Of all the welcomes they had received in the Netherworld, this was the most delightful.

"I'm afraid that I became rather err… busy in the last few weeks chasing portals," he continued. "Very uncanny I have to say, never seen so many rogue portals," he said distractedly. "Well anyway, I'm here now and we need to get you home."

"Yes please," replied Saul quickly.

Ambrose raised his eyebrows. "And where is *home*?"

"Edgings Burrow."

"Curchester Mansion?"

"Yes," replied Saul hesitantly. They had never heard it referred to like that before.

"I'll begin preparing the portal before Solaris sets. Be in the gardens by then," the children nodded excitedly. "You'll probably have to wait a bit, the mansion's always difficult to pinpoint."

Saul, Ruby, and Henry nodded in unison.

"One more thing," he said. "Could you see the portal that brought you here?"

"Yes," said Henry.

"What did it look like?"

"Well. A bit like a thin mist spreading over the floor in the landing—"

"It seemed to spread up to the ceiling," remembered Ruby.

"You're sure you saw it?"

The children nodded.

"Was it clear?"

They nodded. "It hurt," added Henry.

"Yes, that was because you hadn't taken the portarix serum," continued Ambrose Dunster thoughtfully. "This doesn't make sense."

He stood in silence for a moment with a knotted brow, his left eye twitching now and again. "Well not to worry, off you go."

"That was strange," remarked Henry quietly as they walked up the stairs to their room. "But I suppose it shouldn't surprise us anymore. Do you remember all that stuff about *can you see us* and now he's going on about *was it clear?*"

"I think the thing is that *ordinary* people shouldn't be able to walk through portals," suggested Ruby. "And if portals start opening up willy-nilly around Edgings Burrow, there could be huge problems and—"

"Jordan, Jessy! It's time to go!" boomed a voice behind them. Caleb was walking speedily towards them. "We have to get back to the mines. Vince, you're coming with us."

Their hearts sank. Saul, Ruby, and Henry knew Caleb was desperate to get back but had not thought it would be so sudden.

Caleb turned to Saul, Ruby, and Henry. "I can't thank you enough for what you've done." He put his arm on Henry's shoulder. "I'm forever indebted to you. I'm sorry we have to leave so suddenly, but we have to return to the mines."

The last few weeks flashed in front of their eyes. The burden of being in the Netherworld had been made lighter through the friendship with Jordan. Moreover, rescuing Jessy and Vince and seeing them safe and sound gave Saul, Ruby, and Henry a reason for being in the Netherworld.

Now they were separating, Jordan's burden began to weigh heavily on them. Although proud of finding his sister, they were worried about his mother and that the search would be a long and frustrating one.

"I'm sure you'll find your mother soon," said Ruby emotionally as she hugged Jordan.

"We will. We're so much closer thanks to you," he replied. "I suppose we won't see each other again will we?" he asked quietly.

"I don't know but…" Ruby did not finish the sentence. Deep down she knew this was the last time she would ever see Jordan, Jessy, and Vince.

"We've had some wonderful times, haven't we?" asked Saul. "Lots of good memories that'll stay with us forever."

"Yes. That's one thing we can hold onto forever," returned Jordan with a shaky voice. He wiped a tear from his eye.

"I wish we could have spent more time together," said Ruby as she hugged Jessy.

"Jordan has told me all about the time you've spent together. I wish I could've been with you," she said quietly.

A little while later, Caleb, Jordan, Jessy, and Vince walked to the stables at the back of the hall. Even later still, Saul, Ruby, and Henry heard the familiar whooshing sound of four krays shooting up into the night sky before disappearing away into the distance.

*

Saul, Ruby, and Henry sat in the bedroom with mixed feelings. They were keen to get home but were already missing Jordan.

Henry was stuck in deep thought. He was worried about Bowman. Although desperate to get home, he wished he could stay and search for Bowman and be sure that he was safe.

"I've been meaning to say something," he began. "Something weird happened when I was locked in the cellar,"

Saul and Ruby looked up attentively.

"Well, I was really scared and kind of lost my temper."

"You do that all the—"

"This was different," snapped Henry. "I screamed and something happened to Edgerton. He fell on the floor screaming, holding his head in pain."

"You reckon you did that to him just by screaming?" asked Saul after a pause.

"Yes. I felt a really strange sensation go through my body. Like a rush of freezing cold blood. I thought I was going to faint."

Saul and Ruby thought long and hard about this.

"I think there's something strange happening to all of us," said Ruby. "I mean me talking to krays is a bit weird right?"

"And now I think about it," began Saul. "When you rescued me during that battle, did you notice the soldiers falling backwards, I mean almost flying off their feet?"

"Yes, but I thought the sorcerers—"

"No. I did that. I'm sure of it. I just raised my hands and… well I can't explain it." Saul stood up and raised his hands. "I just," he pointed his hands at the jug of water. "Well I—"

CRASH.

The jug of water smashed against the wall. Saul, Ruby, and Henry watched awestruck as the water trickled down the wall.

"Crikey..." muttered Henry. "That's amazing."

"Do you think we're sorcerers?" asked Ruby.

"No," said Saul. "I think the Netherworld has done that to us. When we go back, we'll just be *normal* I reckon."

"Should we tell anybody?" asked Ruby.

"No, let's not complicate anything," replied Saul. "Let's just get home."

For a while longer, the children pondered over the strange circumstances. They were convinced they had experienced an onset of special powers but were at a loss to explain how this had happened to them.

*

The evening drew on. Saul sat in the garden watching Solaris setting behind the orange valley. The garden behind him was filled with the murmur of busy conversations.

"I hope Jordan and Jessy are reunited with their mother soon." Ruby walked up behind Saul and sat down.

"And Vince with his family."

"It feels so strange to be going back," murmured Ruby.

"We've been so desperate to go home and now the time is finally here, it feels a bit weird doesn't it?" responded Saul.

"I wonder how long we've got left," Henry walked along and perched himself next to them. "Rufus said we have to see Rabin before we go."

A soft breeze rustled through the branches and carried a mixture of beautiful scents across the garden. A steady busy murmur rose from the garden as sorcerers congregated in small groups.

The children reminisced on the adventures, misadventures, and agony of the last few weeks. They knew they would miss the Netherworld. Despite the trials and tribulations, the Netherworld was a remarkable place. Now, so close to returning home, a strange air of sentiment overcame them for the friends they had come to know, as well as the plight of the Netherworld.

Ambrose Dunster stood at the edge of the garden. He waved his arms over his head in a circle and muttered something unintelligible. Now and again, a small light appeared in front of him, it shone for a moment before disappearing into nothingness. After a while, he stood looking satisfactorily at a faint steadfast white light in front of him, this time it did not disappear but steadily became stronger and bigger.

"Are you taking this with you?" asked Ruby holding up Saul's sword.

"Yes, why not? It's a souvenir."

"Who do you think the traitor is?" asked Henry looking lazily at the hive of activity in the garden.

Saul raised his eyebrows. The question caught both him and Ruby by surprise. "Does it matter? We'll be gone in a little while and I'm sure the council will deal with whoever it is."

"It matters to me Saul," insisted Henry determinedly. "Our lives were put at risk more than once because of the traitor."

From time to time, this question had niggled at all three of them, but they had seemed continually distracted with one thing or another to have given it any serious thought. Saul and Ruby turned around and looked at the groups of people in the garden.

"Well, how about Doe Festers?" Ruby proposed. "He's a bit too quiet for my liking; you just can't tell what's going on in his head, can you?"

"Was he in the meetings where the plans were being discussed?" asked Henry. Doe Festers stood in the distance with a wine glass in his hand celebrating in a small huddle. His scarf flayed gently in the soft breeze.

"I think so," said Saul.

"I'm not sure we can suspect him just because *he's too quiet.*"

"Good traitors normally are," Ruby replied cynically.

"I reckon it's Siraf," offered Saul. "My bones chill every time

I see him. His brother turned to the dark side remember? I'd probably outcast my brother if I had one for something like that. Instead, Siraf is constantly fretting about him."

Siraf stood in a small crowd with two more vampires, both as skinny, tall, and pale-skinned. Two sorcerers listened in and a giant peered down trying to submerge himself in the conversation of this macabre group.

"And now I think about it, he had that little scuffle with Jarrett when we were last here. He wanted Jarrett to tell him a secret or something."

"But how did he get to know about the Gelatonian regiment?" asked Ruby. "You said he wasn't in all the meetings."

"He was in the important ones," said Saul. "I'm sure he joined the meeting where we planned the raid. He knew everything and could easily have tipped the Gelatonian regiment off."

"Well as spooky as he seems, I get this gut feeling that he's genuinely on our side," replied Ruby. "He probably regrets what his brother's done. I doubt he'd betray the council. Anyway, why didn't Jarrett report that scuffle and have it dealt with?"

"Well, what about Junus?" proposed Ruby. "He was so eager to get into the mines and leave us stranded. And how convenient to have left his weapons behind, he didn't need them did he? He's been an absolute pain since we entered the Netherworld hasn't he?" Henry was quiet throughout the whole conversation. He watched the crowd carefully, seemingly in a world of his own.

"From before we entered," Saul chipped in.

"True. And what about when… Henry what are you doing?"

Henry had grabbed Saul's sword and was walking towards the hive of activity in the middle of the garden. His walk turned into a trot and then into a determined run.

Then, a few feet away from a small group, He pulled the sword from its hilt and launched his foot into the legs of someone standing with his back to them.

Jarrett landed flat on the floor, the drink in his hand spilt onto the grass.

"Henry! What the…!" shouted someone

Jarrett turned over and Henry lined the tip of the sword carefully against Jarrett's neck.

"Child!" cried someone. A busy commotion surrounded him.

"What are you playing at Henry!" cried another.

"It was your voice!" shrieked Henry. "I've been racking my brains trying to figure out who it was. It was your voice I heard outside the carriage."

"Henry what are you—?" began Jarrett.

"You *heard* me banging on the carriage, didn't you? But you ignored me," a crazed contorted look sat on Henry's face as he said this.

"W... what the... Henry?" shrieked Jarrett trying not to move in case the tip of the sword dug into his neck.

"Saul was a hundred yards away waving at you, trying to draw your attention. But you ignored him and stood by as the cart took me away," Henry pushed the sword a fraction closer. *"You could've stopped the cart, but you let it go! You didn't even bother looking for me and Saul, did you?"*

Ruby and Saul had caught up now and were standing at Henry's side.

"Henry, what's possessed—" began Saul.

"And I reckon your little excursion to find us a lodging at Kirk Heidengaard was your opportunity to tip off the searchers wasn't it?"

"Don't be silly Henry I would never—"

"That's how the searchers got to know we were there with Rufus, wasn't it? And then your little *tour* into the depths of the Catellan Mines. You didn't need to go that deep, but it bought more time for the Gelatonians to cause havoc."

Henry saw Jarrett's hand twitch softly. At any moment, he would raise it and strike a bolt of lightning at Henry. Instantly Henry pushed the sword softly.

"Don't you dare move a muscle!" Henry cried with a mad look on his face. There was a trickle of blood on Jarrett's neck and a painful grimace on his face.

"Child!" cried Mistie Herma running towards them, Rufus close behind her. "What ARE you're doing? For crying out loud someone get that blade away from the stupid—"

"Shut... up!" Henry cried.

"Henry," Ryder spoke softly at Henry's side. "That's enough. We'll take it from here." He put his hand comfortingly on Henry's shoulder.

The pressure was piling on, twenty faces were transfixed between Henry, the sword and Jarrett. Henry did not want to pull the sword back, far from it. Everything he had been through with Edgerton and Rankin in the rickety old house flooded through his mind making his blood boil.

Then, for a split second, Henry felt a tiny glimmer of regret. This was silly. Stupid. Why would Jarrett, the man who had shared a tent with them, who had made them laugh every evening during the journey to Kirk Heidengaard, why would he possibly betray them? The flicker of regret turned into a sense of disappointment. Henry had to put the sword away. He had to apologise profusely and hope that somehow, Jarrett would find it in his heart to forgive Henry, and…

"You stupid… stupid fool," muttered Jarrett slowly in an unrecognisable timbered harsh tone. Henry noticed a faint black smoke emanating from his mouth. Dozens of people watched and listened attentively.

"Pesky... stupid... child," continued Jarrett. "I should have disposed of you pests in Kirk Heidengaard when I had the chance."

There was a collective intake of breath. The noise at the periphery of the garden fell to a whisper and the crowd shuffled to let more people see.

"The master doesn't need me to hand you three brats over. He'll find you wherever you are," the mention of Baron Von Valak sent a collective chill through Saul, Ruby, and Henry's bones. There it was again, a very faint smoke, so faint that if Henry had not been standing so close, he would not have seen it. The smoke seemed to twirl gently around the tip of the sword. "He wants you and he *will* find you, all three of you. There's nowhere to hide. *Nowhere!* You think you're safe and well in the Upperworld but his reach goes beyond the Upperworld."

"And that goes for all of you," continued Jarrett angrily. "None of you are safe from the reaches of the dark master. *Join him while you can and you'll be spared!*"

"Henry," said the calm voice of Ryder. "We'll take it from here. Take the sword away."

Henry did not move. "No," he said quietly, his arm shaking. "I'm going to finish it right here right now."

"It's not for you to finish," said Ryder. "You've done the right thing. We hadn't a clue it was Jarrett. We'll take it from here."

"You heard what he just said, he—"

"Yes," Ryder interrupted. "But *we* have to deal with this."

A long moment passed away. Steadily, Henry pulled the sword away.

Instantly, Jarrett shot up, raised a hand and a bolt of white light shot out, missing Henry by an inch. Ryder and two sorcerers shot a bolt back, Jarrett screamed and fell back to the floor.

"Is he—?"

"No," said Ryder. "We've stunned him. He'll be fine."

Jarrett was carried away and it was a while before calm was restored in the garden.

"Let's go inside Henry," suggested Saul holding Henry's arm softly.

Without another word, the three children headed back into the hall, shocked and moved by the whole incident.

*

"I had no idea," muttered Saul angrily as they stepped into the lobby. "But it all makes sense now."

"Did you notice the look on his face when he came out of the mines?" asked Ruby. "He was shocked, maybe he didn't think anybody would still be alive when he walked out?"

"Now I think about it," added Saul. "He did hear me calling him in Kirk Heidengaard. He looked straight at me and—"

"It doesn't matter." Henry had an angry determined look on his face as they walked up the stairs. "We need to see Rabin and leave."

They passed the war room and then knocked on a door and listened carefully.

"Come in," came the quiet voice of Rabin.

They entered a dark room, lit up softly by two table lamps emanating a soft glow. Rabin sat quietly in an armchair. His gaze was fixed on a painting above the mantelpiece.

"Take a seat my children," he said quietly.

Saul fumbled in his pockets, pulled out the wooden box and handed it to Rabin.

"My diary," Rabin said with an excited smile.

"That's a diary?" asked Saul, finally getting around to ask a question that had been on his mind.

"Indeed it is," replied Rabin sliding his finger over four sides of the box. Instantly the box clicked open. A small book sat inside. "Aha," said Rabin satisfactorily.

The door opened to let Rufus and Celia in. They bowed to Rabin and then sat down opposite the children.

"To think the traitor was Jarrett. One of our most trusted companions," began Rabin. A disappointed grimace filled Rufus' face as he looked across at Rufus and Celia in turn.

"Was it a possession?" asked Celia.

Saul raised his eyebrows in confusion.

"Doe Festers is looking into it," replied Rufus. "But he didn't give the signs and..." Rufus and Celia looked at each other nervously. "Master, we had all the protections in place."

"I think," began Henry. "I think I saw some black smoke around his mouth, does that mean that he was, well, possessed?"

"Quite possibly, but how?" said Rufus after a while.

"Let's not worry about that now," said Rabin.

There was a knock at the door.

"My Lord," began Ambrose walking in. "You called for me?"

"How much time do we have?"

"About an hour."

"Splendid, we'll have them back in the garden by then," said Rabin with a soft nod.

"Could I have a word?" whispered Ambrose.

"Of course."

"You said they came through a portal."

"Yes."

"And they saw my homing beacon."

"The lamp, yes."

"That's impossible. People from the Upperworld have never seen the beacon, or portals, let alone walk through them."

"Let's not worry Ambrose," Rabin looked searchingly at the children. "The important thing is to get them back safely."

Ambrose walked out. The lamplight flickered sporadically, and an occasional laugh filled the silence from the garden below.

"Ambrose is right," said Rabin after a while. "You shouldn't have seen the beacon or the portal, and you certainly shouldn't have been able to walk through it. We didn't expect you back so soon."

"Back?" queried Ruby.

"Yes. We've kept a deep secret from you for long enough," announced Rabin looking at all three children in turn. "But circumstances have changed, and we have to reveal it to keep you safe."

The children sat up attentively, Rabin's voice had adopted a serious tone. He was smiling. The corners of his eyes wrinkled together in a friendly way, and there was a familiar twinkle in his eye.

"Your lives are more closely linked with the Netherworld than you could ever imagine."

Saul raised an eyebrow and Ruby and Henry looked dazed.

"I can't blame you for looking confused. Let me tell you something I should have told you weeks ago. Your lives are in danger."

"Danger?" murmured Saul.

"Yes," replied Rabin quietly. "Allow me to take you back to the darkest period in the history of our five states to a time when Petonia and Goran were locked in a long and bitter war. Tens of thousands were killed, countless families were made homeless, and the war created thousands of orphans."

This story and its depressing undertones were not news to the children. They had heard it many times in the last few weeks. But when the words came from Rabin, they adopted a deeper vivid meaning.

"Ninety-five years after the start of the war. The ancient prophecy, that the House of Royal Druids would bring the long war to a decisive end, was being fulfilled. The King of Petonia, the last of the druidic kings, finally entered the battlefield. Petonian fortunes changed, and they won battle after battle. Legions of Goran armies were destroyed on the battlefield and the King led the Petonians through momentous victories.

"The Goran chamber, that's the Goran Parliament, became anxious. If something wasn't done, Petonia would crush them. The only way to bring the war to a quick and decisive end in their favour was to assassinate the King. This became their primary objective. That didn't worry us. While we, the council, remained the guardians of the royal court, nobody could possibly harm the royal family."

The story of the *Druidic King* sent an exciting shiver through Saul, Ruby, and Henry. Although they didn't understand why it was so important for Rabin to tell them moments before they returned home, they listened nevertheless.

"But there was a problem. The noblemen were jealous of our privileged position as personal advisors to the king. Despite decades of plotting and conniving to expel us from the court, their gossiping and idle complaining reached deaf ears. That was until we were sent by the king to deal with the Goran invasion of Semantia.

"The battle lasted three months. During the lonely tiring journey back to the palace, we received the terrible news that devastation had wrought the palace."

The children were gripped by Rabin's words. They had heard snippets of this story in the last few weeks, but now, the story adopted an intriguing undertone.

*

One dark misty night, six steragon tore through the tranquil Petonian countryside. They galloped through the beautiful country lanes and villages, lit up welcomingly by the warm glow of street lamps, and clattered through the pebbled streets of the great cities.

On any other day, the cities and villages would be brimming with busy life. But today, the state was in mourning. The villages were quiet, derelict, and felt abandoned, almost as if an epic plague had sucked the soul out of them.

Eventually, the great palace appeared in the distance. The travellers slowed down to a trot. They entered the palace grounds. Rabin, Rufus, Darius, Celia, and two of their apprentices climbed off the steragon.

"The stables are at the back," said Darius patting his steragon. The two apprentices nodded and led the steragon away.

A horrible aura of death and destruction filled the palace grounds. The sorcerers felt overwhelmed by the misery and sadness that seemed to hang in the air.

"By the beards of the druids," said Rabin. Rufus, Darius, and Celia followed his gaze to the far side of the palace.

The palace was smouldering from a recent fire. A trail of smoke rose into the evening sky. The sorcerers watched this for a moment before scurrying up to a huge wooden gate. Rufus knocked loudly. There was no answer. He knocked again. Eventually, a palace servant came to the huge door.

"Speak your business!" he barked rudely through a hatchet in the door.

"My dear Blaine," said Rabin quietly.

A brief silence was followed by a frantic rattling and clunking from behind the door before it was finally opened.

"Master!" cried a stout chubby round-face man. "Forgive me. The palace is in turmoil, everyone has lost their senses, it's madness I tell you madness," replied Blaine sobbing. "Follow me," he said looking around cautiously.

Blaine led the visitors into a quiet room in the servant's quarters. The room was barely big enough for them to sit. He lit a candle and pulled some chairs.

"We have to be careful. Javier Cass would have my head if he knew I'd let you in," began Blaine quietly.

"Javier Cass?" quizzed Rabin.

"Yes, haven't you heard?"

"Heard what?" asked Celia

"He's the crowned king."

"Crowned king? It's only been three days since the burial."

Darius sighed. "The royal protocol dictates that—"

"Please," stressed Blaine lifting his hand. "We have to be quiet." He ran to the door, looked around anxiously and then closed the door. "If Javier had his way, he wouldn't be the crowned king. He resisted, you know Javier is, dare I say it, completely irresponsible and doesn't want to be burdened with responsibility. But Winfred, Stergo, and Kayla argued that the peace of the land would be in tatters if a king wasn't crowned immediately. They assured him that he was a *caretaker* king until more *permanent* arrangements could be made."

"Winfred, Stergo, and Kayla. Our nemesis. They've been scheming our downfall for years," sighed Rufus slowly. "What better *permanent arrangements* than to have a puppet king ruling the kingdom for them?"

"And take the heat for their decisions," interjected Darius.

"Enough," sighed Rabin putting his hand up. "Where are they now?"

The candle flickered wildly adding to the dark, cold, and sombre atmosphere of the room.

"They left with a contingent of soldiers this morning, in pursuit of the assassins."

"Why was the burial held so quickly?" asked Celia. "A king's burial is always held on the thirteenth day and a queen's on the fifteenth. In the presence of the elders of the kingdom and—"

"Everyone in the kingdom had a right to be there," interrupted Rufus. "The druids established these protocols. Couldn't they wait?"

"It wasn't my decision," began Blaine after a brief silence. "I pleaded with them, but the faces..." Blaine's voice shook. "It was a brutal murder. The faces were... disfigured. Javier believed that if the citizens saw them lying in state like that, there'd be chaos, it would become difficult to maintain peace and order."

"The citizens were already angry that your calls to increase security had been ignored. Following each assassination attempt, the King ordered you be called back from the battlefield. He was ignored each time. A week before the assassination, he sent the message to recall you."

"I think the noblemen felt that if the citizens saw the King and Queen lying in state, they might rebel and hold the noblemen responsible. So, in their *infinite* wisdom, they decided to hold the burial as quickly and quietly as possible."

Rabin shook his head slowly at this. "Or they heard that we were on our way and held the burials before we got here," he suggested with a scowl. "How did they die?"

"A fire broke out in the West Wing in the middle of the night. Everyone fled there to put it out. Hours later when we returned to the royal quarters, we were met by Stergo at the entrance. He was in a terrible state. *They're dead! They're dead!* he repeated like a madman."

"The King and Queen had been assassinated," Blaine sighed. "And the heirs had been kidnapped by the assassins." Blaine's voice began to shake again. Rabin put a hand on his arm.

"Did you see the King and Queen?" asked Darius.

"Yes. I saw them as they lay in the bed. They were mutilated, unrecognisable. Killed in cold blood."

"Can you lead us to the quarters?" asked Celia after a while.

"Of course," replied Blaine. "But there's nothing to see."

"We'd like to see the quarters," insisted Celia.

"We have to be quiet," he whispered anxiously.

Blaine led them up a series of stairs, corridors, and landings. They arrived at a set of beautiful jewel-ridden doors which opened into a magnificent sitting area. A few doors led into a study, some living rooms, and a washroom. The royal bedroom stood at the far end.

The study and living rooms were well kept and tidy, nothing had been disturbed from the night of the assassination. A contrasting scene awaited them in the bedroom. The room had been turned upside down, wardrobes were ripped down and emptied onto the floor, drawers were strewn face forward and the bed sheets were a mess. There were blood stains on the bed. The room carried a terrible deathly smell.

Darius squirmed and pulled a handkerchief to his face.

"Why didn't the guards rush in? They must have heard the commotion," asked Celia.

"They were all in the West Wing dealing with the fire."

"Of course they were," Celia muttered sarcastically. "We'll be a while. Could you keep a lookout?"

Blaine nodded and scurried out of the quarters into the landing.

"It's all yours," Rabin said looking at Celia. He stood back with Rufus and Darius and watched at a distance.

Celia was a scentia. As a child, she had discovered that she had supernatural instincts, and could see and hear things that nobody else could.

Celia walked over to the bed and wiped a handkerchief over the blood. Next, she walked to the three doors leading out of the room, the main entrance, the door to a washroom, and the door to a library and carefully inspected the door frame and the handles. She inspected each corner, careful not to turn anything over. Then she lifted the drawers and moved clothes around.

"What were they looking for?" she asked herself. "Two people entered the room… and went out of the window," she mumbled as she sniffed and touched the window frame, the curtains, and the floor around it. She looked out of the window onto the balcony carefully scrutinising the floor and metal guard that surrounded it.

"This door was opened for them... no signs of forced entry... maybe someone they trusted," she muttered sporadically a few moments later as she inspected the door into the bedroom.

Celia's investigation went on for a while. She came in and out of the bedroom, into the library and the washroom, and then back into the bedroom. As this went on, Rabin, Darius, and Rufus waited anxiously, worried they might be interrupted.

"Listen," whispered Celia suddenly. She stood still. Her head turned thoughtfully to one side.

Darius squinted his eyes and tried to listen carefully. "I can't hear any—"

"Shush," Celia raised her hand. "There again... A wailing sound... like a cat," she whispered. "It's coming from... the library."

Celia trotted into the library closely followed by Rabin, Rufus, and Darius.

The walls of the library were lined from floor to ceiling with bookshelves. At one side, a grand step ladder led up to the top shelves reaching out to the hundreds of old books spread across the shelves. A study desk sat by the window with a clutter of papers riddled across it untidily.

"Behind this bookshelf," Celia announced turning her head to one of the walls.

"There must be a passage behind it," suggested Rufus eyeing the books and shelves very carefully.

"Did you hear that?" asked Darius quietly.

They listened attentively to a faint wailing sound echoing in the distance somewhere.

"It's behind here somewhere," urged Darius.

They fumbled around the bookcase unsuccessfully. There was no opening.

"Shall we break it down? Nobody'll notice more mess," proposed Rufus fervently.

"No," replied Celia. "The noise will wake up the palace. Besides, if there's something to be found, we don't want anybody knowing we found it."

Rufus, Darius, and Celia continued fumbling and feeling around the bookshelf. Meanwhile, Rabin sat behind a desk and surveyed the room thoughtfully. He eyed the paintings, the table, and the bookshelves. Presently, his gaze stopped at a wall lamp. It was an old Trangorian piece made of iron with curved rods protruding out and upwards towards the candle holders.

He walked to the lamp and inspected it carefully. One of the rods was dislodged slightly from the iron plate holding it in place. He pulled it down there was a clicking sound from the bookshelf. The bookshelf became loose at one end.

"Bravo," said Celia excitedly.

Together, Rufus, Darius, and Celia pulled the bookshelf forward. It moved forward with a loud clumsy grating sound. Behind the bookshelf was a small opening leading down into darkness.

Almost in unison, the sorcerers smacked their staffs onto the floor with a clutter. A light shone out from the top to reveal a stone staircase leading down into the darkness. They stepped downwards. With each step, the wailing sound became louder.

At the bottom, they were met by a tunnel separating into two directions. Without a word, Darius and Celia set off in one direction and Rabin and Rufus in the other.

Sometime later, Rabin and Rufus heard a clear distinctive cry in the distance ahead of them. A baby! They picked up the pace and tore through the passage, the sound of their shoes echoing through the tunnel like the gallop of a steragon.

"By the beards of the druids," sighed Rabin stopping still in his tracks.

A toddler, probably a year old, lay flat on the floor making quiet unintelligible noises. He looked up at Rabin and Rufus, reached up and then began sobbing. The child's face was smeared in grime, his nose was running, and his hair was covered in soil and dirt. His knees were scratched and bruised, he had probably tried to crawl through the dark tunnel for the best part of the last few days.

Rabin put the child to his shoulder and consoled it.

"There there," said Rabin soothingly as the child closed his eyes and laid his head on Rabin's shoulder.

Soon Darius returned carrying a second child and Celia returned with a third.

*

Rabin paused and looked longingly at Saul, Ruby, and Henry. His eyes told them the rest of the story. They were oblivious to the room, the fire, the table lamps, the noise outside, and everything else around them. The only things they seemed to see and hear were the eyes and voice of Rabin.

"The child I picked up was you Saul," Rabin looked deep into Saul's eyes.

"M... me?"

"And the two babies that Darius and Celia found were Ruby and Henry Anan. In that maze of tunnels, we found the heirs to the throne of Petonia, the descendants of the Druidic House of Anan."

Saul raised his eyebrows and Henry dropped his jaw. Ruby sniffed quietly and wiped a tear as it trickled down her cheek. They were lost for words.

"But that's... silly," began Saul. "I mean our parents are at home, we were born in Edgings Burrow and—"

"That's what you were told," interrupted Rabin. "You've been raised up for the last twelve years to believe that. But think. Your bond with the Netherworld is much deeper and stronger than you can imagine. It was only a matter of time before you returned to your rightful home."

"Rightful home?" murmured Ruby quietly to herself.

"I have to keep reminding you that people from the Upperworld can't even see the portal, let alone walk through it. They can't see the lamp in the mansion, a lamp that Ambrose lights to act as a homing beacon for the portal. But you saw it.

"Finding your way back here wasn't an accident, you were meant to be here. Somehow, the Netherworld brought you back. If you hadn't accidentally run through the portal, it would have happened another way. This, my children, is your home," Rabin said warmly.

There was a long silence.

"But we had a few problems to solve," continued Rabin. "Firstly, how had you ended up in the tunnels? Was it a kidnap gone wrong? Had the King and Queen sensed danger and put you there? If so, why didn't they keep running and escape instead of hiding you there and returning to meet an inevitable doom in the royal quarters? We've never really answered these questions and even today all four of us have different opinions.

"We had to get you out of the palace without being seen, not even by Blaine. We figured that the tunnels came down so deep for a reason, not to hide people but to act as an escape route. There had to be a way out.

"The second problem was, what to do with you once you were out? We had to get you away from the palace. Whoever assassinated your parents wanted you dead as well. If the Netherworld came to know that the heirs are alive, hope would pervade.

"When the noblemen returned to the room, there was no trace of you. They announced your death, but in the back of their minds, Javier, Winfred, Stergo, and Kayla still believe that you're alive. Secretly they've been searching the Netherworld to find you because in you rested, or should I say still rests, the last remnants of a glorious kingdom which has thousands of years of rich magical heritage. We couldn't possibly risk losing it.

"As the years progressed, they became less worried. If you were alive, you'd be found by now," continued Rabin. "However, they will never be totally convinced until they find your grave or meet someone who witnessed your burial. They haven't found such a person yet, so the thought continues to niggle at them.

"But the problem is that it's not just the noblemen that are intrigued by the legend of the heirs," the children looked up. "Baron Van Valak is deeply intrigued by the legend that the heirs to the Druidic Throne are still alive."

"So, what were we to do with you? Your lives in the Netherworld would be at continual risk, you'd never be safe here. We couldn't guarantee your safety. The sorcerers were under attack, many of us had been captured and imprisoned by either the Gorans or the noblemen. We had to hide you in a safe haven until you came of age. That *safe haven* was the Upperworld.

"The tunnels were huge and seemed to span for miles. Nobody knew when these tunnels were built, or where they led. But after hours of walking through endless twists and turns, we reached a hatch. We were stunned to discover that it led to the Forest of Petonia.

"Our association with Edgings Burrow goes back three centuries. Your guardians, Samuel, Jefferson, and David are old, reliable, and trustworthy allies of the council."

"Our guardians," muttered Henry to himself.

"Placing you into the guardianship of Samuel, Jefferson, and David was an inspired decision. I was imprisoned, Darius was exiled, and Rufus and Celia went into hiding. You were much safer in the Upperworld than here." Rabin looked thoughtfully at Saul, Ruby, and Henry as if a weight had been taken off his shoulder.

"This means... we're siblings, right?" asked Ruby after a while.

"Of course," replied Celia smiling.

The children should have been celebrating this revelation, but the news that their parents were dead, and they were heirs to the throne of Petonia was too much to comprehend.

"You've been safe in the Upperworld," started Rufus. "But last year, I learned that two searchers had found a portal into the Edgings Burrow. I became worried about your safety."

"That's why you came to Edgings Burrow," said Ruby.

"Yes. To look over you and make sure no harm came to you."

"Returned?" asked Saul.

"Yes, I've been twice before, each time because I was worried you might be discovered. It turned out Arak and Trenton weren't actually a threat to you. They had accidentally found a portal. They went in and out a few times and got bored. But then Arak discovered I was in the Upperworld, and in Edgings Burrow of all places. My cover was blown. You see, there are two bounties on my head. I'm wanted by both the Goran searchers and the noblemen. The Baron wants to recruit me into his gaggle of miscreants, and the noblemen just want to finish all the sorcerers off, especially me.

"Arak set out to recruit me into the Baron's army. If I didn't join, he said, he and Trenton would return with an army of searchers. I was in a conundrum and decided to leave. But I made a remarkable discovery on my way into the forest. I saw the homing lamp in the mansion. You won't believe how excited I was to discover that the council was meeting there."

"I…" began Saul after a moment. "I should have told you this sooner. But I met Darius Algar," Rufus and Celia raised their eyebrows. "I didn't mean to meet him, it just happened when I was lost between Kirk Heidengaard and Port Newton. I didn't know where to go and somehow, I ended up in Beezel Mount. He was very helpful and... well not just to me but to Caleb as well because Darius led us to Jessy and Vince and," Saul realised that he was speaking too fast. "I remember, he called me *Saul Anan*. Without him, I don't think I would have survived," he finished more slowly.

"That's the second time he's saved your life," smiled Celia. "It was his idea to put you in the care of Samuel, Jefferson, and David, and he promised that given the opportunity, he would be a father to all three of you," remarked Celia. "Unfortunately, his circumstances changed dramatically and much as he'd have liked to, he hasn't been able to honour that promise."

"Will Darius ever be released?" asked Saul.

"We'd like him to be released," began Rabin after a short silence. "But it isn't straightforward. The mount is, as you know, protected by numerous spells and beasts which even with all our powers we'd find difficult to overcome. But added to that, he's a desperately contentious and unpopular figure and extremely unpopular amongst the council. Many believe that his altercation with Lord Deeson led to the entrenched position of the noblemen resulting in our extended troubles with them."

"Shouldn't we just stay here?" suggested Saul after a brief silence. "I mean if this is our rightful home perhaps, we should just—"

"Not yet," interrupted Rabin sharply. "The time isn't right for you to return for good. Petonia needs visible heirs to inspire the citizens. But we're still regrouping, and we need to keep you safe for a while longer. Evidently, we can't keep you safe here yet.

"The raid on the mines is the first step in our preparation for war. It's a small victory in a bigger plan. We've only entered a small handful of mines and there are many more places to get to. We've shown our hand to the enemy, and they'll be much more prepared now, especially when they discover that I'm alive. Your presence here puts you in more danger than ever before I'm afraid."

"It's time," announced Celia glancing out of the window at the steady bright glowing circle.

Rabin collected his staff and led everybody out of the room.

As they walked out of the entrance of Kirby Hall, they heard a buzzing sound followed by a crackling crash. This was followed by the strange sight of Ambrose being thrown from the glowing light. He landed unsteadily on his feet, shook his arms and shoulders, patted his jacket, and walked to Rabin as if nothing had happened.

"Ready when you are master," he said humbly. "It's a bit rough on the journey back I'm afraid."

Rabin looked longingly at the children. Once again, they saw that wonderful bright glint, the lovely warm look which made them value the aura around his presence.

"You should say goodbye. We don't have long," he smiled.

"Fifteen minutes," added Ambrose sternly.

After wandering around for a few minutes, the children found Althea, and it took a few more minutes before they managed to say a sentimental goodbye to Berto Manser, Doe Festers, Ryder Hestrung, Mistie Herma, and the many others they had met briefly in their adventure. Even Junus Palfrey, so hostile those many weeks ago, hugged them and said goodbye with a croaky voice.

Back in the garden Rabin, Rufus, and Celia were waiting with Ambrose.

"This way please," he gestured. "Take a swig of this otherwise you'll have terrible chest pains."

"The portarix serum," remembered Henry taking a bottle from Ambrose.

In turn, they sipped the cordial and coughed profusely as it hit their throats.

"I'll stand behind the portal. Look at me and walk straight through towards me with your eyes closed, the light might make you dizzy," he advised. "Rabin and Rufus will see you through," he said nodding at Rabin and Rufus.

Saul, Ruby, and Henry turned to Celia, smiled, and waved before lining up, closing their eyes, and walking successively through the misty. As they walked through the light there was a small bang and then complete silence.

*

The children landed with a thud on the wooden floor of the mansion. A moment later Rabin walked out of the portal followed by Rufus.

"We don't have much time," he urged.

"Sir we can make our way back from here," said Saul.

"We have to speak to Samuel," suggested Rabin. "There are certain *safeguards* we need to put in place now," he added cryptically.

As they stepped through the hallway, some of the wall paintings seemed to come alive. The desperate scenes depicted in some of the paintings seemed to make vivid sense. The children could relate to many of them now.

Moments later they trudged quietly away from the mansion through the snow of Edgings Burrow towards Gibbets Lane. For weeks, the children had been desperate to return to their cosy homes, to sit in front of their warm fires with their parents, but now it felt strange. They should have felt relieved and excited, but all they could feel was a strange numbness. Innumerable memories flooded back of their experiences in the Netherworld.

They were shrouded in these thoughts when suddenly Saul realised that he was only a few yards away from his house. Ahead of them, Samuel was clearing the snow from the front path.

He had started to look older thought Saul. The first signs of grey hair had appeared, and he had started to complain about sleeplessness and a few mild ailments.

Samuel turned his head towards the five travellers searchingly and then slowly raised his eyebrows. His face lit up.

"Oh my," he began. "Rabin, I thought you were—"

"Dead?" suggested Rabin. "My dear friend."

Samuel and Rabin embraced quietly. They spoke in friendly tones and queried each other's health and how they had kept themselves *all these years*.

"The picture," began Saul excitedly. "The picture in the dining room is—"

"Rabin," interrupted Samuel with a smile. "My long and dear friend Rabin," he added with a twinkle in his eye.

"And the man with him is Darius," suggested Saul excitedly.

Rabin and Samuel smiled as he said this.

"I'm afraid that the heirs came home a bit earlier than we had anticipated," said Rabin holding Samuel's hands and looking him in the eye.

"There was a... err… accident and they ended up in the Netherworld," explained Rufus.

"The children will explain, I'm sure. But for now, there are a few things we need to discuss," continued Rabin in a serious tone.

"Saul, could you walk Ruby and Henry home?" asked Samuel. "And ask Jefferson and David to come over this evening," he added in an urgent tone.

Saul nodded. The children turned to Rabin and Rufus and embraced them for a few moments. Henry removed his glasses and wiped a tear, and Ruby sobbed quietly.

Saul, Ruby, and Henry turned and walked away. At the corner of the lane, they turned around and paused to look once more at Rabin and Rufus in quiet conversation with Samuel.

*

When Saul returned to Gibbets Lane half an hour later, the snow was coming down steadily, the lane was still and quiet. He was met with two pairs of footsteps leading away from the cottage into the distance. Rabin and Rufus had gone.

For a moment Saul stood and looked at the cottage thoughtfully. One day they would return to the Netherworld to assume a tremendous responsibility. When that happened, he would be ready.

Printed in Great Britain
by Amazon

35645337R00162